Midnight's Edge:

The Possession Book 2

David Chappuis

&

Michael Klinger

Published by
Melange Books, LLC
White Bear Lake, MN 55110
www.melange-books.com

Midnight's Edge: The Possession
Copyright © 2016 by David Chappuis and Michael Klinger

ISBN: 978-1-68046-248-7

Names, characters, and incidents depicted in this book are products of the author's imagination or are used fictitiously. Any resemblance to actual events, locales, organizations, or persons, living or dead, is entirely coincidental and beyond the intent of the author or the publisher. No part of this book may be reproduced or transmitted in any form or by any means, electronic or mechanical, including photocopying, recording, or by any information storage and retrieval system, without permission in writing from the publisher.
Published in the United States of America.

Cover Art by Becca Barnes

A special thanks to Vanessa Leavitt, our editor, and friend, for making suggestions and giving us great feedback.

Acknowledgement

We'd like to extend our thanks to Nancy Schumacher, who not only assisted with editing but provided us with an opportunity to get our work in front of an audience.

sought to destroy him.

Damon Sheilds—A mortal, but gifted man who can transcend between the mortal and spirit realms. Damon shares a past with Lucy and Carol.

Freddy Wickcliff—The son of Shelly and Rory.

Rory Wickcliff—The deceased husband of Shelly.

Pit Bowen—The estranged husband of Rebecca, who has found himself entangled with the Wickcliffs.

Greta—The Wickcliff maid.

Chapter 1

The concept of time is different in the spirit realm than it is in the mortal one. It's not measured by hours or even minutes. Although time has gone on, it feels like I've been trapped in one long, endless nightmare since my suicide and transition to the spirit realm. I can't gauge how long it's been now, but that doesn't matter. All that matters is I've found myself trapped in the attic of the Wickcliff mansion, where I ended my life, with no apparent way out.

In an instant, I, Shelly Hawkins-Wickcliff, the younger sister of Ethan Hawkins and daughter to Carol and Jeffrey Hawkins, ceased to exist. I can still connect with my family and friends in my mind. I can see the events of the mortal realm unfolding like a movie. I've seen my father murdered by Jeremy Wickcliff, the same evil, vile spirit who'd gotten inside my mind and coerced me into taking my life. He'd returned to the mortal realm using Midnight's Edge, a time of night where the veil between the living and the dead ceases to exist and inhabited the body of Reed Withers, who soon became trapped in the spirit realm with me after his mind and body were possessed. At the age of twenty-five, the same age as me, it appeared that his life was over just as mine was.

Reed's a fighter who refuses to accept that his life as he knew it is over. Having him in the spirit realm with me has helped me realize that like him, I can't sit back and let Jeremy get away with what he's taken from me. Reed's determination to reclaim his life has reignited the fighter in me, the person who no longer wishes to be a victim. I've become determined to make Jeremy pay for the suffering he's inflicted on me, my late husband Rory, and the rest of my family, although I'm still figuring out how.

David Chappuis & Michael Klinger

The one connection I still have to the mortal realm is through Kasey Menze, one of my closest friends and my brother's lover. While no one in the mortal realm knows of my presence there when I go there in my mind, Kasey's the exception. He has special abilities, psychic abilities. He can hear me when I speak to him. I've also been able to give him visions, visions of my death and turmoil that I now face. While he's doing his best to shut me out, afraid of what I've shown him and desperate for a normal life with my brother, I know I've got to keep trying to connect with him. He's the only hope I have of warning my loved ones of the impending danger they face as a result of Jeremy's presence in their world.

I turned to look out the window, peering out at the town below, before shutting my eyes and attempting to make contact with the mortal realm. I saw Kasey outside his mother Gracey's house, who'd just encountered Jeremy, who he thought was Reed. He thought the encounter odd, as he couldn't figure out why Reed was there or why he'd left as suddenly as he'd appeared. He hadn't known that Jeremy had shown up to coerce Gracey into telling him who his son was, the son he'd blamed her for helping his wife, Lucy, keep from him his son's entire life. He wouldn't even have known about his son's existence if it hadn't been for his paying off an old gypsy woman that Lucy once knew to tell him the truth.

Kasey hadn't realized the extent of the danger his mother was in as he went up to her kitchen door and entered the house without knocking. She'd told him to come over in a hurry, and while Kasey was only five years older than me, the worry I saw as I studied his face made him appear much older than he was.

"Mom, I got here as quickly as I could. You sounded so strange on the phone. I could tell by the tone in your voice that something's wrong. What is it?"

Gracey stood up slowly and pointed to Hilda. "Kasey, this is an old friend of mine, Hilda. You remember her."

Kasey gave Hilda a nod, acknowledging that he did remember her. Hilda was one of Gracey's dearest friends, but he hadn't seen her in fifteen years. No one had until recently after she'd taken an extended absence from Sleepy Meadows. Much like his mother, he'd noticed that she hadn't aged well. Her gray eyes still showed the kindness he'd always remembered she had, but now the shade of her hair, pulled back in a bun, matched. Her skin had withered, and while he hadn't known what happened in her life while she was away, it was obvious that her experiences had weathered her. She appeared weaker and more frail than he remembered.

"Yes, I do," Kasey said, smiling. "Mom talks about you all of the time. It's nice to see you again."

"I haven't seen you since you were a teen," Hilda said, her voice lower and not as feminine as Gracey's. "I didn't expect you to remember me at all. Your mother didn't tell me what a handsome young man you've become."

He blushed. "Thank you."

"Please sit down," Gracey said. "I need to talk to you." He sat. "Would you like something to drink?"

"What I'd like is for you to stop stalling. I know that something's bothering you, I always know. Just tell me what it is."

Gracey smiled. "We do have a special connection, don't we, son?" She lost her smile and winced.

"Are you alright?" Hilda asked.

"My leg's bothering me," she said, sitting down. "I'll be fine."

Kasey began to stand up. "Where's your pain medication, Mom?"

Gracey put her hand on his arm, and he sat down again. "Don't worry about that now. It makes me groggy. I need to talk to you clearly about this. All those years I spent taking care of you as a boy, I never expected that the roles would be reversed. You take such good care of me."

He patted her on the knee softly. "I figure I owe ya one…or two…or fifty. When Ethan left, and I started drinking more, you were the one that was there for me."

She rubbed his hand that was still on her knee. "I know what a burden I've become."

He shook his head. "No, you haven't. I do what I do because I love you."

"And I love you, son. That's why I need to tell you the truth now, for your sake."

He removed his hand. "The truth about what?"

"About your biological parents, and how I became your mother."

His eyes widened. "I've asked about them before, and you never gave me a straight answer. Why do you want to talk about them now?"

She sighed. "I've kept the truth from you because it's what your mother asked me to do. When you were born, she made me promise to take you and keep you safe. However, you're a man now, Kasey, and you can protect yourself. To do that, you need to know where you come from."

He turned to Hilda. "Did you know my biological mother too?"

She nodded. "Let your mother finish, Kasey."

He looked back at Gracey. "What were you keeping me safe from?"

She took his hand. "Not from what. From whom. Your mother was afraid of her husband."

"Who was she? Why was she so afraid of my father?"

"Your mother's name was Lucy Sheldon. She married a Wickcliff. He was ruthless."

"I know the story of Lucy Wickcliff." He took his hand back, exhaled sharply, and looked away from the women for a moment. He ran his hands through his dark hair, remembering the story he'd heard as a child about how she'd died. "She was married to Jeremy," he said, meeting eyes with them again. The next thought he had sickened him. "Are you telling me that he's my father?"

Gracey shook her head. "You aren't Jeremy's son. That's why your mother was afraid for your safety. If Jeremy had discovered that, he would've killed you. He would've never accepted that his wife had a child with another man."

He sat back in his chair, relieved. "That's how I ended up with you?"

She nodded. "Your mother was pregnant with you when she married Jeremy, but he didn't know that. He went away to Europe for several months and so he never knew about her pregnancy. When she had you, she told no one. I was her midwife, and she asked me to keep you and raise you as my own."

"Why would you do that for her?"

"I did it for both of you. Lucy, Carol, Hilda and I were sisters in a coven. Lucy was taken in by Jeremy's charms, but it didn't take her long to discover what a mistake she'd made in marrying him. She soon realized how despicable he was. Your mother loved you, and she gave you up to save your life."

"Ethan's mother was part of your coven?" He looked back and forth between Hilda and Gracey, who gave him another nod. "She's a witch?"

"You care about Carol's son a great deal, don't you?" Hilda said. "I can see it in your eyes."

"Never mind that now. I want to hear the rest of the story. Did Lucy die in a car accident as the legend says?"

"Our coven was trying to help rid the town of Jeremy's evil," Gracey said. "We were unsuccessful. He tried to eliminate us all, and we fought back. That's how I hurt my leg. Lucy took it upon herself to end his life, but in the end, she lost hers too. They were both killed when their car went over Lover's Bluff."

"If he really loved Lucy, he wouldn't have hurt me. She would've had to know that."

"Jeremy doesn't know the true meaning of the word. If he finds out that Lucy's your mother, the ultimate revenge on her would be to have you killed. I'm sure he blames her for the accident that caused his death."

He rubbed his forehead. "Wait a minute. You're talking about him as if he were still alive."

Gracey's face fell. "We believe that he's used Midnight's Edge to return to the mortal world. You must remember the stories I used to tell you about it."

"That's exactly what I thought they were. Stories."

"You have abilities, Kasey. You inherited Lucy's gifts. You understand that there's more to this world than what we can see, that's beyond all logic."

"And you believe he's coming after me? How do you know this?"

"Your mother came to Hilda in a vision with a warning. That's why Hilda's here."

He turned his attention to Hilda. "You've seen her?"

"I see many spirits," she said. "It's part of my gift."

He stood up. "If Jeremy's here, it could explain a lot."

Gracey's eyes narrowed. "What do you mean by that?"

He sighed. "I told you about the terrible vision I had in the bar, but that's not all. After I left you, I had another one about Ethan's sister, Shelly."

"What sort of vision?" Hilda asked, intrigued.

"I went up to the Wickcliff's to check on her after I'd heard that she wasn't returning any of her family's calls. I heard her call out to me, and suddenly, I was in a vision. I went up to the attic in the mansion and saw her hanging there. She was dead, and it looked like she'd committed suicide."

Hilda gasped. "Good heavens. Are you sure?"

He nodded with a grim and remorseful expression on his face.

Gracey turned in her chair to face him. "Oh, darling, how terrible for you. Did you tell anyone else what you saw?"

"I went to Sheriff Withers. I saw his son, Reed, on the Wickcliff grounds with Pit Bowen. They were carrying what looked like a body toward the mausoleum. He said he'd investigate, but I think he thought I was off my rocker, or at the very least drinking again. I don't blame him."

"That can't be. I've spoken to Carol since Jeffrey's wake," Gracey said. "She mentioned that Shelly showed up and explained her absence."

He shook his head. "When I touched her, I could feel that she wasn't the same. I can't explain it, but she was different. I feel it in my gut. I don't know who that is, but it isn't Shelly."

"That's quite possible," Hilda said. "If the real Shelly's gone, she may have been inhabited by another force, just as Jeremy's inhabited a mortal."

"So he's back, but he couldn't come back in his own form?" Kasey asked.

"Only his spirit's remained alive," Gracey said. "He has no mortal body to come back to, so he had to find a mortal host that he could possess."

"Reed," Kasey said in sudden revelation, his eyes shifting away from the ladies.

"I beg your pardon?" Gracey said.

He paused before meeting eyes with her. "Reed's been acting so strangely. First, I find him creeping around the Wickcliff cemetery in the middle of the night barking orders at Pit Bowen. I thought that strange enough. Then I just ran into him outside right before I came in here. He acted as if he'd never seen me before. What if Reed's the one that Jeremy's possessed?"

Hilda turned her attention to Gracey. "If that was Jeremy outside, he may have heard us. He may know that Kasey's Lucy's son. I fear that you're both in more immediate danger than I thought."

"If Jeremy's possessed the Withers boy," Gracey said, "I suppose he was here to seek revenge on me for my part in his destruction. I'm not surprised. I knew it was only a matter of time before he came looking for me. If he heard us, he knows you're here too, Hilda."

Kasey rubbed his mother's arm. "Don't worry, Mom. I won't let him get to you as long as I'm still breathing."

"That's my greatest fear," Gracey said, her eyes searching his. "I'm not worried about myself. I'm not without my powers. Even if he did come after me, I'm an old lady, and I've had a good life. I wouldn't hesitate to give up my life if it meant saving yours."

They hadn't realized that although Jeremy had overheard their conversation that he'd misunderstood it. He'd assumed he was Kasey's father because Lucy was his mother. This didn't keep Kasey out of danger, but Jeremy needed him alive as he needs to inhabit someone of his own bloodline if his spirit's going to remain in the mortal realm permanently.

"Don't say that," Kasey said, holding his hands in front of him as if to stop her. "Don't even think it. I'll protect you from him. I promise." He exhaled. "I'm not even sure that Reed's the one Jeremy possessed, but it makes the most sense given his behavior. My first instinct is to warn Sheriff Withers about his son, but he'd never believe me, not now that he thinks I was wrong about Shelly's death. It's too fantastic of a story."

"Sit back down," Gracey said, gesturing to the chair he'd sat in before. "There's more to the story."

He sat, and grabbed her hand for emphasis. "Mom, do you know who my father is? Did Lucy tell you?"

She nodded. "Your father was a friend of ours, a mystical teacher named Damon Shields. He was working with us to try to bring down Jeremy as well. Your parents were very much in love."

I felt that Damon Shields was the same Damon I'd heard my mother talking about. Had Lucy and my mother been in love with the same man? If he'd been in love with Mom, why was he involved with Lucy? I suddenly remembered the bald man in the monk's habit that Kasey had seen in his vision at The Hook. My instincts told me that the man was Damon reaching out to Kasey. I continued to listen to their conversation, hoping for answers.

"You said he *was* a friend," Kasey said. "Does that mean he's dead?"

"I believe he's alive," Gracey said. "But he's been in seclusion."

"My father just left me?"

"He doesn't know about you. He's a good man. If he'd known about you, things would've been different."

"If he'd known about you," Hilda said, "he would've wanted to be part of your life. He probably still would want to be."

He stood up, unable to take it all in. He didn't know if he should be thankful or angry. The woman he'd trusted the most had kept everything about his parents from him. He was silent for a moment before meeting her eyes.

"You should've told me who my parents were a long time ago. I had a right to know."

"As I told you, Lucy asked me to keep your identity secret for your sake. I saw no reason to cause you any more pain by telling you your mother was dead. Things are different now that Jeremy's back."

"If this is true, if he's back, I'll kill him myself. I swear it."

"You can't," Hilda said. "If you destroy him, whomever he inhabits will parish as well whether it be the Withers boy or another. Our only hope is to exorcise him back to the darkness from where he came."

"I want you to promise me that you won't seek him out," Gracey said. "You don't know what you're up against, son. He's more powerful than you realize."

He took a deep breath, trying to maintain his composure. "So now what? I can't stand by and do nothing."

"You can and you will. I've fought him before. I know what to do.

You don't."

"Mom, you aren't in any shape to confront him, and you know it."

"Your mother isn't alone," Hilda said. "She has me, and she has Carol. We're family, and we'll protect each other just as we always have."

He bent down so that he was at Gracey's level and touched her cheek. "You're the only mother I've ever known. If anything were to happen to you, I'd never forgive myself."

She looked into his eyes. "You have to trust me, Kasey."

He sighed. He was upset with Gracey for keeping the truth from him, but he understood. In his heart, he knew how much she loved him, and he was convinced she'd done what she thought was best.

He didn't verbalize it, but he made a vow that he'd stop Jeremy before he could do any damage to anyone he cared about. Gracey had protected him his whole life, and now that she was withered and broken, it was his turn to protect her.

I was worried for Kasey's safety. Gracey was right, he didn't know anything about Jeremy. He had no idea of the cruelty that Jeremy was capable of.

Chapter 2

I shifted my thoughts away from them and was back in the attic with Reed. I kept my back toward him for a moment, not wanting to take my eyes off of the brilliant moon in the sky. Its light was the only illumination in the room. I didn't want to face my surroundings, the chair that I'd stood on or the noose that still hung from the rafters mocking me. I still can't face what I've done.

I rubbed my temples, finally turning around. Making contact with the mortal realm exhausted me, and as I looked into Reed's light blue eyes, I knew that he'd have endless questions for me, ones that I wasn't up to answering and most that I had no answers to.

He stared at me perplexed. "Now what's happened? You look upset."

"I just overheard Hilda and Gracey tell Kasey about his biological mother. It's Lucy, just as I thought. Jeremy knows. Before Kasey got there, the women were talking about it outside. He hid in the bushes and overheard them. Jeremy thinks that Kasey's his son."

"So he's not?"

I shook my head. "Kasey's father's name is Damon Shields. He was the man that my mother was in love with. I can't figure out why she was in love with him if he was involved with Lucy, but that doesn't matter now."

He ran his hand through his red hair. "So Jeremy's son has to be Jason."

Jason Beckett, the mysterious stranger who had recently arrived in Sleepy Meadows and had become involved with Rebecca Bowen my brother's childhood friend, was the other possibility I believed to be

Jeremy's son. The crazy old man who had given him a ride had accused Jason of being a Wickcliff. He'd said he'd seen it in his eyes. Jason hadn't known his family, but when I looked into his green eyes, the same color as Jeremy's, it reminded me of the intensity I'd seen in Jeremy's every time he'd drawn me to his portrait that kept me mesmerized.

"I believe so." I sighed. "There's something else. Kasey's figured out that Jeremy's inhabited your body."

"Are you kidding me? That's fantastic." He noticed my less than enthusiastic expression. "Isn't it?"

"It's not going to accomplish anything. It's not like he can go to your dad or anyone else. He starts talking about possession and he'll be locked up for being insane." I shook my head. "Poor Kasey."

"Poor Kasey? What about poor Reed?"

"This might not be paradise, but at least we're safe here. Kasey's in real danger."

"If Jason's Jeremy's son as you say, Kasey's not the only one in danger if Jeremy finds him. This whole town's screwed."

"I don't know enough about Jason to know whether or not he can be trusted. He may not be like Jeremy at all."

Reed shrugged. "If you ask me, I think it's freaky just how close Rebecca and Jason have become in such a short amount of time, at least that's what I gather from what you told me about their relationship. He could have Jeremy's powers. He could be screwing with her head. We need to figure out how much he knows and what his motives are."

I nodded. "You're right. I'm worried for Becca. I can see the longing in her eyes every time she looks at him. She wants him. I know she does. He's already got a hold over her."

I turned my back on Reed and looked out the window. During the time that Reed and I had been speaking, daylight had come, and the sun shone brightly in the sky. It saddened me that I could no longer feel the warmth of its rays on my skin. It wasn't as though I got out much in the last few years of my life, and the feeling of wastefulness I had for locking myself away added to my sadness. I exhaled deeply and shut my eyes, attempting to shut out my self-pity.

* * * *

I focused all of my energy on Jason and saw him down on the docks.

The wind was kicking up off the ocean and dampness filled the air around him. He put his hands in his pockets and patiently waited for Rebecca to meet him there as they'd agreed to do at Dad's wake. It wasn't long before I saw her approach him.

I could feel Rebecca's mixed emotions as she approached him. While she was attracted to him, this much she was sure, a part of her felt guilty for being so because she was already married to Pit Bowen. She hadn't loved Pit for a long time and wasn't sure that she ever did, but the religious upbringing that she was subjected to had taught her to be faithful, regardless of her unhappiness or attraction to someone else. Although the marriage was over, she still felt pangs of guilt.

Jason smiled widely at her, drew her to him, and kissed her passionately. "I missed you. I thought you'd never get here."

She laughed, wiping a piece of her brown hair out of her eyes that matched. "You called me and told me to be here before noon because you couldn't wait to see me and it's still not soon enough for you? You just saw me yesterday."

"That doesn't matter. An hour away from you feels like forever." He tried to kiss her again, but she pulled away. "What's wrong?"

"We're moving too fast here. We just met, and I'm still married."

He put his hands around her waist, pulling her closer to him again. "Married or not, you can't tell me that you aren't attracted to me, that you don't want me."

She tried to pull away. "This is wrong."

"Tell me you don't want me. Tell me that you love Pit. Look into my eyes and say that. If you can, I'll leave right now and never bother you again."

She looked away. "I can't do this."

He turned her head to face him. "Yes, you can. You told me yourself that your marriage was over. I saw how you interacted at the wake. There's no love lost on either side. This feels so right. I know you feel it too. I see it every time you look at me."

They kissed again. The whole time Rebecca tried to make sense of what it was about this man that had her so spellbound. As the passion overtook her, she stopped trying to figure it out.

She broke away and took him by the hand. "Come with me."

"Where are we going?"

"I want to take you to the place I was telling you about. It's very special to me, and I want you to see it."

He nodded and walked with her to her car. She'd planned to take him to the meadows, and I followed them as she drove. I saw the way that he looked at her, and I didn't know what to think. It was obvious that he wanted her, but I couldn't tell if it was genuine desire or if he was just using her for another purpose.

When they arrived at the meadows, she pulled over on the side of the road and turned off the engine.

Jason looked around. "Where are we?"

"This is called 'the meadows,' a quiet, peaceful place. This is my other special place beside the docks. I like to come here and think when I need to get away." She faced him. "Would you like to have lunch with me?"

"Where are we going to get lunch?"

She pointed to the back seat.

He looked back and saw a picnic basket. "Well you've just thought of everything, haven't you?"

She winked. "I try."

They got out of the car, and Jason took out the basket and blanket. They found a nice spot and set up. It was a beautiful day, sunny and much warmer than it had been.

I continued to study Jason's face, sensing vulnerability in him. While Jeremy had an arrogant, self-centered sense of importance, Jason was just struggling to find his place in the world and didn't know yet where he fit in. He had a physical resemblance to Jeremy, but they seemed to have different personalities.

Rebecca sat there staring into Jason's eyes as a warm breeze brushed her cheek. She smiled.

He smiled back. "Can I take that smile to mean that you don't regret being here with me?"

She took his hand. "I'm the one that brought you here. If I had any second thoughts about being here with you, I wouldn't have shown you this place."

"If you feel like we're moving too fast, we can slow down a bit, okay?"

She put her hand up. "I didn't mean what I said on the dock. I know my marriage is over. I never really had one to begin with. I was raised to believe that you stayed faithful to your partner regardless of the circumstances. I was told that it's the moral thing to do. Doing the right thing is what got me into trouble in the first place. I long for so much more. I can't tell you how much it means to me to have someone who desires me. It makes me feel special. I've never had that before."

He put his hand on top of hers. "You deserve to feel special because you are. I can't understand why Pit doesn't appreciate you. I think you're right about him. He does have an IQ of two."

She took her hand back. "I don't want to talk about him right now. I just want to focus on us, on being here with you."

"Can I ask you a question, Becca? There's something I need to know."

"You can ask me anything."

"Why did you marry a man you didn't love? Don't you realize that you're worth so much more? That you deserve so much more?"

She looked down. "I'm not proud of this, but shortly after I met Pit, I got pregnant. I come from a very religious family, and they insisted that we get married." She met eyes with him again. "It was the biggest mistake of my life."

"You have a child?"

"I lost the baby."

"I'm sorry. I didn't mean to bring up painful memories for you. I'm even sorrier that you had to go through that."

She wiped a single tear away. "Don't worry about it. In a way, it feels good to talk about my baby. I can't ever talk to Pit about the loss. He just gets infuriated. He blames me for our baby dying even though the doctors said there was nothing I could've done to prevent it." She exhaled. "I can't believe I'm telling you all this."

"I should've never asked such a personal question. I feel like an idiot."

"You're not. I made the mistake of getting into a loveless marriage, and I've got to deal with the consequences."

"You're not alone anymore, Becca. You don't have to be alone." He touched her cheek tenderly. "You need a man who will respect you in the way that you deserve. I feel a connection with you. I never knew my parents, and never had a stable home or many people to depend on. I've built up walls to protect himself from getting hurt. I never let anyone get too close, but I feel that changing."

He leaned in and kissed her, a long, soft kiss. I could feel her desire for him growing. She felt a connection to him that she'd never felt with anyone. She couldn't explain why she felt as if she'd known him her whole life. At the moment, she didn't want to try.

They stopped kissing and caught their breath.

"I know you don't love Pit, Becca. There's no reason for you to feel guilty about this."

"I don't want to anymore. I'm tired of the guilt, of the loneliness. As of this moment, that part of my life is over."

"Good because I don't believe he loves you. He looks at you as a possession. I'm not like that."

"I believe you."

"I know how to treat a woman with respect, with kindness. I treat people as human beings, and I don't degrade them like he so readily did at that wake. When I'm in love, I want the whole world to know it."

"You've been in love before?"

He nodded. "I was once, but she died. I vowed never to let another person get close to me. When I met you, everything changed."

"I'm sorry."

"It's alright. It took me a long time to accept that life has to go on, but I finally have."

They ate lunch and enjoyed a glass of Sangria before the formally brilliant blue sky became gray. Dark clouds began to form, and they heard thunder in the distance.

"I guess I didn't think of everything," Rebecca said, starting to pack up the basket. "I didn't check the weather forecast."

Jason put his hand on her arm. "You don't need to pack up yet."

"But the rain's coming."

He shrugged. "So? You aren't afraid of a little rain are you? I like storms. We can watch it come in."

"I don't want to get stuck in it. You aren't from here. We can get some pretty wicked ones this time of year."

He snickered. "Scaredy cat."

She hit him on the arm. "I am not. I just think we need to leave before we get caught in…" A crash of thunder disrupted her, and the rain started coming down in buckets. She shrieked.

Jason laughed. "Too late. Where the hell did this rain come from? It was so nice a minute ago. Weird weather."

"Welcome to Sleepy Meadows." She wiped the wet hair away from her forehead. "There's nothing normal about this place."

He pointed towards the Love Shack in the distance. "Let's pack up. We can seek shelter in there."

Seeing the shack made her think about the time she'd come to the meadows to be alone only to find Kasey and my brother there. Neither he nor Kasey knew she'd seen them together, but that's when she'd realized my brother would never love her in the way she'd wanted him to. All she wanted to focus on now was making new memories in this place.

They got to the shack, opened up the door, and peered inside. It was dark due to the rain, but there was a kerosene lamp on a table by the door and a box of matches beside it. Jason got the lamp lit and glanced around the room.

"I thought this place was abandoned, but it looks like someone's been here."

"We're soaked," she said, poking him in the side. "I told you we should've packed up."

His teeth chattered. "I don't think I've ever been this cold. How embarrassing."

"Take your clothes off."

His eyes widened, and he smirked. "Excuse me?"

She motioned to chair in the corner. "There's a blanket over there. It'll help keep us warm."

She watched as he removed his shirt, taking notice of what great shape he was in. She grabbed the blanket, took off her shirt, and wrapped it around them.

He gazed at her noticing the rain still dripping from her hair.

"What is it, Jason?"

He looked away. "Nothing."

The Possession

She put her hand on his chin and turned his face towards her. "Something I think. It's okay. I want this too."

He pressed his hands against her back and pulled her closer to him. He pressed his lips to hers, kissing her with an aching need.

I knew where this was going, so I looked away. Once they'd finished making love, I looked upon them again; still not convinced that I could trust Jason to be alone with her.

"That was amazing," he said.

She chuckled. "You're telling me. I've never experienced anything quite like that."

As they laid there listening to the rain, my curiosity about Jason continued to be piqued. I didn't think that he could be trusted by Wickcliff association. I wondered if he was like Rory, a good man who only wanted to make her happy, or if he really was his father's son.

Jeremy had promised Lucy a life full of happiness and love only to destroy her. I didn't want to see the same thing happen to Rebecca.

Chapter 3

I looked away from Rebecca and Jason and faced Reed again. "She slept with him. What was she thinking?"

"Becca?" Reed said. "She probably wasn't getting any satisfaction from Pit, so she stopped thinking altogether and got some action elsewhere."

I nodded. "I can understand the need for affection, but she doesn't even know anything about him. What if he's just like his father? I can't believe she'd be so desperate."

Reed smiled deviously.

I put my hands on my hips. "What's that smirk for?"

"Pit's done nothing but treat me like crap. Forgive me if I take a little bit of pleasure in the fact that his wife's screwing around on him. It's the best news I've gotten since I've been trapped in this prison."

I shrugged. "I feel sorry for him. He started to show some sympathy for me when Gaul and Jeremy tried to cover up my death. He may be rough around the edges, but I'm not convinced that he's all bad."

"Trust me. Pit Bowen's a selfish bastard that doesn't care about anyone but himself. If it weren't for him dragging me to this house, I wouldn't be in this situation."

"Pit doesn't matter. I've learned that you can't trust the Wickcliffs. I have to get back to the mortal realm, and not just in my mind. I need to be there for my son and my family."

"And how do you propose to do that? Jeremy had his painting taken downstairs. We don't have the portal anymore."

"I'm not sure, but if Jeremy can do it and if he can bring Rachel back, there's got to be a way."

Reed sighed heavily. "There it is."

My eyes narrowed. "There what is?"

"I was waiting for the time to come when you were going to ditch me, just like everyone does. My mother, Kasey…"

"Your mother died, she didn't ditch you, and while Kasey doesn't love you like you want him to, neither did he. I could see how much he cares for you when he talked about Jeremy possessing you. You aren't alone, Reed. We're in this thing together."

He scoffed. "Yeah right. You know, you asked me to trust you. You promised me that if I did, you'd find us a way out of here. We've been up here for days, and it's driving me nuts. If you can figure out how to get out, go ahead and leave, but I'm not going to stay here alone."

I put my hand up. "I'm not going to abandon you. Where I go, you go. I know this is hard for you, but please, you just have to be patient a little bit longer. My powers are getting stronger every day. It'll only be a matter of time before I figure a way out of here."

"Well, I don't have time to stand around here and wait. The longer I'm stuck here, the greater the chance that I'll never make it back. I'll find my own way out."

"Reed, don't do anything stupid."

He stuck out his chest. "So now I'm stupid? Just because you threw away your life because of some psychopath doesn't mean that I don't want to get my life back. Just because you wanted to die doesn't mean I've got to."

His comment stung me, and I couldn't hide the hurt in my eyes. "I didn't want to die. Jeremy tortured me for years. I fought against him for as long and for as hard as I could until I couldn't stand it anymore."

He groaned and ran his hands through his hair. "I'm sorry. I didn't mean that. I'm scared, and I'm taking it out on you."

I pointed to my chest. "I'm scared too, but we can't turn on each other. We need each other. Don't worry, I'll get us out of here. Time's of the essence for you especially."

"I know that, but something else is wrong. I can see it written all over your face. What is it that you aren't telling me?"

I didn't know how to tell Reed that I'd heard Hilda mention that Jeremy's spirit was eventually going to die in his body, making his chances of returning bleaker. He was upset enough. I didn't see the point in telling him that I wanted to get close enough to Jeremy to be able to save Reed's mortal life, especially since I didn't know if I could.

"I just meant that I know how important getting your life back is to you." I gave him a reassuring look. "Trust me?"

He slumped his shoulders forward. "I suppose."

"I want you to promise me that you won't try to find another way out of here. We don't know what's out there, and I don't want to have to worry about you. I've got enough on my mind as it is."

He sighed. "I promise."

I gave him a nod and a half-smile. "Good."

I went back over to the window and gazed out upon Sleepy Meadows. If I was going to find out Jason's true motives, I had to put aside my fears about trying to get back to the mortal realm and my worry for Reed. I cleared my mind and focused all my attention on Rebecca.

* * * *

I hadn't seen it because I was talking to Reed, but by the time Rebecca came into focus, she'd already left Jason and was home. The feeling of elation that she'd had from being with Jason lessened with every step she took closer to the door. Dread replaced it, because even though she'd ended things with Pit, she couldn't avoid seeing him again if she wanted her belongings.

She opened the door of their small house and found him sitting in his favorite, worn recliner chair in the living room.

He pushed the mute button on the TV and stood up. "What the hell are you doing here? Did you come to gloat some more about your boy toy?"

She set down her purse and keys on a stand near the door. "I'm not here to fight with you. I just wanted to get some of my clothes." She went toward the bedroom.

"Haven't you done enough by humiliating me in front of half the town at the wake?" he said, following her. "I bet you just came to rub it in."

She turned to face him. "You did that all by yourself. You didn't need any help from me to make yourself look like a fool. You never did.

Now leave me alone. It's obvious we have nothing left to say to each other. You wanted me to get my stuff out, and that's all I'm here for. This sham of a marriage is over."

"It's only a sham because you made it that way. You never even gave me a chance. You never even tried."

"I want more, Pit, and that isn't you. It never was. You were right about Jason and me."

He scoffed. "What happened to 'we're just friends'? What crap."

"That was then, and this is now. I'm falling in love, and I won't allow you to stand in the way of my happiness anymore. Do you understand?"

He looked away.

She stood there waiting for some response. "What's the matter? Don't you have anything to say? Don't you want to tell me what a whore I am? That was always your favorite thing to say to me when you talked to me at all. I have an idea. Why don't you try to hit me again?"

He glared at her, and I could feel his contempt for her growing. "I'm not going to fight with you anymore. It's not worth it."

Rebecca put her hands on her hips "What's wrong with you? You're acting even stranger than normal. First you cause a scene at the wake because Jason shows up, and then when I tell you it's over, you don't even react." She sighed. "I get it. You don't care if I leave you at all. The little display you gave at the wake was just to try to humiliate me in public. You don't care about how I made you look. Everyone knows how you've treated me and they don't think very highly of you anyway. You just did it to embarrass me in front of my friends. You had to get in that one last dig, didn't you?"

He chuckled. "There you go again thinking that you're the center of the universe. I'm not going to fall apart just because you're leaving. I'm not the same man I was. The things I've seen and done would change any man."

She squinted. "What are you talking about?"

"Don't worry about it. You don't care about me anyway. You never did. Now get your stuff and get the hell outta my house."

She grabbed his arm. "Not until you tell me what's going on. You're in some sort of trouble, aren't you? I shouldn't be surprised."

He yanked himself away. "It doesn't matter. Nothing matters anymore."

She studied his face closely. "I've never seen you like this. You look genuinely afraid of something. I didn't think anything could scare you."

"Why are you so insistent that I talk to you about this? It's too late to start acting like you care about me now. I'm just the man you hate."

"I don't hate you. I feel sorry for you. That's part of the reason I stayed. But I can't do it anymore."

"Promise me something. You have to stay away from Jason. He's dangerous."

Her eyes widened. "Excuse me?"

"Stay away from him, Becca. I've come face-to-face with pure evil. I see the same look in his eyes. It's unmistakable."

She scoffed. "There it is. I was just waiting for the other shoe to drop. I knew that this reformed man act was nothing but a crock. You resent me because I'm happy for once. I'm sure the only evil you see is when you look in the mirror."

He grabbed her arms, shaking her. "You don't understand. This is serious."

She shoved him away. "What I understand is that you're a cold, unfeeling, jealous, shallow man who's so miserable and insecure that you want everyone around you to feel the same way."

Pit lowered his eyes. "Don't say I didn't warn you. When the sick bastard cuts your throat in the middle of the night, don't expect me to shed a tear."

She clapped her hands. "I've got to give you credit. I almost believed that there was something different about you, but I can see that you're the same. You're the one that's the sick bastard. I loathe you."

"You just said you didn't hate me."

She started to walk away. "Temporary insanity."

He grabbed her arm and made her face him again. "You're so smug, aren't you, you little bitch? You deserve whatever you get."

She yanked her arm away at the same time Pit's cell phone rang. He took it out of his pocket. The caller ID read 'Reed'. He stood there, frozen.

"Aren't you going to answer that? It's probably one of your drinking buddies that got arrested again, lookin' for bail money."

Pit grasped the phone tighter in his hand. "I don't know why I even bother. You never listen to me. If you know what's good for you, get as far away from Sleepy Meadows and Jason as you can. It isn't safe here, and you aren't safe with him."

She turned back around. "I do know what's good for me, and that's why I'm getting the hell away from you." She headed towards the door. "Goodbye, Pit. You'll be hearing from my lawyer. I'll arrange a time to come get my stuff with the police."

"Why would you need the police? You don't trust me at all, do you?"

She laughed. "You said that, not me. You threatened to throw my stuff in the street. I'd hoped that we could do this civilly when I came here, but it's obvious I'll need backup. I should've known better."

"You're afraid of the wrong man. Your trust in Jason is idiotic."

Rebecca turned, glared at him, and walked out, saying nothing more. After a moment, the phone rang again and this time, Pit answered it.

"I'm disappointed in you, Mr. Bowen," Jeremy said, on the other end. "I warned you what would happen if you didn't make yourself available to me when I needed you. Don't make me say it again. There's nothing I find more tedious than repeating myself."

"I did what you wanted. Please, just leave me alone." He tried to hang up, but Jeremy kept on.

"We're not done until I say we are. Get over here. I have a job for you. Oh, and Mr. Bowen, don't think about running because I'll find you. If I have to chase you, I'll make you beg for death."

Hearing Jeremy say that to Pit reminded me of the night I'd taken my life, how I'd preferred death over his torture. I'd never known anyone could be so incredibly ruthless. I began to think about Jason, and what Pit said about seeing evil in his eyes. Was it true that Jason was like his father or was it a lie concocted by a jealous husband in an attempt to keep he and Rebecca apart?

David Chappuis & Michael Klinger

Chapter 4

I got nervous when I heard Jeremy summon Pit to the mansion. I could feel that it had something to do with his plan for Kasey, and although he wasn't Jeremy's son, Jeremy didn't know that, and it put Kasey in grave danger. I wanted to warn him, but he was still finding a way to shut me out. After encountering Jeremy's sister, Rachel, at my father's wake, he was convinced that everything I'd shown him was real. She may have looked and sounded like me, but her whole demeanor was different. He knew she wasn't me, and knew that he'd have to learn to trust his visions. That was the problem. He was afraid of his visions and didn't want to accept them.

I thought about who else might be able to help me warn Kasey. Hilda was strong and was able to see spirits, and although she hadn't seen or heard me before, I thought I'd try again. She knew that Jeremy was back but didn't know Jeremy's plans for Kasey.

Night had fallen, and as Hilda came into focus, I saw her lying in bed in the cozy guest bedroom at Gracey's house. The room was filled with antique walnut furniture including an armoire and pictures of their coven covered the walls. This made Hilda feel at home. Before I could say a word, I heard the faint sound of another woman's voice whispering her name.

Hilda stirred and sat up in bed, waiting for the voice to call out again. She wasn't afraid. She'd frequently been awoken by spirits, and this wasn't anything new. Her instincts told her that Lucy was attempting to make contact with her again.

"Lucy, I know it's you. Please speak to me."

She waited for an answer, and when one didn't come, she lay her head back down on her pillow. It was only a moment before we both heard the voice again.

"Hil...da..."

She sat up again and spoke softly. "Let me see you. I can feel that your spirit's restless. It has something to do with Jeremy. That much I'm sure."

Having never known Lucy, I didn't recognize the voice, but Hilda did. I thought this might be my chance to get through to Hilda. I could do it through Lucy.

"Lucy, if you can hear me, I need you to listen. My name's Shelly Wickcliff, and I'm a friend of your son, Kasey. He's in danger. Jeremy thinks the two of them are father and son since you're his mother. Jeremy needs to possess someone of his bloodline if he's going to remain alive, and he's going to use Kasey. Kasey has abilities. He'll be able to hear you. Otherwise, you can tell Hilda, but I need to get him this message."

I waited to see if Lucy would respond, but I got nothing. I knew she could hear me. She's a spirit just as I am. Why was she not responding to me?

"Please, Lucy, respond or, at least, tell Hilda what I'm telling you. She can get the message to Kasey."

Still getting no response, I turned my attention back to Hilda. She turned on a lamp by her bedside, got out of bed, and put on her robe. She shivered and ran her hands over her arms.

"I can feel that you need help coming through," Hilda said. "I want you to listen to the sound of my voice. Block out everything else and concentrate. I'm going to bring you through. I call upon the powers of goodness and light to help me communicate with this lost soul. Let the wind carry my voice and help me transcend the barrier between the living and the dead. I call upon the Earth, the Moon, the Sun, the sky, and the stars to allow our two worlds to become one tonight. Speak to me my dear Lucy."

Lucy's voice, at first, faint, had grown stronger and more distinguished. "I need your help, Hilda. Yours, Carol's, and Gracey's. I need my sisters."

By the window, Lucy's specter appeared. She was young, radiant.

The Possession

Her long blond locks fell on her shoulders softly. Her blue eyes sparkled as she spoke.

Hilda reached out to her, her eyes filled with tears. "You know we'd do anything for you. What is it?"

"I need to come back to the mortal realm during the next Midnight's Edge. I can fight Jeremy. I can stop him as I did before, but I can't do it alone. I need your power."

"So you know what Jeremy's planning to do?"

"My sons are in danger. Jeremy's presence in the mortal realm, and, in particular, Sleepy Meadows jeopardizes their very existence. He's already returned Rachel from the depths of darkness. If he's not stopped soon, there will be others."

Hilda put her hand on her heart. "It's happening again, isn't it? Just as it did ages ago."

Lucy nodded. "I know you feel as though you have to confront them, but you can't. You're not strong enough to do it on your own. None of us is alone. We have to stick together, use our powers as one. I want you to promise me that you'll keep your distance until we can confront him together." Lucy began to fade away. "My time's short. I need you all to go to Lover's Bluff where I died tomorrow night during Midnight's Edge. I need my sisters to help me rise from the depths of the sea. Wait for me, dear friend, wait for me..."

"Lucy wait," I said. *"What about Kasey?"*

Lucy vanished, and Hilda called out. "Please don't go, not yet."

I called out to Hilda, but she didn't respond. The connection she'd had with Lucy had been so strong that she had no room for me. Connecting with Lucy had also taken a toll on her, and I could feel her exhaustion. Now was not the time for me to get through. Hilda wiped her tear-filled eyes and got back into bed. She finally fell asleep and spent the rest of the night having nightmares about Jeremy, Rachel, and the rest of the Wickcliffs returning to Sleepy Meadows.

I was discouraged that Lucy hadn't acknowledged me and that Hilda hadn't heard me, but I did learn one important thing. I'd learned that Lucy had more than one son. If that were true and if Jason was Jeremy's son, then Lucy was most likely his mother. That made Kasey and Jason half-brothers.

*　*　*　*

Once daylight came, I focused my attention on Hilda again. The sun shone brightly, but the fear that she had inside her made her feel like it was as dark and cold as midnight. She felt it surround her whole being.

She got out of bed and groaned. Her joints hurt, very much like Gracey's did, and it concerned her. When they'd fought with Jeremy for survival decades ago, she'd been younger and healthy enough for the fight. The years hadn't been kind to her. She was weaker, frailer, as Kasey had observed. There were times where her mind felt foggy and confused, and she wondered if she'd be strong enough to help bring Lucy back. She was overwhelmed at the prospect of telling Gracey and Mom about Lucy's visit, and what they'd have to do tonight.

Hilda entered the kitchen and saw Gracey sitting at the table drinking tea.

"Good morning, sleep well?" Gracey asked.

"Hardly at all," Hilda said, approaching the table.

"Me either. I've had a terrible feeling all morning, and I can't stop thinking about our conversation with Kasey. I thought I'd feel better once I told him the truth about his parents, but I don't. I'm worried that he's going to go after Jeremy himself even though I specifically told him not to."

Hilda sat down. "Speaking of Jeremy, I need to talk to you about him, but Carol should be here as well."

"Why?"

Hilda took Gracey's hand. "Please. There's very little time. Just call Carol."

Gracey called Mom who said she'd be right over.

*　*　*　*

Mom was at our family home with my grandmother, Edith, who was becoming increasingly suspicious about Mom's behavior since Dad died. Gram wasn't stupid, and she knew that the reasons why Mom had been so distant towards her had more to do with than just being a grieving widow. She could always tell when Mom was hiding something, and it wasn't going to be long before she confronted her with it. I found them in the kitchen, which was towards the back of the house that led to a side porch, the most used entrance to the house.

"Who was on the phone?" Gram asked, catching Mom just as she was about to leave. She had an inquisitive expression on her face.

Gram may have been in her eighties, but she was still strong and spunky. She knew Mom was hiding something. She didn't know it had to do with Jeremy, but she was going to be like a dog with a bone until she found out. I learned that the night I'd died when she'd come to the house to ask Jeremy's mother, Irma, the only surviving member of the family about my whereabouts.

"Out," Mom replied.

"Where, may I ask?"

Mom released her hand from the back kitchen door and faced Gram.

"To Gracey's place, if you really must know."

Gram sighed. "Caroline, you know I don't like you hanging out with that woman. Must you go?"

"Honestly, Mother. I'm fifty years old, and you're still trying to tell me who I can associate with. I'm not a child."

"Then don't act like one and I won't treat you like one."

Mom put her hands on her hips. "What's that supposed to mean?"

"Don't think I haven't noticed the secret telephone calls and your distance with me. I know you're up to something. I'm not as senile as Irma's pretending to be. I know something's wrong."

Mom didn't say anything about Hilda being back in town. I got the feeling that Gram didn't care for Hilda much. While she didn't care for Gracey much either, she tolerated her.

"Everything's alright, Mom. Stop worrying."

Gram watched her leave from the back porch. She and Mom never had the ideal mother and daughter relationship. Despite the strained relationship due to Mom's pursuit of witchcraft, she never stopped loving Mom.

"You're hiding something, Caroline," she said to herself once Mom was out of sight. "I just pray that whatever it is doesn't destroy us."

* * * *

Back at Gracey's, Hilda appeared restless as she and Gracey waited for Mom to arrive. She kept looking out the window anxiously. It wasn't long before Mom arrived and walked up the path. Gracey let her in, and she approached Hilda, who was sitting at the table.

"Now what's happened?" Mom asked brushing aside a piece of her short, black hair. "This is the second time you two have asked me to rush over here in a hurry. Does this have something to do with Jeremy?"

"In a way," Hilda said. "I've discovered that Jeremy's planning to return all of the Wickcliffs to the mortal realm. He's obviously powerful enough that he can do so since he was strong enough to return during Midnight's Edge. He's already returned his sister, Rachel, although I'm not positive of the form she's taken. His powers have grown tremendously over the years that he's been gone, and I fear what it means for us and everyone we love. No one would be safe if he succeeds."

Mom crossed her arms. "Did Lucy tell you this?"

"Her spirit's restless. She's convinced that the longer he stays here, the more unstoppable he'll become. She's going to help us."

"I don't know how she can help us. She's in the spirit realm. We're alive."

"If things go according to plan, she will be too."

Gracey's eyes widened, and she sat down. "What are you saying?"

"Jeremy still loves Lucy even though part of him resents her for what she did to him. She's his vulnerability, and we need her. Tonight's Midnight's Edge, and we're to go to Lover's Bluff where she died."

Gracey put her hand up. "If you're talking about resurrecting her, I don't know if I have the strength. I haven't used my powers in so long. I'm weak. I can barely get around."

Hilda's eyes expressed sympathy and understanding. "I know you're scared, Gracey, so am I, but we can't bring Lucy back without you, and if we don't succeed in doing that, we don't stand a chance against Jeremy. We have to stick together. She knows what his motives are, and has insight that we need."

"The bastard killed my husband," Mom said. "I won't let Jeffrey's death be in vain. So we meet at the bluff near Midnight?"

Hilda nodded. "As you may remember about Midnight's Edge, the ritual has to be completed by midnight or it won't work." She looked at Gracey and clasped her hand. "Please, you can't stand by and let him take over this town."

"I'll do what I can," Gracey said. "My son's in grave danger due to Jeremy's presence here. I'll do anything to protect him from that monster, even if it means sacrificing my very soul."

* * * *

Kasey had no idea what Jeremy had in store for him and for some reason, the woman I'd recently learned was his mother, wouldn't help me warn him. Maybe she wanted to be the one to protect Kasey like she had when he was a baby, but I wasn't sure if I had faith in Lucy's plan to return to the mortal realm. From the conversation I'd overheard between her and Hilda, she was confident that she would be able to stop him if given the opportunity, but her prior attempt resulted in her losing her life. I couldn't count on Lucy and the coven. There was no way of telling whether their attempt to resurrect Lucy would even work. I had to warn Kasey in my way and to do that I needed to find out what Jeremy's plan entailed.

As the parlor of this house came into focus, I noticed that the morning sun poured through the windows of the room, which was near the front door. It was the most light I'd seen coming into the house in years. Everything in the house had seen its better days. Although everything in the house was expensive and rare, the furniture and draperies were worn, dusty and soiled, and the musty smell of mildew penetrated the air. There was a chill that seemed never to leave, although the sun did seem to help some.

I saw Rachel there peering out the window, still incredulous that Jeremy had been successful in bringing her back to life. She never thought she'd see the sun again. She stood with her dark hair pulled back against her pale skin. Every time I see Rachel, it's still a shock. It's like looking into a mirror, but the difference is I know that it's not me staring back at myself.

"What a glorious morning," she said. "I'd almost forgotten what it felt like to be alive, not like I had a real life before. I have a shot at a life now. Isn't it grand?"

"It certainly is," Jeremy said, entering the room behind her. "It's even grander to see you so happy." His smile broadened, a smile once belonging to Reed. It faded when he noticed that she'd become melancholy. "Rachel, what is it?"

"I asked you not to call me by that hideous name." She sighed heavily. "I just can't help but think about all those years I spent alone locked in the tower room. It was so lonely, so dark and cold. I was a grotesque monster then. I'll never forget the countless days, weeks, years that I spent in that place feeling unloved." She turned to the window again and grimaced. "I would've never been able to experience a day like this before. I went up to that room when I was on my way to see Mother, yesterday. I saw myself in the mirror, my true self. I don't ever want to see that hideous sight again."

He approached her and met eyes with her. It was the first time I saw any hint of compassion in his eyes. "It wasn't real. You know that, don't you?"

"I want to believe that."

"Well you can, and believe this too, you were never unloved. You had me."

"And Gaul." She didn't believe Jeremy any more now than she had the first time he'd said it, but she didn't let on. "He was always so kind to me. You always said he wasn't capable of that kind of emotion, but you were wrong. He did care. He'd talk to me, entertain me, anything I wanted. He made it a lot less lonely."

Jeremy raised a brow. "I had no idea that Gaul ever did that."

"He was always loyal."

"Still is." He tugged on her arm and smiled. "Come on. You don't have to be sad anymore. You aren't the same. You can go out among others without stares and snickers. You can go into the sun without getting deathly ill. You don't need to be quarantined. You have a second chance at life. We both do."

She smiled. "I suppose you're right."

"Have you seen Mother this morning?"

"No, I haven't seen her at all yet. I got distracted yesterday after my experience in the tower."

He frowned, noticing her forlorn expression again. "I wish you'd stay out of there. There's nothing for you there except painful memories. Why don't we see Mother together?"

She shrugged. "I suppose we could. I suppose she'd think I was Shelly if she even remembers her at all. From what you said, she doesn't remember much. Seeing her in such a sad state might make me forget all about my horrible experience in the tower. I have to focus on the positive things in life, one of which I consider seeing our mother weak, senile, and frail."

He shook his head. "She remembers you. She mentioned you the last time I spoke to her. In fact, she remembered you and not me."

Her eyes narrowed. "Really?"

He nodded, not telling her that what Irma said about her was negative. I got the feeling that Rachel was pleased just to be remembered at all. Despite how she'd insulted Irma, deep down I felt the need she had for her mother's approval.

Jeremy gestured with a wave of his hand. "Come now. It's a new day. Maybe seeing us and knowing we've come home will bring her back to reality."

They went up the stairs together and intercepted Gaul in the hallway who was heading to Irma's room with a food tray. Jeremy took the tray he was holding. "I'll take Mother her breakfast. Thank you, Gaul."

Gaul nodded, turned, and walked down the hallway without speaking a word. They went into the room to find Irma awake, sitting up in a chair by an open window. It was the first time since Jeremy had been back that he'd seen her out of bed. He took that as a sign she was recovering. He walked up to her and took her hand.

"Mother?"

Irma turned her head to face him. In the daylight, she was an even more frightening sight. Her hair was white and spiked all around her head, in wild, crazed fashion. Her bright eyes bulged out from her sunken in, wrinkled face.

"Jeremy? You came to see me last night, didn't you?" She nodded. "I know you did. I remember. I thought I was having a nightmare. Why are you here?"

His face fell. "I was hoping for a warmer welcome than you referring to my return as a nightmare." He bent down so that he could lock eyes with her. "It's a long story, one that you probably wouldn't even begin to understand, but I've taken on the body of a mortal so that I could come back to this world and take care of you."

She stared him up and down and groaned. "How did you do it?

What did you have to sacrifice to come back from the pit of hell?" She paused. "Forget it. I don't want to know."

"It's time that I reclaim the life stolen from me, Mother. You have to remember what Lucy did to me."

Irma scoffed. "You made that poor girl miserable from the day that she moved into this house. You got what you deserved if you ask me." She rolled her eyes and looked away. "Just when I thought I'd gotten rid of my psychopathic, pathetic son, here you are again." She looked up at the ceiling. "The universe is cruel. Why must you torture an old woman?"

As he glanced at her, I saw a vulnerability I'd never before seen in him. He appeared genuinely hurt by Irma's rejection.

He cleared his throat. "You aren't the least bit happy to see me? I don't understand why you'd say these things."

She turned back to face him and snickered. "Happy? I was until now. Face it, Jeremy. You've always been two bricks shy of a full load. You get that from your father's side of the family."

He stood up and crossed his arms. "You've always spoken your mind, Mother. I always admired you for that. But, I don't appreciate your tone or your insinuations."

"And I don't appreciate you coming back right when I'm at the height of my sexual peak. I've spent my entire life looking out for you spoiled, crazy, ungrateful children. I finally have the ability to go out and find myself a strapping young buck, and you had to go and ruin it. No man wants to be tied down to a woman with children." She stifled a sob.

Rachel, who had been silent, spoke up, looking at Jeremy. "And she calls you crazy."

Irma turned to her and scowled. "This is a family matter between me and my son, Shelly. I'll thank you to keep your opinions to yourself."

Jeremy put his arm around Rachel. "Mother, this isn't Shelly. Shelly's dead."

Irma grunted and waved her hand to dismiss him. "I know who she is." She put her hands on the sides of her head. "Stop trying to confuse me."

"Mother, this is Rachel. She's come back and survives in another body just as I do."

The Possession

Chapter 5

Irma gasped and put her hand to her cheek. "Rachel? How? Why? When?"

"I'll explain it all later. The point is we're here, and we can be a family again."

"Take me now," Irma said, looking up towards the ceiling. "I'm ready."

Rachel scoffed and stepped towards her. "It's nice to see you too, Mother. Do you have any idea how many women would give everything they have in the world to get back a child they lost? You should count your blessings."

Irma glared at her. "Some blessing. You children were nothing but a curse since the day you were born. Especially you, Rachel."

Rachel's face tightened. "I know what you think of me, Mother. You proved it every day when you kept me locked up like some diseased animal. You could've at least pretended to give a damn about me."

Irma sighed heavily. "It's not my fault that you were an ugly child even before you became ill. People used to tell me that you had a face only a mother could love. I responded by saying that wasn't true in every case."

Jeremy put his hand up. "Mother, stop."

"Let her speak, Jeremy. Let her try to justify what she did to me while she lied to everyone and said I was away at school."

"We couldn't very well tell people that you had a fatal illness," Irma said. "Think of the scandal, dear. I wanted to send you away where they could deal with monstrosities like you, but your father resisted, too guilt-ridden over what he'd done."

Rachel glanced at Jeremy. "What's she talking about?" He didn't answer, so she looked back at Irma. "What does Father have to do with what happened to me?"

"Pay her no mind," Jeremy said, firmly. "She obviously doesn't know what she's saying."

Irma chuckled. "I know what I'm saying. It was no accident that Rachel was so grotesque." She pointed to the door. "Get out of my sight, both of you."

"You call me grotesque?" Rachel said, leaning into her. "Do you have any idea what the hell you look like, old woman?"

Irma's eyes widened. "What do you mean? I'm radiant. All my suitors tell me so."

Rachel got closer to her and bent down to stare into her mother's eyes. A twisted smile crossed her face. "Your suitors, huh? You think you could get one to be interested in you now?"

"Of course." Irma raised her nose in the air.

"Of course," Rachel said, mimicking her and standing straight up. She clapped her hands and laughed. "You're right, Mother. There are tons of men out there attracted to senile, crotchety, old bitches that are bound to wheelchairs, are diaper dependent, and reek of piss. I can see the attraction. I'm surprised they aren't lined up for miles."

Irma's upper lip stiffened, and she sat up straighter in her chair. "That isn't true. I'm vibrant and beautiful."

Rachel guffawed. "You're delusional."

Jeremy pulled Rachel away. "Let's just go."

"Get out, I said!" Irma pointed to the door again.

Rachel pushed away from Jeremy. "When was the last time you looked in a mirror, Mother? I bet it's been awhile."

"Rachel, stop it," Jeremy said.

She turned to face him. "No way am I going to miss this chance."

"I may be getting on in years, but I still look better than you," Irma said. "Always have, always will."

"Oh, yeah?" Rachel turned back around, went over to Irma's dressing table, and picked up a handheld mirror. She went back to her and put it in front of her mother's face. "Look at this."

Irma let out a shriek, grabbed the mirror, and threw it at the wall shattering it.

Rachel snickered. "Tsk. Tsk. That's seven years bad luck, Mother. Lucky for you, you won't be around that long."

"That wasn't me," Irma said, trying to catch her breath. "You children are playing a cruel joke."

Rachel shrugged, laughing. "Why would we want to do that to such a loving and devoted mother?"

Irma began sobbing hysterically. "I look like the walking dead." She placed her hands on her cheeks. "I'm going to be alone for the rest of my life!"

Rachel wiped a tear from her eye and tried to stifle the laughter. "I think you can hold out for a month, maybe two at the most, don't you?"

Irma glared at her children for a moment before beginning to scream. "Who are you people? What are you doing in my room? Harold help, call the police!"

Jeremy led Rachel out of the room. "Let's just go." When they entered the hallway, he faced her. "Was it necessary for you to be so cruel to the woman who bore us?"

Rachel was still chuckling. "Come on, you have to admit that it was fun to play with her." She nudged him. "She did it to us enough when we were kids. Sorry, but, as they say, payback's a bitch, just like her."

As I watched them walk down the stairs and back into the foyer, I wondered what Irma meant when she said that Harold, her deceased husband, and Jeremy and Rachel's father, felt guilty for his actions regarding Rachel. I didn't understand what he had to do with what happened to her in life, and given Irma's state, whatever she said must be taken with a grain of salt.

* * * *

Outside of the house, I saw Hilda coming up the overgrown, brick path that led to the door. Despite Lucy's pleas for her not to confront Jeremy alone, she was determined to do it.

I could see by the expression on Hilda's face that she was in pain, but she wasn't going to let Jeremy see that. She knocked, and waited patiently for someone to come to the door.

Hilda blamed Jeremy for Lucy's destruction. If he hadn't needed to be stopped, Lucy would've never felt the need to sacrifice herself. She knew that he killed my father too, and at that moment, although concerned for her, I was also envious of the opportunity she had to confront him because that's all I wanted to do.

Greta answered the door, with a stern expression on her face as usual.

"Yes?"

"Good afternoon," Hilda said. "Is Mrs. Wickcliff here?"

"I don't know who you are or what you want, but I'm sick of people coming here to harass Mrs. Wickcliff. She's not well, and is no longer receiving visitors."

Greta tried to shut the door, but Hilda put her hand on it. "No need for hostility. I just want to come in for a moment."

Greta sighed. "If you don't want hostility, leave. Mrs. Wickcliff's not lucid, and I'm terribly busy. There's no reason for you to be here."

Greta tried to shut the door once more, but Hilda put her other hand up, commanding her to stop. "I didn't want to have to do this, but you don't leave me any choice. Keep looking into my eyes. You can't look away."

Greta was unable to take her eyes off Hilda. "You're going to do as I tell you, aren't you?"

Greta nodded slowly, dazed. "Who are you and what are you doing to me?"

"Don't worry. I'm not going to harm you, just step aside and let me in."

Other than the day that my father died, and I first found out my mother was a witch, I hadn't seen any of their powers at work. Granted that getting Greta to let her into the house may have been simple, it showed Hilda's powers were strong enough to manipulate the maid's will. Seeing this gave me a shred of hope that if the witches worked together, they might be strong enough to fight Jeremy.

Greta stepped aside, and Hilda entered the foyer. Greta shut the door behind her. Hilda glanced around the room taking in her surroundings. It had been decades since she'd been in the mansion, and she was shocked by its condition. The once shiny marble floor had become dull and dingy. The exquisite art that hung on the fabric layered walls in the foyer was covered with dust and cobwebs. It didn't look like the house she'd remembered at all, the one envied for its beauty and feared for its secrets.

She turned to the left and entered the parlor. Greta remained silent following behind her. The first thing Hilda noticed was the large portrait of Jeremy on the wall, and she turned to face Greta. "Where's Jeremy?"

Greta feigned innocence. "Mr. Wickcliff's dead. Everyone knows that."

"Please don't lie to me. This will go much smoother if you just tell me the truth."

"I'm not lying."

Hilda clenched her fists tightly, and a sharp gust of wind forced a window open, blowing over a glass vase that shattered on the floor.

Greta gasped, and her eyes widened. "I knew there was something different about you when I answered the door. Now I'm convinced that I was right. You aren't human. What are you?"

"It's none of your concern. Tell him that Hildagarde's here. He'll know me."

"I already told you. There's no Jeremy here."

Hilda heard footsteps approaching, looked past Greta, and saw Jeremy standing at the door. She hadn't met Reed, but she didn't have to. She felt Jeremy's presence. It was evident in his demeanor. The way he stood and grinned at her in a cocky manner that was his trademark. It made Hilda's body turn cold, her bones rigid, and her stomach sour.

"That will be all, Greta," Jeremy said.

Hilda stood silently for a moment studying him. He stood with his chest puffed out and his head high, with the same arrogance he'd always had. His eyes bore into her with pure hate. He tried to downplay it, but she knew better. He could take on a new body, but he couldn't change his soul.

"I'd hoped that I'd never see you again, Jeremy, and here we are."

He smiled and approached her. "I'm afraid I don't understand."

Hilda put her hand up. "Don't come near me. I know who you are. There's no need for this flimsy ruse."

He shrugged. "Ruse? There's no ruse. I don't believe we've met before, ma'am."

"Save it. I know it's you. I'd recognize you anywhere."

The Possession

He nodded and exhaled. "I see. I'm sure you realize that this knowledge puts you in an extremely dangerous situation." He sauntered in front of the fireplace and picked up his wine glass from the mantel, taking a sip. "I wondered how long it would take for one of you old bitches to show up."

Before Hilda could respond, Rachel entered the room, not realizing that Hilda was there. She stood there speechless for a moment, her eyes moving rapidly from Hilda to Jeremy not knowing what to say. "I'm sorry. I didn't know you had a guest."

Hilda stared at her. She saw the same evil, the same madness in Rachel's eyes that she saw in Jeremy's.

"You must be Rachel, I presume? I heard that you'd returned too."

Rachel exchanged a glance with Jeremy before she met eyes with Hilda and smiled. "I don't know to whom you're referring. My name's Shelly Wickcliff. Who might you be?"

Hilda gasped. She hadn't seen me since I was a young girl, so she hadn't recognized Rachel as me when she'd walked in, but now she knew that what Kasey said about my death was true. "You can't be her."

I couldn't help but feel relieved at that moment. Now that Hilda knew the truth about my fate, it wouldn't be long before Mom, and the rest of my family knew. While it was sad to think about what the news of my death would do to them, it was satisfying that at least now, Rachel couldn't pass herself off as me any longer. She wouldn't be able to take over my life and most importantly, wouldn't be able to pretend to be my son's mother.

Jeremy took another sip of his drink and looked at his sister. "You needn't bother denying the truth to this woman. She's one of the ones responsible for my demise. She's no ordinary mortal. She's a witch, and she knows the truth."

"I know the truth alright. I know what you've done to the Withers boy." Hilda shifted her eyes to Rachel. "And you aren't Shelly. I see what I needed to see. I'd hoped when you first said you were her that she was alright, but if you were her, you'd know that her mother and I were dear friends when she was a child. I haven't seen her in years, but she'd remember me. She's no longer part of this world. I know that to be true. I didn't even tell her mother because I wasn't sure until this moment, but now I can't deny it."

Jeremy swirled his glass, chuckling. "Neither will we. There's no point. We disposed of her, as we will you."

Hilda balled her fists. "There's nothing humorous about this situation."

Jeremy tilted his head. "I disagree. What I find the most humorous is that you've come here to confront me even though you're frail enough for me to break in two. I can tell just by looking at you. In fact, you look so pathetic that I just may allow you to live. It's obvious you can't stop us."

There was Jeremy's arrogance at work again. He thought himself invincible and unstoppable. Hilda may have been frail and old in body, but in spirit, she was strong. I felt that. It was his arrogance that led to his undoing before, and I was banking on it leading to his downfall again, especially if the witches could be successful in bringing back Lucy.

Rachel put her hand to her chest and turned her attention to her brother. "What did happen to Shelly? You never told me."

Jeremy smirked, not giving her an answer. He took one final swig of his drink and then looked at Rachel. "It doesn't matter what happened to that sniveling bitch. You're here, and that's what matters."

Hilda put her hands on her hips. "You two don't belong in this realm. My sisters and I are going to make sure you get sent back to where you belong."

Jeremy met eyes with her. "I doubt that. You couldn't defeat me last time, and you were younger and stronger then. Lucy had to do your dirty work for you. You poisoned her against me."

Hilda's brow arched. "I did no such thing. You did that yourself with all your lies and manipulations."

"I loved Lucy, more than…" Jeremy hesitated, and his eyes seemed to change. They softened, and he looked away as not to show his feelings to Hilda. I saw in his expression that Lucy was his weakness after all. He'd really loved her, and her betrayal had torn him apart. He regained his pompous composure. "If you couldn't beat me then, you sure as hell can't do anything now."

Hilda didn't back down. "Did you think that you could just come back here and we wouldn't find out about it? Did you think that we'd let you bring those soulless creatures you call family back from the dead and not lift a finger to stop you?"

Jeremy approached her. "Well, well. You think you have it all figured out, don't you? What you don't know is how I plan to do it."

She shook her head. "It doesn't matter how you plan to do it because you won't last long enough to try."

He grabbed her by the wrist making her wince. "You tried before, and you failed, old woman. Maybe I was too quick to show you mercy. You almost died last time. Stay out of my way or this time, you will. I guarantee you that if you try to stop me, your death will be more painful, more torturous than you could ever imagine. You'll beg for me to kill you."

Hilda grimaced and jerked her wrist out from his grasp. "I'm not afraid of you. You made a mistake coming back here." She then looked at Rachel. "Both of you did. You belong to the darkness, and my sisters and I will make sure you're sent back there if it's the last thing we do."

Jeremy glared at her. "It will be. Do you honestly think that I'd be afraid of a pathetic old hag like you? You're about as dangerous as my mother who can barely move."

"Appearances can be deceiving, as well you know. Lucy was able to deceive you, wasn't she? She didn't love you. She loathed you as much as the rest of us. Unfortunately for you that you didn't find that out until it was too late. We will not fail again. You're running out of time."

He shot her a venomous stare. "You're a simple, stupid twit. You're the one that's running out of time."

"Am I?" She glanced at his arm and pointed. "I can see what's happening. You haven't much time left. Your host body's dying."

He put his arm behind his back. "It's just a bruise."

She grinned, knowing she'd caught him. "You know that isn't true and so do I. The Withers boy is dying because his body is without its rightful inhabitant. I implore you to give him his body back before it's too late. Stop this madness now. If the body dies, there will be nothing for his spirit to come back to."

"I've never felt stronger," Jeremy said, pushing his chest forward. "I've come back to get revenge on everyone in this town who hunted my ancestors down like dogs. They didn't want us here just because our last name was Wickcliff. They were all jealous and continue to be. No one is going to stop our family from taking our rightful place in this town and in this realm."

"It had nothing to do with your name," Hilda said. "It had to do with your motives. You people brought nothing but tragedy and despair to this town. It followed you like a dark cloud, and it still does."

"Spew your hate all you want old woman. I was willing to let you go if you promised not to stand in my way. It's too late for that now. If it's a battle you want, it's a battle you'll get. My return's going to be the end for you and the rest of those old crones you call family. Mark my words."

"We shall see, won't we?" Hilda turned to walk away. She stopped and rotated back around to face him. "I should've known better than to try to reason with you. You're obviously insane, and you can't reason with the unreasonable." She pointed to Rachel. "And by the looks of it, time's running out for you too."

Rachel crossed her arms. "What do you mean?"

"Take a look in the mirror, my dear."

Rachel went to the mirror and gasped, placing her hands on her cheeks. Her face was pallid, and veins protruded in her forehead. They were dark in color, almost black. She touched her face all over.

"What's happening to me? What's wrong with my face?" She whipped around to face Jeremy wanting an explanation. He lowered his eyes.

It was hard for me to look at her. When I looked at Rachel, I couldn't help seeing myself and it was too disturbing. I continued to listen.

"You really should tell her," Hilda said. She waited for Jeremy to respond, but he didn't. She looked at Rachel. "You're a foreign entity in a body that's not your own. You can't be here without paying a price, neither of you can."

Rachel stomped her foot like a spoiled child. "What does she mean, Jeremy?"

"Ignore her!" He glared at Hilda and pointed to the door. "Leave."

Hilda smiled and stood tall. "I'd like to see you make me."

"This is your last chance old woman. I'd kill you now, but it would take the fun out of the others watching you die."

Still distraught, Rachel approached Hilda. "What did you do to me?"

"She did nothing," he said. "She has no power over us."

"If that were true," Hilda said, "then why do you suddenly seem so nervous?"

"I'm not nervous. I'm bored with you and won't waste my time or energy on you any longer. Now get the hell out of my house."

Hilda gave him a nod. "Very well. I've found out what I needed to know. I'll go, but be prepared. I've been around the block a few times since we last met. I'm stronger now. We all are."

He stepped closer to her. "You're nothing but a pathetic old bag."

"I may be old, but with age comes wisdom. And that will give me all the power I need over you."

He shrugged. "I doubt all your friends are as confident. How about Gracey? She always seemed so much weaker compared to the rest of you. How's she doing? How's that leg of hers holding up? Maybe I should pay her a visit, hmm?"

Hilda lost her confident expression and got in his face. "Stay away from her, or you'll pay with more than your life."

"You and your friends will pay for keeping secrets from me and for the part that you played in my death. I'll always believe that you soured Lucy against me. Double crossing me was a mistake, a fatal one."

"Just get rid of her," Rachel said, having turned her back on them. "Don't just talk about it."

"All in good time."

Hilda knew that Jeremy overheard that Kasey was Lucy's son and that's what secret he was referring to, but she didn't let on. She went into the foyer, and as she was about to open the door, she turned back to them one last time.

"I'll give the two of you fair warning. What you think you have here will be short-lived. Enjoy it while it lasts, because soon you both will go back to the darkness you came from and this time, you'll never escape again."

She opened the door, stepped outside, and breathed in deeply when the door closed behind her. She walked down the steps and back towards her caravan, wondering how she'd tell Mom that I'd been inhabited.

Chapter 6

With the confrontation over, I returned to Reed in the sparse attic. "I think I may have some good news."

He put his hands on his hips. "Well, that would be a welcomed change. What is it?"

"For one thing, Hilda's found out that Kasey was telling the truth when he told her and Gracey that I'd died. My family should soon know. It doesn't make me feel good to know how much pain it'll cause, but they deserve the truth."

"And?"

"Hilda's confronted Jeremy and Rachel. She's stronger, more confident than I've given her credit for. She truly believes that she and the other witches can stop him. Listening to her speak made me believe in her. We finally have hope that the Wickcliff's will be destroyed."

He shrugged. "Forgive me if I'm not as enthused. We're going to need more help than from two old ladies and your mother."

I smiled. "We'll have it. Lucy's planning to return tonight during Midnight's Edge with their help. I've seen her in my visions. She appears to be young and strong. Jeremy's still in love with her despite what she's done to him. I feel it when he talks about her. She's his vulnerability, the missing piece of the puzzle that can destroy him."

"I don't want to get my hopes up, but I can't wait to see that bastard go down. I want my life back for myself obviously, but I feel bad for my dad too. Ever since Mom died, it's just been the two of us. I'm all he has."

I bit my lip. "I don't want to discourage you, but I feel like you deserve the truth. Jeremy appears weaker, and the bruises on your skin look worse. Hilda noticed it too. He tried to cover, but I could tell that he's worried. The longer he remains in your body, the less your chances of returning."

He nodded. I could see that he was crestfallen. "I know. That's why I'm so anxious to get out of here. I might as well be honest about it. Even if I can find a way out of here, there's nothing I can do. The witches are our only hope."

"There is another option. If he doesn't find out Jason's his son before his spirit gets too weak to hold on, you might be able to go back."

"That's not good enough."

I gave him a sympathetic look. "I'm going to go back and check on Jason. I can't shake the feeling that I shouldn't take my eyes off of him for too long. He seems innocent enough, but the key word there is seems."

* * * *

I turned my back to him, closed my eyes, and focused on Jason. I saw Rebecca in his room at the Moonlight Inn. The Inn dated back to the 1800's, and its rooms were small, comfortable and inviting. It was one of her favorite places, unlike her home with Pit. She loved the four poster bed, the antique furniture including a lacquered trunk with leather straps at the end of the bed covered with a handmade quilt. There was a smell of furniture polish in the air, combined with old wood and cinnamon from the scented, twig broom hanging at the door.

After her latest go-round with Pit, she'd gone straight to Jason. She was in bed, thinking about how uncomfortable it was. While the décor was lovely, the furniture left a lot to be desired. It wasn't the best accommodations, but it was still better than having to share space with Pit. She was relieved to have cut ties with him, and I felt her happiness growing as she thought about her potential future with Jason.

Rebecca groaned as she got out of bed. She went to the bathroom door and knocked. "Jason, hurry up! I told Ethan we'd meet him by five, and it's already four."

"Sorry," he said, opening the door, "I tried to hurry. How do I look?"

She eyed him up and down, looking at his dingy khakis and faded polo shirt. She struggled to find the words not to hurt his feelings.

"I know it isn't much. But this is the best I can do right now."

She put her hand on her chin. "You look great. Ethan's my best friend and a jeans and t-shirt kinda guy. He's not going to care if you don't have a suit."

He shrugged. "Are you sure? I really wanna make a good impression."

She winked. "You're going to knock him dead. Let's go."

After our dad's wake, Ethan had talked to Mom about what to do about our parent's business. Guilt-ridden over the fact that he felt he abandoned his family and because he didn't want anyone to lose their jobs, he'd agreed to stay and run things until Mom found a suitable replacement. It was clear to me that that was the last thing on Mom's mind, but Ethan hadn't realized that.

Rebecca had arranged a job interview for Jason as she'd promised to do. A few minutes later, she pulled up in front of the Golden Crescent Diner where they'd agreed to meet Ethan. Jason hadn't said a word the entire way. She shut the ignition off and turned to him.

"Are you ready?"

He nodded. "I suppose so."

She raised an eyebrow. "Are you okay? You look kinda flushed."

"Just nervous, I guess."

She opened the door, and they both got out. "Don't be. Just be yourself. Ethan's a great guy. He's easy going. He'll love you."

When they got inside, Rebecca searched the restaurant for my brother. He sat in a booth by the window.

She pointed. "There he is."

"Hey, Becca," he said, as they approached his table. He rose to give her a peck on the cheek. He turned to Jason and smiled. "So you must be Jason Beckett?"

Jason nodded. "It's nice to meet you. I've heard a lot about you. I feel like we already know each other."

The three of them sat down. Ethan's blue eyes that seemed sad at first brightened a bit.

"Weren't you at my father's wake?"

"I was there to see Becca. I wanted to come over and express my condolences, but I wasn't sure how appropriate it would be coming from a stranger."

"I appreciate your concern."

"Of course," Jason said, extending his hand. "I want to thank you for taking the time to talk to me."

Ethan shook his hand. When he did, his demeanor changed. Although he couldn't place it, he got an odd feeling when he shook Jason's hand. He didn't know that Jason had Wickcliff blood running through his veins, but his instincts told him that Jason wasn't who he appeared to be.

Rebecca noticed the change. "Hey, you okay?"

"Fine," Ethan said, turning to her before looking back at Jason and forcing a smile. "So, Mr. Beckett…"

"Call me Jason."

"Jason. You have to bear with me. My father always took care of meetings like this. He would meet with potential employees and make all the business decisions. This is new to me. Becca tells me that you worked for a fishing company in your town."

"Yes, that's true."

"What did you do there?"

"A little bit of everything. We were short-staffed, so I did several jobs. I guess you could say I was a multi-tasker."

"Was there any one job in particular that you did the most often?"

Jason stumbled. "Oh…uh."

"You okay, Jason?"

"I'm sorry. I'm just nervous. The bottom line is that I'm the hardest worker you'll ever have. I come to work early, stay late, don't call in sick. Look, the truth is that I need this job. Working on boats is all that I know how to do, and there isn't an abundance of opportunity out there."

Rebecca looked at Ethan. "What do ya say, Ethan?"

He looked Jason directly in the eyes. "You've got a job."

* * * *

After finishing the meeting with Rebecca and Jason, I followed my brother to the docks. As he stood there, a breeze brushed up against his cheek, which he delighted in. It helped to dry the beads of sweat that were forming on his brow.

He knew immediately that hiring Jason was a mistake, although he didn't understand why. The only reason he'd hired him was that he knew how much it meant to Rebecca. He was worried his first business decision would be a disaster. For the last five years he'd been away, he'd supported himself by doing odd jobs. He didn't feel particularly skilled in one area and would do any suitable work that came his way. He liked the idea of being able to do a variety of different jobs. He found it exciting because he constantly had new experiences. Now he was back in a place where he felt trapped.

"I'm struggling here, Dad. Your death was so unexpected. I feel saddled with the burden of trying to hold our family as well the business together. I never wanted this responsibility and would've certainly never asked for it."

I understood his feelings. Our parents worked tirelessly to build up the Hawkins Fishing Company from one boat and one employee to the largest employer in town. This was on Ethan's mind as he continued his conversation with Dad.

"I don't have the skills and the judgment to be your successor. My greatest fear is that I'll let you down by losing the business that you dedicated your life to. I don't have what it takes to make the business work. As soon as I'd get comfortable and believe in my ability to do something, that voice in my head would begin again, telling me that I'd never be good enough. I've always felt like a failure for leaving. That I left you, Mom and Shelly."

He paused, looking out at the clear water. "I can't do this, Dad. I'm not as strong as you were. I've screwed up everything I've ever touched." The early evening sun shone on his face, and he felt slightly comforted by its warmth but not comforted enough. "You wanted me to stay here, learn the business, and follow in your footsteps. But I left because I was afraid. Afraid of everything. I've let everyone down."

I wanted to tell my brother that what happened wasn't his fault and that he didn't let us down by leaving. Dad believed that Ethan had left to make it on his own, and he was proud of him. But Ethan didn't know that.

He decided that he was going to go to The Hook so he could forget the guilt. My brother was falling apart for many reasons, and I was the only one who knew what all of them were.

Chapter 7

"Don't keep me in suspense," Reed said, disrupting my thoughts. "What's going on?"

I turned to him. "Nothing's happening."

His shoulders fell. "You mean that you didn't see anything?"

"All I saw was my brother offering Jason a job. Jason still doesn't know who he is or who his parents are. That's good news for us I suppose."

Reed shook his head. "No. It's good for you. I'd rather have them find each other. At least Jeremy would have another host to go into, and I could get back to my life. If they don't find each other, I'll never get back. You said so yourself." He waved his hand. "What do you care? Your life's already over. You don't have anything to lose."

I took a deep breath and let it out slowly. "First of all, I never said you'd never get back. I just told you what I'm seeing and secondly, I've got plenty to lose. I already have. I'm worried sick about my son whom I've left in the mortal realm with the Wickcliffs, and then there's the rest of my family."

"I don't mean to be cruel, Shelly, but you don't know much of anything. What kind of spirit are you if you can't even figure out how to get out of here? Aren't ghosts supposed to be able to go wherever they want?"

I shot him a look. "I'm doing the best I can with no guidance. There wasn't a handbook left for me here. I've not only had to accept that my life's over, but I've had to learn how to use these powers I'm developing. It hasn't been easy."

"I know that, but my life's on the line. I can't wait for you to figure it out anymore. It's obvious that I can't depend on anyone but myself. I'm getting out of here." He went over to the window and tried to open it. It was a futile attempt. His hand passed through just as mine had.

"You know that's not going to work."

He turned to me. "I don't know anything anymore. I've got to at least try again to get out of here."

I put my hands on my hips. "Even if you could, where would you go? We don't know what's out there. I thought we agreed we'd stick together."

"No, you agreed, and I went along, but I'm running out of time and out of patience."

Before I could say anything else, I received a sharp pulsating sensation in my head, similar to the one I felt the night I first got inside Kasey's head at the bar. I groaned and put my hands on both sides of my head.

Reed stared at me, deeply concerned. "Shelly? What's wrong?"

I shook my head. "I don't know. It's almost like a vision, but I'm not trying to connect with anyone. It's not clear what I'm seeing. It's foggy, almost like a dream." I groaned again. "I feel like my head's going to split in two."

I closed my eyes and took a deep breath. I shut him out and all my surroundings and focused my attention on what I was seeing. The fog began to lift the longer I concentrated, and I saw a door that opened away from me. Beyond the door was a set of steps.

I opened my eyes and turned back to Reed, with urgency. "We need to go to the door and try to open it again."

"It didn't work before, and neither did the window."

"This time, I think it will. I saw it open in my vision. I think we're finally going to get out of here."

We went to the door, and I focused all my energy on forcing the door open. The knob turned by itself and the door opened away from us. A creaking sound filled the air.

Reed turned to me and grinned. "How did you do that?"

"I kept trying to open it with my hands. I've got to remember that I don't have a body anymore. I've got to use my mind."

I started for the steps, but Reed stopped me. "What if you're right, and there's something dangerous out there?"

"It can't be any worse than being stuck up here. Let's just stick together. No matter what we encounter out there, we don't separate. Agreed?"

He nodded. "Agreed."

We went through the door and down the steps slowly and silently. When we got to the bottom of the landing, Reed spoke up.

"Everything looks the same. Is this what the afterlife is supposed to look like? I mean, where are the angels and harps and all that stuff?"

I laughed. "Very funny." It was the first time I'd laughed on this side, and that made him laugh too. "Jeremy said that there were many realms in the afterlife, more than just heaven and hell as we were always taught. This is just one of them."

"But it looks just like our world. Does that mean we're back or…?"

"How am I supposed to know? I'm not an expert by any means, but I doubt that returning to the mortal realm would be as simple as descending a staircase. After what I did, I'm probably stuck in purgatory forever."

"But I shouldn't be. I didn't kill myself, and I didn't die. I'm probably just going crazy after what happened to me."

"You're not crazy, and neither was I. We're victims, but Jeremy's not going to get away with what he's done to us."

He grimaced in pain and rubbed his arm.

"What's wrong?"

"My arm's killing me."

"Let me have a look." He stopped rubbing it and held it out. The skin had changed color. It looked as it did in the visions I'd had of Jeremy.

"Your spirit body is revealing what your mortal body's experiencing. How do you feel otherwise?"

"Confused and scared."

"I am too. It's going to be alright. We're going to figure this out together."

He gave me a comforting look. "I'm glad I don't have to go through this alone."

As we reached the hallway, we took each other's hands. I didn't feel like we were in any imminent danger, but I didn't know who or what we were going to encounter. At the top of the stairs that led to the foyer below we paused.

He looked anxious. "Should we go down there?"

"Why not? What do we have to lose?"

"Do you think there are others like us?"

We heard the piano being played in the parlor. My eyes widened. "Maybe there is, or maybe it's just Jeremy or Rachel."

"Do you think they'll be able to see us?"

"Only one way to find out. Let's go."

When we reached the foyer, we saw Greta walking towards us. She didn't acknowledge us. She walked right through us and disappeared down the hall.

His eyes widened, and he met eyes with me. "I guess that answers my question. This is freaky as hell."

"Those in the mortal realm can't see us. I suppose that means we're free to move about this house as we see fit."

I walked towards the parlor door and gasped when I saw Jeremy and Rachel sitting inside. Although I'd seen them in our bodies in my visions, it was even more surreal to walk into a room and see myself sitting there.

Reed walked up behind me. "What is it?" He glanced at Jeremy and Rachel standing in front of us. "Holy shit."

"That's one way to put it," I said, a wide smile encroaching on my face.

Because Reed couldn't see what I'd seen in my visions up in the attic, he was glancing upon Jeremy in his body for the first time.

"If this is a nightmare, I'd like to wake up now."

"It's a nightmare alright. But there's no waking up from it."

He met eyes with me and for the first time, I saw the anguish in them. "I'm never getting back, am I? I wanted to believe I could but seeing him standing there...I can't take this."

"I know this is hard."

His face went red. "Jeremy you sick bastard! I'm right here! I see you, and I'm not going to let you get away with this. Do you hear me?"

We watched as Rachel stopped playing the piano. Jeremy smiled at her. She got up, and they turned around to walk towards the door. We stepped aside and watched them walk out of the room and down the hall.

"Hey you!" Reed said, trying to get Jeremy's attention. "Over here."

Neither one of them heard us. I put my head down. "It's no use. They can't hear you."

Reed sighed. "Now what?"

We entered the parlor and sat on the sofa. "We'll have to figure that out. I just wish I knew where to start."

"You have to start from within yourselves," a man's voice said, filling the room.

The voice startled us. It was familiar. It took me a moment to place it, but eventually, I recognized it as the voice of the man Kasey had seen in his vision at The Hook. He was the man I'd thought about when Gracey had told him who his father was.

We turned to the doorway, and I saw the man standing there. He wore the same monk's cloak that he'd had on before.

He put his hands up. "I'm sorry. I didn't mean to startle you. There's no reason to be afraid. I'm not going to harm you."

"You can see us?" Reed asked.

The man nodded.

"You're Damon Shields, aren't you?" I asked, standing up. "I've seen you in my visions."

"I am," he said, taking down his hood and revealing his bald head. "I've come to help you. If you both look inside yourselves, things will start to become clearer. You'll find the answers you seek."

I approached him. "Are you dead too?"

"No. I'm a mortal, but I'm also a spirit guide. My spirit can transcend the different realms, Shelly."

I tilted my head. "You know my name?"

He nodded and gave us a smile. "And I know you too Reed. I've been watching you and am aware of what Jeremy's done to you."

"I know about you. Or of you. I heard Gracey speak of you. You're Kasey's father, aren't you?"

"I didn't know about him at first, but I've learned of his parentage over the years. There's a part of me that's always wanted to know my son, but I live in seclusion in the mortal world. Too many years have gone by to develop a relationship I'm afraid."

"And you know my mother, Carol Hawkins. I never heard her speak of you until I crossed over."

When I mentioned Mom's name, his eyes lit up. "Yes, I know Caroline very well. At least I used to."

"Why did you appear to Kasey at the bar?"

"I'll explain all of that in time."

Damon was preoccupied with the bruises on Reed's arm and touched it. "I see it's starting."

Reed winced. "Is it true that the longer I remain here the harder it will be to get back?"

Damon nodded. "I'm afraid so. The mortal body dies slowly if it's not inhabited by its intended host."

Reed's eyes bulged, and he swallowed. "So I'm going to die for sure?"

"Unless we can force Jeremy out while your body still has life in it."

"Jeremy's son is Jason Beckett, isn't he?" I said. "He's got to be. He's got Jeremy's eyes."

"That's not important right now. What's important is getting this young man back to his body while there's still time."

Reed looked at him, his eyes filled with hope. "You can help me do that?"

"I'll do my best," Damon said. "But you have to trust me."

He eyed Damon. "I've never met you before and I'm not sure I can trust you, but I'll try anything at this point."

I was starting to worry for Reed more and more. Seeing Jeremy inside his body and knowing that his body was dying for certain seemed to be too much for him. He was beginning to sound desperate, and that scared me. When people are desperate, they do things they would never normally do. I understood that better than anyone.

"What can we do to help him?" I asked.

"There's a ceremony that can exorcise Jeremy's spirit from Reed's body and allow Reed to go back," Damon said, "but it's not a simple one. I'll do all that I can to help, but if it fails, Reed may be stuck here permanently." His eyes moved to Reed. "Is that a chance that you're willing to take?"

Reed stood there for a moment silently and then nodded. "We have to try. It's my only hope."

I looked at Damon. "I have so many questions for you. How did you get here and why are you here?"

"I'm a guardian of sorts. The Wickcliff's evil is strong. They have many powers, and I watch over the Wickcliff cemetery and mausoleum to make sure they remain bound there. They know about Midnight's Edge. I always have to be one-step ahead of them. If they escape during that time, they can get into the mortal realm. They've made deals with the demons in the dark realm before and have been given the power to come back, so I must be on my guard constantly. That's why I live in seclusion in the mortal realm. I can't have any distractions."

"How are you able to do this?" Reed asked. "You said you were just a mortal. How do you have the power to keep the Wickcliff spirits contained?"

"I'm a mortal, but I have the ability to enter an altered state of consciousness to make contact with the spirit world. That's why you see me now. I have spirit guides that show me things when I enter my trancelike state. It's how I was able to make contact with Kasey."

"How did you learn to do that?" I said. "Could I learn?"

"Possibly," Damon said. "But it takes years of practice and meditation. I learned my craft from a Native American shaman, and it's taken me years to build up my abilities. I was chosen to guard the Wickcliffs when he died to make sure that none of them escape."

"Why them?" Reed said. "What's so different about them that you have to stand guard? Aren't there spirits everywhere?"

"They're not just evil, Reed," Damon said. "It's because of where they got their powers. They gave up their souls to demons for the promise of power and life everlasting. When they lost their souls, they lost everything that made them human. They're selfish, vile, unfeeling creatures. If they escape, they'll wreak havoc on this realm and the mortal one."

"Jeremy's plotting to return them all to the mortal realm," I said. "He forced me to commit suicide so that he could return, and he used my body to bring his sister, Rachel, to life. He's not going to stop until he's brought them all back."

Damon looked at me with a warm expression. "I'm sorry you were victimized by a madman like that. At least your pain's over now."

I chuckled softly. "My pain isn't over, Mr. Shields."

"Please, call me Damon."

"Damon. I have to exist with the guilt of what I've done and the pain I've inflicted on my family and my son. It's not easy to deal with."

"Your son's going to be fine. Your mother's a wonderful woman. She'll be sure to give him a good life. You can take comfort in that."

"How well did you know my mother? I overheard a conversation she had with my grandmother. From what I could gather, you were close to say the least."

"We were once." His eyes drifted to the side. "That was a long time ago."

"This is all fascinating," Reed said, sarcastically, "but I'd rather we talk about what it's going to take to get me back to my life."

"If I'm going to focus on helping you," Damon said, turning to him, "I need to find someone else on this side that's as strong as I am that can keep watch over the cemetery while we prepare for the ceremony."

"I still don't understand their power," Reed said.

"What Jeremy did to you was only a sampling of their powers. As I said before, the Wickcliff's sold their souls to the dark for power, but the forces of good sought revenge on them for it. Their spirits were sentenced to remain trapped in the Wickcliff cemetery in the large stone cenotaph. It's not impossible for them to escape, and that's why it's my job to prevent it."

"Why were you chosen?" I asked.

"The guardian needed to be someone who's the opposite of them. I'm an honorable man with a pure heart and unselfish motives. That's why I was chosen as the guardian."

Reed groaned and grabbed his arm again. He sat back down on the sofa.

Damon looked down at Reed's arm. "We're running out of time. We have to hurry."

Reed met eyes with Damon. "Do you think it's possible that it's already too late?"

Damon's expression was grim, which made Reed throw his hands up in the air. "I don't believe this! That son of a bitch stole my life and by the time I realize I can do something about it, it's already too late."

"I didn't say that," Damon said. "It depends on how much damage has been done to your body. I'm not going to guarantee you that we'll be successful. All we can do is try."

I sat down next to Reed and tried to comfort him. "It's my fault you're here. My death set this whole thing in motion. If I'd been stronger, if I'd been able to fight him, this would've never happened to you. I'm sorry."

Reed grabbed my hand. "It isn't your fault. It's like you said before, we're both victims."

Damon came closer to me. "Reed's right. Jeremy's very powerful, and he knows how to exploit a person's vulnerabilities."

I met eyes with him. "I still feel responsible."

He sat next to me, putting his arm around me. "You can't blame yourself. The Hawkinses and the Wickcliff's were always enemies. Jeremy would do anything to destroy your family, and he used you to help him do it. The rivalry goes back generations, long before you were born. It's not your fault. You were just a means to an end for him."

"He can't continue to destroy innocent lives. He has to be stopped." I said.

"He will be." Another voice said, filling the room.

We turned to the doorway, and I glanced at the man who had entered the room quickly, not believing my eyes. My chest tightened, and I could feel the tears welling up in my eyes. I stood up to face him. It was my husband.

"Rory? Is it you?"

He opened his arms and nodded enthusiastically. "Hello, darling."

I ran to him and embraced him. I touched his face and peered into his brown eyes that sparkled with kindness as they always had in life. He was as handsome and regal as ever.

"It is you," I said. "I don't believe it."

"I've missed you so much." He broke the embrace still smiling and wiped the tears from my cheeks. "I know what Jeremy did to you, to both of us. I'm sorry that I wasn't able to protect you."

"That wasn't your fault. You didn't know what was happening, and

I couldn't tell you. He wouldn't let me."

He cupped my face with his hands. "It doesn't matter now. You've made it to us. We're together again, and nothing's going to tear us apart." His eyes moved from me to Damon briefly. It was obvious that they had a connection. His gaze met mine again. "Jeremy took our lives away from us, darling, but he won't go unpunished. We're going to see that he gets what's coming to him." He embraced me again. "I promise you that."

I stepped back from him after a moment and put my hand on my head. I suddenly felt dizzy.

"What's wrong?" he asked.

"You need to continue with your visions so we can see what's happening in the mortal realm," Damon said. "We'll need your gift of sight."

"Can't you do that?" I asked.

"I can't see everything. I can see what's happening in the cemetery, but since I'm not a spirit like you, my vision's limited. Even if I could see the mortal realm, I can't stay here. I have to get back to keeping watch over the cemetery."

I glanced at Rory.

"It's alright," he said, giving me a half-smile. "I'll be here when you come back."

I didn't want to leave and take the chance that Rory would be gone when I returned, but I turned away from all of them and took a deep breath, trying to focus my energy on the mortal realm. I thought about my friends and loved ones, and before I knew it, I was with them again.

Chapter 8

In the time I'd left the attic, met Damon and reunited with Rory, night had fallen, and I found myself at Lover's Bluff where Mom, Hilda, and Gracey stood at the edge of the cliff looking out at the ocean crashing on the rocks below. The salty smell permeated everything around them. Midnight's Edge was fast approaching, and I felt the trepidation in each of the ladies. Mom and Gracey hadn't used their abilities in years and weren't sure if they'd be strong enough to bring Lucy back. Hilda, while confident when she'd confronted Jeremy, wasn't as sure of her ability to succeed as she'd wanted him to believe.

This was the first time that Hilda had seen Mom since learning that I'd died. I wished that she'd tell her, but I could feel that she wasn't going to. All three of them needed to be strong and undistracted if they were going to have any chance of success. If Mom knew about me, it would interfere with what she had to do.

Gracey shivered and ran her hands over her arms, finally breaking the uncomfortable silence between them. "It's been so long since I've used my powers. What if this doesn't work?"

"It will, dear friend," Hilda said, trying to convince Gracey as well as herself. "You have the power within you. If you look deep inside yourself, you'll find it again."

The three women converged and formed a circle by taking each other's hands. Mom grasped Gracey's hand and squeezed, meeting eyes with her. "I believe in you, and so does Lucy. She wouldn't have asked for our help if she didn't believe we had the power."

"It's almost Midnight," Hilda said. "The moon's full in the sky but there are no stars. Midnight's Edge is upon us. We haven't any time to lose."

Mom looked into Gracey's eyes. "Please, do this for Jeffrey and for all the other people whose lives will be in danger if Jeremy isn't stopped."

Gracey nodded. "I need to protect my son from Jeremy at any cost. I'll try."

In the center of their circle, they gently wrapped strands of Lucy's hair that Hilda had kept and combined it with dried lilacs, herbs, and oils. Gracey pulled out a black-handled dagger from her bag and pricked her finger. She winced and passed the blade on to Mom, who did the same. Hilda then followed. Each put a single drop of blood into the wrapping.

"Our blood is an offering," Hilda said, holding it up in the air. "Our sister Lucy must live again to stop an evil spirit from destroying all that is pure and good about this town and the people who live here. Lucy was, and still is a member of our coven, our family. We are sisters in the way that nature intended us to be, and our blood is her blood, our breath her breath, our light her light. On this night during Midnight's Edge when the veil between the living and the dead ceases to exist, we have come to the place where Lucy Wickcliff left this mortal realm and ask for the power of good and light to be with us now as we return her to life from the depths of the sea."

Hilda kissed the bundle and threw it out over the cliff, into the water. They all grasped each other's hands again.

"Please let this work," Mom said. "Please."

* * * *

Suddenly, I was no longer with the witches on the bluff. It was as if I were in the water, and it was freezing. I could feel it touching my skin.

Amidst the crashing waves, I heard Lucy's name being called, but it wasn't by the women on the bluff. It was an unknown voice, a whisper in the wind. Then before me, I began to see the most amazing thing I'd ever seen. I was witnessing Lucy's rebirth under the water. The ritual was working.

The blood from the ladies in the bundle expanded in the water and slowly those particles developed into her brain, spine, bones, organs, and skin—all that was Lucy in her previous life. There in the ocean, she grew from an infant to the woman I'd seen in my visions of her. Lucy, who had previously existed only in spirit, was now a living, breathing human being. I fantasized briefly about the same happening for me, but it was quickly squashed by the reality that Rachel inhabited my body.

After watching her rebirth, I was now inside her head and could read her thoughts as I did with the others. She was confused at first. Her thoughts scattered. She remembered her visit with Hilda and realized what had happened. She began to panic, realizing that she had to get to the surface quickly so that she could breathe.

Moving her arms wildly, she swam desperately to reach the surface, making it to the top, purely on instinct and adrenaline. Once she'd reached the surface, she popped out of the water, gasping for air, choking, and taking in gulps of the salty water.

Once the initial shock was over, her senses kicked in. She felt the ice-cold water for the first time on her skin like a thousand needles. It was so cold she had a fleeting fear that she wouldn't make it out of the water onto land. She pushed the fear from her mind and used every ounce of strength she had to swim until she reached a point where the large waves could no longer reach her. By the time she'd reached the ledge of the cliff and began climbing it, she was fatigued, in pain, and bleeding from where she'd cut herself on one of the rocks. If she'd doubted at any point that her return to the mortal realm was real, she didn't now. She thought as she continued to climb about how she'd spent so much time as a spirit that she'd forgotten what it felt like to be a mortal.

Lucy stopped to rest a moment. She sat on the ledge of the rocks, naked and trembling. She was so transfixed by the beauty of the reflection of the moon off of the surface of the water that she almost forgot about the cold and the pain. After a minute, she continued to climb. It didn't take long before she could see the trees at the top in the distance.

"Look," Hilda said, walking over to the edge of the cliff. "I see her. The ceremony worked."

Mom ran to the ledge and got down on her knees.

"Lucy, it's Carol. I'm going to extend my hand to you, and I want you to grab it so I can pull you up, okay?"

I watched as Mom pulled her up. Lucy lay on the ground beside her for a moment, gasping for breath. Gracey approached them with a blanket.

"Are you alright?" Gracey wrapped the blanket around her.

Lucy shivered. "I think so unless I catch my second death of cold."

Hilda laughed and began to tear up. She wiped the tears away. "If I'm being honest, I wasn't sure it would work. It's been years since we used that kind of power. I should've known that you'd fight like hell to get back to us. You were always the strongest willed of us."

Mom touched Lucy's face, smiling. "I can't believe that you're here. It feels like a dream. A pleasant dream, but a dream nonetheless."

Lucy returned her smile. "It's real. I'm here." She took a moment to take in her surroundings. "It's been such a long time."

Gracey chuckled. "It's been almost 30 years. I can hardly believe it. You look just as you did before you died. You're just as young and beautiful as you ever were. Spirits don't age."

"Not us," Mom said with a tinge of jealousy in her voice. "We've changed a bit."

"The three of us have been around the block a time or two," Gracey said.

Lucy didn't lose her smile. "Nonsense, you all look wonderful. I've missed all of you."

Mom helped her to her feet. "And we've missed you more than words can say. Come on. Let's get you out of this cold and get you some clothes."

They helped Lucy to Mom's car. She lied down in the back seat and laid her head on Hilda's lap. Mom started the car, turned on the heat, and began to drive.

"I'm so grateful that you all came here tonight to bring me back," Lucy said, "and that we're together again. I knew I could count on you. You've never let me down."

Gracey, who sat in the passenger's seat, turned her head to face Lucy. "We're a team, kiddo. We're always going to be there for each other. It doesn't matter how much time passes. We're always going to be family." She looked over at Hilda and then turned her attention to the front to Mom. "Aren't we, girls?"

Hilda and Mom nodded in agreement. "I don't think I've been this happy in a long time," Hilda said. "The pain of losing you was too much. It'll be different this time."

The four of them were all in tears now as the joy of being together again overtook them.

Lucy sat up, wiping away a tear. "As overjoyed as I feel right now, we can't forget the reason I've come back. We need to start planning how we're going to rid Sleepy Meadows of Jeremy."

"Don't worry about that now, dear friend," Hilda said. "It's late. We'll take you to Gracey's where you can have a warm meal and get some rest. You're too exhausted to think about Jeremy. I think we all are. It's been a long night."

"We don't have time to waste," Lucy said.

"I agree," Mom said, clutching the steering wheel. "He's killed my husband, and we can't give him any more time to destroy more lives."

Hilda looked at her but didn't say anything. Poor Mom didn't know about me yet. As angry as she felt about Dad dying and despite how determined she was to prevent Jeremy from harming anyone else, she didn't realize it was already too late. When she found out, she'd be a force to be reckoned with. I spoke with Lucy when she was in spirit form too. Had she heard me? She never acknowledged me, so I didn't know if she knew of my fate or not.

"I'm sorry about Jeffrey," Lucy said. "I wish I could've prevented that from happening. I could see what was happening, but I couldn't intervene."

"Thank you," Mom said. "I know you would have if you could've. Did you see him before you came back? Is he alright?"

Lucy shook her head. "As you know there are many realms. I didn't see him. I'm sorry."

Hilda put her hand on Lucy's back and rubbed it. "Don't think of that now. You need to conserve your strength."

Lucy sighed and leaned back. The car became silent. She stared out the window, watching everything she once knew pass by her. Her heart sank as the mansion on top of the hill came into view, a place of unhappiness for her in life, a place that became a prison to her, just as it had been for me. Lucy and I had that in common.

Mom pulled into Gracey's driveway and shut the ignition off. She got out and opened up the door in the back. She took Lucy's arm and helped her inside.

After a warm meal and some reminiscing about old times, Lucy yawned, prompting the women to insist that she get some rest. Hilda helped Lucy to bed and pulled the covers up over her.

"We'll talk more in the morning, dear. Sleep well." Hilda got up and started towards the door, but stopped when Lucy called her name. She turned around again. "What is it?"

"I asked you not to see Jeremy, but you did. I saw you when I was in spirit form."

Hilda went back over to the bed and grasped Lucy's hand. "I had to. I'm sorry. I needed to confront him and look into his eyes to see what we're up against. He's so powerful, Lucy. More than before. Of course, I didn't let him know I thought this. We're going to be in for quite a battle. Fortunately, his mortal body's weak." She sighed and patted Lucy's hand gently. "We'll talk about it tomorrow."

Lucy's eyes became heavy and began to close. "Hilda, will you sit with me until I fall asleep?"

Hilda sat down next to her. "I will."

Lucy thought about the battle ahead of them and closed her eyes. The last thing she remembered before falling asleep was Hilda's smile. Once Lucy was asleep, Hilda went out into the kitchen where Mom and Gracey sat talking.

"The poor dear's exhausted," Hilda said. "I can't even imagine how she feels."

"She's probably just as overjoyed and overwhelmed as we all are," Gracey said.

Hilda went over to the table and sat down. "I need to talk to you both. I didn't want to bring it up until the ritual was over, but I went to the mansion and confronted Jeremy today."

Mom's eyes widened. "You did what?"

"Don't you realize what a dangerous situation you put yourself in?" Gracey said, staring at Hilda. "Or all of us in? Now he knows we're onto him."

"He would've found that out sooner or later. I had to tell him we knew that he was back and that he wasn't going to get away with what he's planning."

Mom's face turned grim. "Who does he inhabit?"

Hilda thought of me, but once again, she decided not to talk about that with Mom. "Kasey's suspicious of this boy named Reed Withers. I haven't seen the boy for over 15 years and even before that, I only knew the sheriff and his family in passing. I wouldn't recognize him even if I saw him, but Kasey's confident."

Mom nodded. "I knew that Jeremy was responsible for Jeffrey's death. You just gave me the confirmation that I needed. Ethan mentioned that Reed was at the hospital the day Jeffrey died. That wasn't Reed. I wonder how he got involved in this mess?"

"That's not all," Hilda said. "Rachel's back as well. She was the first one he's returned from the grave. They admitted it."

Gracey gasped and put her hand on her heart. "Oh good God in heaven."

"Who is she?" Mom asked, her eyes searching Hilda's. "Who has Rachel inhabited?"

Hilda diverted her gaze from Mom and met eyes with Gracey. "That's not important right now. I needed you to know that Jeremy isn't alone. We have to prepare ourselves for the battle ahead."

I was beyond frustrated. Hilda again had the opportunity to tell Mom my fate, but once again, she kept it quiet. She believed that if they were going to be successful in defeating Jeremy, they would all have to be at the top of their game. She didn't want to hurt Mom, and she didn't want her to be distracted either. She surmised that learning that I was dead so shortly after losing Dad, could be too much for her.

Regardless of Hilda's reluctance to tell Mom the truth, I felt more confident than I ever had about Jeremy and Rachel's defeat. I knew how great his evil was, but with Lucy's return and Damon's help, we had our strengths. I was no longer trapped in the attic. I was with my husband and my new friends. I was starting to have hope again, and it felt wonderful.

* * * *

By the time I turned my attention back to Reed and Rory, Damon was gone. He'd returned to guarding his post in the cemetery. I explained to them how the ritual to return Lucy to life from the ocean had been a success, but I wasn't with them for long until I felt compelled to return to the mortal realm.

Ethan was in trouble. I'd seen earlier on that he was in a dark place, and it felt like his despair was escalating.

I found him at The Hook. The gloomy atmosphere of the bar's interior, with its dark wood and dim lighting, seemed to fit Ethan's mood. He was sitting at the bar with an empty shot glass in front of him. He turned to the bartender, Hal, and demanded another. He was thinking about how much he missed Dad, and how guilty he felt for missing out on the last few years of our father's life. He'd only planned to have a drink to dull the pain, but one had now turned into multiple drinks.

He briefly entertained Dad's claim that the Wickcliffs had returned, but shrugged it off. After seeing Rachel show up at the wake and no longer believing that something had happened to me, he assumed that everything that Dad had said in the hospital was nonsense.

His mind was also preoccupied with thoughts of how good it felt to have Kasey back in his life. He knew in his heart that he wanted to be with him. What bothered him was that Sleepy Meadows is a small, old-fashioned town and although Kasey had been out publicly for years and didn't care what people thought, Ethan did. Our family was well known in town, and Ethan was now responsible for keeping the family business afloat. He was afraid that if the clientele and people that did business with him were to find out he was gay, the business would be destroyed.

The bar door opened and in came Kasey carrying a guitar case, followed by a few other men in his band. He glanced over at the bar and saw Ethan sitting there. He said something to the guys, walked over to him, set his guitar case on the ground and smiled. "I didn't expect to see you here so late. What are you doing here?"

Ethan didn't look at him. "It's a bar. What do ya think?"

Kasey frowned. "You're drunk."

"I've only had a few. I'm not nearly drunk enough." He turned to Hal. "Where's that vodka I asked for?"

Kasey pointed to the empty glass. "How many of those did you have?"

He shrugged. "Hell if I know."

"Hey, Hal," Kasey said, facing the bartender. "I think my friend's had enough."

"If you say so, Kase," Hal said, slinging a towel over his shoulder.

Ethan laughed and looked around the bar. "Ya hear that? Now we're only friends." He turned back to Kasey, finally making eye contact. "That's not what you said when I was—"

Kasey put a hand up. "Stop it."

He looked over at Hal, who shot them a look and walked away.

"That's it," Kasey said, taking Ethan by the arm. "We're leaving."

Ethan yanked his arm away. "I'm not done yet."

"Yes, you are. Let's go."

"You're killing my buzz, Kase. If you insist on staying, at least sit down and have a few."

"I don't drink anymore. I told you about my drinking problem."

Ethan waved his hand. "The only problem you have with alcohol is that you don't drink enough."

Kasey tried to grab his arm again. "This isn't you talking. It's the booze. It's time for you to leave."

"You don't give up do you?" Ethan stood up and pawed Kasey's jacket. "If you insist on taking me home, you'd better crawl into bed with me."

Kasey pulled away. "Down boy, you aren't in any shape."

"You were begging for it before."

Kasey helped Ethan sit back down and sat beside him. "This isn't like you. Why are you doin' this?"

"I have my reasons."

"It's not healthy, Ethan."

"I don't need a lecture. You aren't my father. My father's dead."

Kasey's chin went up. "So that's what this is about. You didn't need to do this. You could've come to me. I can help you get through it. Your dad wouldn't want this for you either. Booze doesn't help anything. I learned that the hard way."

"I disagree."

Kasey shook his head. "I'll be right back. You sit right there." He went over to his band members. After a moment, he came back over to him. "Let's go."

"What about your band?"

"They'll have to manage without me. You're more important."

* * * *

I followed my brother and Kasey to our mother's house. Ethan looked like he was going to be sick the entire way. When they got there, Kasey helped him out of the car and tried to keep him steady as they went up the driveway.

"Lean on me," Kasey said. "It's alright."

As they approached the door, Mom pulled into the driveway and came running up to them. "What's going on here?"

"He's had a little too much to drink, Mrs. Hawkins," Kasey said. "I think he'll be fine. He just needs to sleep it off."

Mom gave Ethan a reprimanding glance. "I see that. Thank you for bringing him home, Kasey. I'll take it from here."

"Are you sure? I can help you get him inside."

She glared at him. "I'll handle it. Now have a good night."

Kasey, surprised by her curt tone, stepped back and glanced briefly at Ethan. "I'll talk to you tomorrow." He walked down the steps and up the path disappearing from sight.

Mom put her arm under Ethan's and led him inside.

"Where were you?" Ethan asked as they entered the kitchen. "It's the middle of the night."

"That's not important. I'd rather talk about you. I'm surprised at you. You've been having a tough time lately. We all have, but going out and getting drunk doesn't help anything."

"I'm going to bed," he said, breaking away from her and stumbling forward.

She gave him her hand to stabilize him. "We aren't finished here."

"I say we are."

She let him go and put her hand on her hip. "What's the matter with you? I haven't seen you in five years, and when you finally decide to come home, you do it in this condition. Why did you feel the need to get drunk?"

He scoffed. "If you're that dense that you don't know, I'm not going to bother to tell you."

"Ethan!" She paused and softened her tone. "Look, if this is about your father, he wouldn't want you doing this. He'd want you to get on with your life."

He chuckled softly. "How?"

"Well, by focusing on keeping the company going and building a life for yourself in Sleepy Meadows."

He laughed. "Yeah, right, and maybe I'll find a nice girl to settle down with?" He turned and stumbled into the living room.

Mom followed him. "What? Is it so ludicrous that a handsome young man like you would find someone? You can't be single forever. It's a shame that Rebecca isn't available. I always thought that the two of you would make a nice couple."

He looked away. "So did she."

"No matter. You'll find someone eventually."

He gazed at her. "What if I told you I already have?"

Her eyes widened. "Why didn't you say anything?"

"I couldn't." He glanced down.

"Sit down here." Mom helped him sit on the sofa. She sat beside him and put her hand on his leg. "What's bothering you? I can always tell when you're upset. Is it about the girl you've met? Do I know her?"

Ethan began to sob.

She rubbed his back. "Honey, whatever it is, you can tell me."

"It's Kasey."

Mom swallowed. "What?"

"It's Kasey Menze." Ethan covered his face with his hand.

Mom put her hands to her mouth. "Kasey?"

"Don't make me say it. I can't."

Mom shook her head and stood up. "I don't believe this. It can't be true."

His eyes were wracked with pain, and he met her glance. He stood up, suddenly sober. "I know how ashamed you must be. I'd understand if you wanted me to leave."

She took him in her arms. "Why didn't you tell me?"

"I can't even deal with it myself."

Mom shook her head back and forth. "This relationship can't go on."

The Possession

He stifled a sob and glared at her. "What?"

She put her hand up. "Not for the reason you think. There's something you don't know."

"Great. You ask me to pour my heart out to you and then when I do, you stomp on it. I guess I shouldn't be surprised."

"You don't understand, Ethan."

He threw his hands up. "Like hell I don't. I'm sorry if my existence embarrasses you so much, but maybe I'm sick of lying to myself and everyone else about who I am. You're already ashamed of Shelly. You might as well be ashamed of me too."

Mom shook her head. "That's not true."

"You're lying. All you care about is your reputation in this town. You just don't want to be known as the mother of the town kook and the town queer."

"Stop!" Mom grabbed his arms and shook him. "Just stop right now!"

He pushed her away and left the room. Mom ran into her room, slammed the door, and plopped down on the bed, crying.

Chapter 9

I wanted nothing more than to comfort my mother and brother. As I watched Mom cry, I realized that it wasn't Ethan's revelation that upset her so much. What upset her was who he was in love with. He was in love with Kasey, whose father was Damon. Then she started to think about me. This time, I wished I couldn't read her thoughts. What I found out next devastated me. She was thinking about how Damon's my father too.

I left her thoughts and returned to Reed and Rory, who were sitting on the couch talking.

"Where's Damon?"

Rory, seeing the look on my face, stood up and approached me. "He's still guarding the gate. What's the matter?"

My throat was tight and hot, and I could barely speak. "Is he my father?"

Rory tilted his head. "Where did you hear that?"

I sighed heavily. "Just answer the question. Is he?"

"I think you need to discuss it with him."

I put my hand up to my mouth. "It's true, isn't it? Damon's my father." Rory tried to embrace me, but I broke away. "Don't. I don't want to be touched right now."

"It's going to be okay. I promise."

"Wait," Reed said, with an obnoxious grin on his face. "So that makes Kasey and Ethan both your brothers and they're hooking up? That's incestuous."

Rory shot him a look. "You're not helping. Kasey and Ethan both have different mothers and fathers. Ethan's father is Jeffrey Hawkins.

They aren't related."

"I know," Reed said, rolling his eyes. "I was just trying to make light of it. This bothers me just as much as it does Shelly."

I looked at Rory with tears in my eyes. "All these years I thought Jeffrey Hawkins was my father. It was all a lie."

Rory wiped my cheek. "He was, in every way that counted, especially in his heart."

"He knew I wasn't his daughter?"

Rory smiled. "It didn't matter. He loved you, just as I love you."

I let him pull me into his arms, and he held me close. It felt so good to be in his strong, loving arms again. After a moment, he pulled away in looked at me. "We need you to keep an eye on the mortal realm. Remember what Damon said."

"I want to remain with you."

"We'll have an eternity together, darling. Right now we need to know Jeremy's every move, and you seem to have the abilities to see everything. That's a special gift."

I gave him a nod and closed my eyes to focus on the mortal realm again. I noticed that in the short conversation I had with Rory, morning had come there.

* * * *

As my vision became clear, I saw Gram going down the hallway at Mom's house with a basket of laundry in her hands. As she approached Mom's room, she heard muffled sobbing coming from inside. She knocked on the door and opened it slowly.

"Caroline? What's wrong, dear? I heard you crying."

Mom was lying on her bed and looked over at Gram, her eyes bloodshot and full of tears. "Not now, Mother. Just leave me alone."

Gram walked into the room and set the laundry basket on the floor by the bed. She sat down at the end of the bed and touched Mom's leg. "Not a chance. Talk to me."

Mom sat up and wiped her face. "I don't even know where to start."

"It's always best to start at the beginning."

Mom choked back the tears and put her hand on her heart. "I feel like the entire world as I know it is falling apart around me, and I can't do a damn thing to stop it."

Gram squeezed Mom's hand gently. "I know you miss Jeffrey. We all do."

"It isn't just that. It's the kids too."

"His passing's been hard on them too. I'm aware of that."

"It's more complicated." Mom took a tissue from the box on the nightstand and wiped her nose. "Shelly's up in that Wickcliff prison wasting away. I didn't even recognize my little girl at Jeffrey's wake. It's almost like she's a different person. And Ethan, it doesn't even make any sense."

Gram stood up. "What doesn't? Will you stop carrying on and tell me what has you so upset?"

Mom nodded and bit her lip. "Ethan told me he's gay and that he's in love with Kasey Menze."

Gram gasped and put her hand on her cheek. "I don't believe it."

"It's true. He made that quite clear last night."

"But Ethan's such a handsome boy. He could have his pick of any woman he wants, like Rebecca."

"He doesn't want them, and she's married. You know that."

Gram shook her head. "I don't understand that boy. What's wrong with this generation? In my day, that sort of thing was unheard of."

"No, it wasn't, Mother. People didn't talk about it as much back then. It doesn't change the man that my son is. I'll always love him unconditionally. It's who he's in love with that disturbs me so."

"You have to put a stop to this, Caroline, right now. Ethan can't be with Kasey. He's practically family. He's Shelly's brother for God's sake."

So it was true. Gram knew all along too that I was Damon's daughter and that Kasey was his son. Kasey had always been like a brother to me growing up, but I never dreamed that he was my biological brother.

Mom got up from the bed. "Don't you think I know that? Why do you think I'm so upset? I just got my son back, and I could lose him again if he finds out the truth. It'll destroy him. What am I supposed to do?"

Gram grabbed the rocking chair behind her and sat. When she did, the shawl that was on the back of the chair fell to the floor. She picked it up.

"It's lovely. How come you never wear this?"

"It isn't mine. It's Hilda's."

Gram raised an eyebrow. "Hilda? What would you be doing with Hilda's shawl?"

Mom snatched the shawl out of Gram's hands. She threw it on the bed. "We were together last night, and she saw that I was chilled."

"She's back in town?" Gram sighed. "I'll never understand why you insist on hanging around with that old crone."

Mom put her hand on her hip. "She isn't an old crone, and she hasn't been here to hang around with. She's been gone for years. She's a dear friend. I was upset when I first saw her after so many years, but it doesn't change the fact that I care about her."

Gram shrugged. "Okay, an old coot then."

"Mother, stop being so rude. That old coot's going to help save this town, and you're going to thank her for it. She came back here to warn us."

Gram's eyes narrowed. "What do you mean save the town? Warn us about what?"

"Jeremy Wickcliff's alive again."

Gram got up. "I think you need to lie back down."

"I know what I'm talking about. Jeremy's returned from the dead."

Gram put her hand on Mom's forehead. "You don't seem to have a fever." She went over to the bed and pulled the covers down. "I think losing Jeffrey and Ethan's revelation may have been a tad too much for you. You'll feel much better after you've had a nice long rest."

Mom stomped her foot. "Don't patronize me. I'm not crazy. If you don't believe me, ask Hilda or Gracey, or Lucy even."

Gram's eyes popped open wider, her mouth agape. "Lucy? I haven't heard that name—"

"We brought her back last night, the three of us. She's going to help us stop him."

Gram clasped her hands together as if she were going to pray. "Oh, dear God in heaven. You're using that witchcraft again." She looked up at the ceiling. "God forgive her."

"I'm not the one you should be praying for. We're not the evil ones. You should pray for the people in this town because if Jeremy takes a hold, we're going to need your prayers."

"You know I don't agree with this, Caroline. What you've done isn't natural. You promised me that you'd stop."

Mom sighed. "I did for a long time, but I don't have any choice. I've got to protect this family. Whatever I promised you in the past doesn't matter at this point. I have enough on my plate as it is without having to worry about how you feel too. I need to stop lying in here crying and get my act together. The four of us need to hatch out a plan."

"How can Jeremy come back to life after everything that happened years ago? I don't understand any of this."

"There's a lot you don't understand, but then again you never cared to. You were too busy judging me. All you need to know is that he's possessed a mortal and that Hilda confronted him at the mansion yesterday. He revealed his identity to her."

"The dead returning to life? Evil spirits possessing the living?" Gram exhaled sharply.

"Don't act so surprised. It's not like it hasn't happened before. This is Sleepy Meadows after all."

Gram ignored her comment. "I hope you're satisfied."

Mom squinted. "What does that mean? We aren't responsible for this."

Gram went over to the bed and picked the laundry basket off the floor. "I've been warning you since you were a young girl about what that craft of yours is capable of. You're going to get yourself killed. If Jeremy's back, you're no match for him, and you know it. Don't you remember what happened last time?"

"That was then, and this is now. Things have changed."

"I doubt that."

Mom groaned. "I can't talk to you when you're like this. I can't stand around here arguing. I've got to get Shelly out of that house. I don't trust him there with her."

Gram didn't say anything and instead walked toward the door.

"Where are you going?" Mom asked.

"To finish the laundry and get breakfast started. It's nearly eight."

"You're going to act like you didn't hear a word I just said?"

Gram turned to look back. "That's exactly what I'm going to do. I refuse to take part in any of this witchcraft malarkey." She shook her head. "I'd be more concerned with your children's problems than what Jeremy's planning. Worry about your own and let the people of this town fend for themselves."

"I'm doing this for my children. If Jeremy's not stopped, this family and many others will be destroyed. Is that what you want?"

Gram's eyes lowered. "Of course not, but I'm afraid for you."

"I survived then, and I'll survive now. I won't make the same mistakes again. I need to do this for Jeffrey. He needs to be avenged. Jeremy murdered him. Do you realize that? You know how the Wickcliffs always blamed Jeffrey's father for Harold's death."

Gram put the clothes basket down again. "He wouldn't want you putting your life in danger for his sake. Your children need you."

"My children are adults, they have their own lives, and if I don't do something soon, we could all be killed."

Gram shook her head. "I don't want you involved. I forbid it."

"Excuse me, Mother, but I'm a grown woman, and I can think for myself. We're the only ones with the power to do battle with him. The people in this town don't stand a chance without us."

Gram gave her a sour expression. "I blame Irma for this. She promised that we'd all live in peace if the townspeople let her stay in that Godforsaken house. Jeremy wouldn't have had a place to come back to if we would've run her off like we should have. She must know that Jeremy's returned. How could she not tell us that he was back? Not give us some warning?"

Gram turned her back on Mom and walked out into the hallway. Mom followed right behind her.

"Now where are you going?"

"Forget the damn laundry and the breakfast. I'm going to march over there and give that old biddy a piece of my mind."

"Leave Irma alone, Mother. It isn't her fault."

"I disagree," Gram said, starting down the stairs. "Just let me do what I need to do. I'll find Shelly while I'm there too."

"Mother, come back here!"

Gram didn't turn around. She went down the stairs, out the door, and to her car. As she got into the car and started it up, she thought about how Irma's son had put Mom's life in danger again. Just as Mom felt like it was her responsibility to protect her children, Gram had the same sense of responsibility. Gram thought that the feud between our families ended with Jeremy's death, but his return had changed everything.

"They have no idea what they've done by reigniting this feud. They're messing with the wrong old broad."

* * * *

I kept my focus on Gram. I didn't like the fact that she was coming to the mansion alone again, and I was afraid of what Jeremy and Rachel might do to her if they found her here. I had to make sure that she was going to be safe.

Gram replayed the conversation she'd just had with Mom repeatedly in her head as her car went around the curve near Lover's Bluff. She wasn't exactly sure what she was going to say to Irma or what she could do to protect her daughter, but when she'd heard that Mom and the rest of her coven were planning on doing battle with Jeremy again, she was filled with confusion, rage, and panic. She needed to take that out on someone.

When she arrived at the mansion, she got out of the car and slammed the door. She hurried up the overgrown path leading to the front door, all the while thinking about how much she wanted to lay into Irma about Jeremy's return. She reached the door and pounded on it. She stood with her hands on her hips waiting for an answer. After a moment, Greta opened the door.

"Ms. Ford. Now what do you want?"

"Where's Jeremy, Greta?"

The maid's irritated expression didn't change. "Who? You mean Jeremy Wickcliff?"

"I don't have time for games. I know he's here, and don't try to deny it."

Greta frowned. "Mr. Wickcliff's been deceased for many years, Ms. Ford. Before I worked here even. You know that."

"Don't give me that. I don't believe you."

The Possession

Greta shook her head. "I don't care what you believe. Look, I don't know what you want me to say, but it's obvious that you're disturbed and that I can't help you. If you'll excuse me, I have much to do today."

She tried to shut the door, but Gram put her hand on it and held it open. "I'm not leaving here until I speak with Jeremy."

"You're insane."

"And you're a liar. By covering for them, you're helping unleash their wrath on this town. If people die, their blood will be on your hands."

She pushed her way past Greta and stood defiantly in the foyer. Greta shut the door behind her and turned to face her. "I'm afraid you're trespassing, and if you don't leave, I'll be forced to call the police."

"You do that. Sheriff Withers has already searched this house once because he was suspicious. I wonder what he'd find the second time around. Go ahead and call. I dare you."

Greta didn't respond. She just glared at Gram.

"If you insist that Jeremy isn't here, I'll just have a little chat with my old pal Irma."

Greta shook her head. "That's not possible. Mrs. Wickcliff isn't well. You saw that for yourself when you were here the other night. She doesn't even know what's happening."

"You sound like a broken record, Greta. Don't you ever get tired of the same spiel? I'm tired of hearing it. She knows a lot more than you think she does about a lot of things, and I want answers about Jeremy's return." She put her hand on her hip. "I'm not leaving. You can either take me up there, or I'll go without you."

Greta sighed. "Very well, but I'll only do it because Mrs. Wickcliff wouldn't like the police nosing around here. If it were up to me, I'd call them."

"If Jeremy hasn't returned, what does Irma have to hide from the police?"

"I don't have time for ridiculous questions," Greta took Gram by the arm. "Come along."

Gram pulled her arm back. "Don't touch me. You're lucky I don't lay you out where you stand. You have no right to grab people that way. Let's go."

Greta reluctantly took Gram upstairs to Irma's room. When she entered, she found Irma sitting in a chair by the window. Although the sun poured through the windows, Gram didn't think that the light did anything to flatter her. Irma appeared just as withered and tired as she always had.

Greta cleared her throat. "You have a visitor again, ma'am."

Irma didn't respond. Instead, she sat rocking back and forth in the chair, humming.

Greta turned her attention to Gram. "She's getting worse." Then she went up to Irma. "Mrs. Wickcliff, please try to focus, dear."

Irma sat unresponsive, continuing to rock and hum.

Greta turned back to Gram again, and her eyes widened. "I don't know what to do. I've never seen her this bad before. She always responds. Her periods of lucidity are becoming less and less. Oh, how terrible."

"Let me handle this," Gram said. She went up to Irma and slapped her in the face. "Irma, snap out of it you senile old bitch!"

Greta gasped.

"Oh," Irma said, her eyes focused on Gram's face. She put her hand on her cheek and rubbed it. "Why did you hit me?" She tried to get up, but her legs buckled and she fell back into the chair. "I don't even know you."

"Of course you do, Irma. It's me, Edie."

Irma shook her head. "I'm telling you I don't. What's wrong with my legs? Why can't I stand up? What's happening?"

"You're upsetting her," Greta said, walking in front of Gram. "You need to leave now before I have you charged with assault." She pointed to the door.

"I'll thank you to remember that I'm still the mistress of this house, Mildred," Irma said. "And if you can't remember that, I'll have to relieve you of your duties immediately."

"She's confused again," Greta said.

"What else is new?" Gram said. "She's talking about Mildred Hamilton, I bet. She used to work here."

Irma glanced at Gram. "You know her?"

"I knew her. We worked together here. She died 25 years ago,

Irma."

Irma put her hands on the side of her head, shaking it. "I'm so confused. Everyone's dying."

Gram's eyes narrowed. "What do you mean everyone's dying? Who's everyone?"

"Why should I tell you? You haven't told me how you even know me."

Greta moved closer to Irma. "I think you'd better lie down, Mrs. Wickcliff. Let me help you to bed."

Irma huffed. "I won't have you tell me what to do in my home. You may go, Mildred."

"But—"

She pointed to the door. "Get out!"

Greta exhaled heavily and turned to Gram with a scowl on her face. "Don't you dare upset her or you'll have to deal with me." She walked out and shut the door behind her.

Gram pulled up a chair across from Irma and sat. "Ok. It's just the two of us now. You can knock off the little game."

Irma gave her a wide-eyed, innocent expression. "Game? What game?"

"Cut the crap, Irma. I know Jeremy's come back, and I want to know why."

Irma's eyes narrowed. "Jeremy who?"

"You know damn well who. Your son."

"I have no son. Harold wants an heir one day, but we're just courting, you know. It would be shockingly inappropriate to bear a child before the wedding. Now if you'll excuse me, I have to get ready for my coming out ball this evening. My parents have been planning it for months, and they'll be extremely upset if I don't make it on time."

Gram grabbed a hold of Irma's arms and shook her. "Oh, for heaven's sake! Don't you know anything anymore? It's me, Irma. Edie Ford, and I think you know that all too well."

A look of clarity entered Irma's eyes. "Edie? What are you doing here? I told you never to come back here."

Gram sighed with relief and let her go. "It's about time you started making sense. I need to talk to you about Jeremy. I know that he's returned, and you needn't bother denying it. What does he want with us?"

Irma grinned, revealing her yellowed teeth. "I don't know, and even if I did, why would I bother to tell you?"

Gram raised an eyebrow. "I beg your pardon?"

"There are times when I don't even remember my name, but for as long as I live, I'll never forget what you and Charles Hawkins did to my beloved Harold."

Gram laughed. "Beloved? You're insane. You loathed each other. You got married for social standing, nothing more."

"That man was the love of my life, and you helped take him away from me. Have you ever heard the expression an eye for an eye, dear?"

Gram shook her head in disgust. "What happened to Harold was an accident. You know that."

"Forgive me if I could care less what Jeremy has in store for your family."

Gram tried to keep her patience, but I could tell that it was wearing thin. "You know how dangerous he is. He's already killed my son-in-law, and there's no telling who will be next. If you help conceal him, you'll be helping him commit more murders."

"I don't care about him, and I care even less about you. Remember what I said, an eye for an eye." She pointed to the door with her long crooked finger. "Get the hell out of my house."

The look in Irma's eye told Gram that she knew what was happening, and she knew what she was saying, just as Gram had suspected.

"Irma, where's Shelly? I didn't see her downstairs. If Jeremy's here, I don't want her in this house with him."

Irma laughed. "Shelly? You're in for quite the surprise, Edie dear."

"What does that mean?"

"I can't very well spoil the surprise, can I?"

Gram didn't move. "You'll pay for this, Irma. If anything happens to any of my family members because of your psychopathic son, I'm going to make you suffer."

"Get out!"

"Irma—"

The Possession

Irma turned back to the window, her eyes becoming cloudy again. "Oh, isn't it a lovely day, Harold?"

Gram realized that she wasn't going to get anywhere else with her, and by the time she'd reached the door, Irma had started rocking and humming again. While her visit to the Wickcliffs didn't exactly go as planned, she'd gotten confirmation that Jeremy was indeed back and that Irma wasn't as senile as she wanted people to believe.

Chapter 10

Since Rory and Damon were depending on me to keep them apprised of what was happening in the mortal realm, I kept my attention focused there. I still wondered how it was that I could see and feel things that happened there. After I'd died, I assumed it was because all spirits could do those things. Rory was a spirit just as I was, and he couldn't see everything. It made me wonder if I had some of my Mom's powers. Maybe I've had her abilities all along, and my death just heightened them. Some of the things I'd discovered about myself were fascinating while others had been hurtful and scary.

I watched as Rachel entered the parlor. She'd waited until Gram left the house to come down from the tower room. She'd figured that Gram would be looking for me, and she was right. Gram had been to my room, Rory's old study looking for me, and interrogated Greta with a million questions regarding my whereabouts before finally giving up and leaving. Rachel didn't know how to explain her appearance and didn't want to try. She wasn't up to the game of passing herself off as me, so she decided to ignore Gram altogether. She didn't know my Grandmother. She wasn't one to let herself be avoided. I knew she'd be back.

Rachel had been despondent ever since Hilda paid her and Jeremy a visit. Hilda had asked her to look in the mirror, and when she did, she was horrified to see that her skin had turned wan, a similar shade of what it looked like when she'd been alive the first time. It made Rachel wonder if the reflection that taunted her had been right, and there was no escape from what she'd been in the past.

She looked in the mirror again, and the circles under her eyes had become darker. Purple veins protruded from her forehead and neck. It was horrifying for me to see my body in this condition, even though it was no longer mine.

Rachel picked up a vase that sat on the mantel of the fireplace, screamed, and threw it against the wall, shattering it. She stood there for a moment, visibly shaken, took in a deep breath and exhaled slowly. While trying to calm herself down, she felt a sharp, searing pain in her abdomen which made her cry out and grab her stomach.

Gaul entered the room. "I heard a crash in here." He paused when he saw Rachel doubled over and went over to her. He helped her stand up straight. "Rachel, are you alright?"

She shook her head. "Something's wrong with me." She rubbed her stomach. "It hurts."

I couldn't fathom what would suddenly cause Rachel to double over in pain, but her skin reminded me of what Reed's looked like the last time I'd seen Jeremy. Rachel was in the same spot he was. She inhabited a body that didn't belong to her. If his spirit was dying, maybe hers was too.

He helped her to the sofa, and she sat down. "Just relax. It'll pass."

She turned to him. "How do you know it'll pass? Do you know what's wrong with me?"

He nodded. "You're having hunger pains."

Rachel's eyes filled with tears. "This is a lot worse than any hunger pain."

He rubbed her back. "It's alright. It'll all be over in a moment."

She sat there until the pain subsided as Gaul said it would. She took a deep breath and let it out slowly. "I can breathe again. How did you know it would get better?" She took another deep breath. "I've never experienced pain like that. I'm not one for doctors but…"

"No doctor can help you. The only way to prevent the pain from recurring is by feeding."

She raised her eyebrows. "I'm not hungry. I'm sick."

"You're not sick. I knew it was only a matter of time before this would happen, but Jeremy made me promise not to tell you until we had to."

She saw darkness in his eyes. "Gaul, what are you keeping from me?" She sat back. "You're scaring me."

"We need to get you some food to sustain you. Otherwise, the pains will start again, and they'll get worse until you satisfy the hunger."

"I don't see how food is the answer. You didn't feel the pain I just felt. It was unbearable. Something's wrong."

"Rachel, you need more than food to sustain you."

She got up. "What are you saying?"

"You're one of the living dead, not alive, not quite dead. The only way we survive is on the flesh and blood of the living. That's part of the condition of you being able to live again."

She began to walk away. "If this is your idea of some sick joke, I'm not amused."

He grabbed her arm. "This isn't a joke. This is serious. Shelly's body isn't yours. You're dead, you only live and breathe because of black magic. You're from the dark realm and those spirits need to feed to survive."

"Gaul, have you lost your mind?"

"You think it's natural that you'd be allowed to return from the grave? There's a price when the dead return to life using the black arts."

"That's ridiculous."

"Is it?" Gaul turned her to face the mirror again. "Take a look at yourself, Rachel. Look at your pallid skin, the dark circles under your eyes, your black lips. What does it remind you of? It looks like death to me."

Rachel broke away from him and turned her back. "Stop it. I don't want to look."

He stepped in front of her. "The reason you look as you do is because you need to feed."

"If that were true, Jeremy would be having these pains too."

Gaul shook his head. "Jeremy inhabited a body that was alive, a living, breathing human being. Shelly was dead. That's the difference."

Rachel put her hand to her mouth, stifling a sob. "So I'm some kind of zombie or something? Is that what you're saying to me?"

He gave her a nod. "I don't know if I would use those exact terms, but in a sense, yes."

Rachel let out a breath slowly. "And if I refuse to feed?"

The Possession

"There's no refusing. If you don't feed, your spirit dies, and you go back into the dark. You may have no memory of that place, but you don't want to go back there."

She turned away again. "I can't live like this. I won't. It's even worse than how I had to live last time and I never thought anything could be worse than that. It's not fair. I finally thought that I had the chance for a normal life. It's all I ever wanted."

Gaul came up from behind her almost touching her. "You can have a normal life. The feeding is just a small necessity. At least we're together again. You have to do this is we're going to stay together. You do want to stay here with me, don't you?"

She turned back to face him again. "Of course, but not like this."

"It's the only way, Rachel." Gaul stepped back and walked to the door. "Follow me."

She followed him out into the foyer. "Where are we going?"

Gaul opened the door and motioned for her to step outside. He followed her and shut the door. "If the pain's as severe as it appears, you're running out of time. You must feed, and I'm going to help you."

Gaul left to get the limo and within minutes pulled up to the driveway where Rachel stood. She got in the back seat. They drove in silence down the winding road past Lover's Bluff. She couldn't enjoy the brilliant pinks and purples in the sky caused by the setting sun because all she could think about was Gaul's revelation.

She wasn't the only one. I had trouble comprehending what I'd heard too. I'd never believed that the dead could return to life, or that they could walk among the living feasting on blood. It sounded more like the plotline of one of Ethan's campy horror movies he'd forced me to watch when we were kids. It didn't seem like reality but after what I'd seen both in the mortal and spirit realms since I'd crossed over, I wasn't sure what was reality anymore. As Gaul continued to drive, Rachel doubled over in pain again.

He looked back at her through the rearview mirror. "Are you alright, Rachel?"

"It's worse than before, Gaul. Please roll down the window so I can get some fresh air." He did what she asked, but it made her feel worse. "I can't stand this pain."

"I tried to tell you. It'll get more intense until you feed."

Rachel writhed in the back seat, clenching her stomach. "Help me, Gaul, please. I'll do whatever you say without question."

"I will. I promise. I know the perfect place to find a victim."

"Victim? You make it sound like I'm a murderer."

"In a sense, you will be. When it comes to survival, it's either yours or theirs."

Rachel groaned. "I don't know if I can do it."

He met eyes with her in the rearview mirror. "Without question, remember? You must trust me." He stopped the car.

"Where are we?"

"This is a drinking establishment."

"A bar? You've brought me to a bar?"

"You need to find people that no one will miss, loners. This is the place to find them."

He got out of the car and opened her door. He extended his hand, and she took it. "You look better."

She nodded. "The pain's starting to subside again."

"We must hurry. Next time it won't."

She didn't say another word. She undid the top button of her blouse and headed inside. Once inside, she looked around the room, filled with cigarette smoke and the smell of alcohol. She was trying to find the courage to approach one of the men at the bar by justifying to herself that Gaul was right. She had a choice to make. It was either her survival or theirs, and she wasn't going to let anything stand in the way of her second chance at life no matter what it took.

Bucky, Kasey's friend, stood behind the bar. "What can I get you?"

She sat down, not making eye contact. "A shot of whiskey."

He cleared his throat. "Forgive me for saying so, but I'm not sure a drink's what you need. You seem like you aren't feeling that well."

She managed a strained smile. "It's nothing that a few drinks and some good conversation won't cure." She waved her hand. "I'm sorry. I seem to have forgotten your name."

He put his hand out. "It's Bucky Loring. It's okay. I don't expect you to remember a common guy like me bein' a Wickcliff and all. You only came in here once. I remember you because you mentioned you're

Ethan's sister."

"That's right. I'm sorry, Bucky."

"It's not a problem." He slung a towel over his shoulder and returned in a few moments with her drink. "Are you sure you're okay? You look like you should be at home in bed."

She downed the shot. "I probably should. I haven't been sleeping well since my father passed away. I think that's why I feel so run down."

Bucky nodded. "I heard about that. I'm sorry. He was a good man."

"Thank you."

She spoke with him for a while and then stood up. "I think you're right. I'm not feeling well. I'd better get going." She put her hand on her forehead and stumbled backward. The pain was starting again.

A burly bar patron caught her. "Hey, you okay, lady?"

"I'm fine, just a little faint."

When he let her go, she stumbled again. Bucky came out from behind the bar and steadied her. "Maybe we should call a doctor."

She shook her head. "That won't be necessary. I just need to rest. That's all."

He gave her a once over. "Is there anything I can do?"

"If you want to help, you can make sure I get to my car safely."

My heart sank. Rachel didn't need help to the car despite the pain. She was luring Bucky to the car and I couldn't to anything to stop it.

Bucky nodded. "Lean on me. I'll help you."

A moment later, they were outside. Dusk had given way to dark now, and the parking lot was only illuminated by the moonlight.

"You shouldn't drive," Bucky said, leading her out into the parking lot.

"I have a driver. I just have to get to the car."

"Which car's yours?"

She motioned with her hand. "Straight ahead."

He looked at it and then back at her. "I should've known you'd come in a limo. I wouldn't expect a Wickcliff to travel any other way. Why did you come here tonight? Not to knock my parent's place, but it's not exactly the kind of place that a woman like you would typically hang out."

"I'm not like that. It gets lonely in that big old house. Sometimes a girl just needs some companionship."

He led her to the limo and opened the door. After helping her inside, she groaned.

"Did I hurt you?"

"I'll be fine in just a minute."

"Where's your driver?"

"I don't know. He said he'd wait for me." She groaned again, and her head fell to the side. She appeared to be unconscious.

"Shit," Bucky said, climbing into the limo. He checked for a pulse. "I knew you needed a doctor."

While he tended to Rachel, Gaul came out of the dark and slammed the door on Bucky's side. Bucky heard the locks click and turned to face the door. He yanked on the handle, but the door wouldn't open. Gaul got in.

Bucky tapped on the glass separating the front from the back. "Hey, driver, we need help back here!"

Rachel sat up, dazed. "What happened?"

He turned to her, his eyes wide. "You fainted. I think you need to go to the hospital to get checked out."

"I'm feeling much better already." She inched closer to him. "You know what I could use? A hug. It's so chilly tonight, and I think that it would make me feel better."

He shook his head. "I should get back to work. If I'm gone too long, the drunks will start stealing booze and my father will kill me." He tried the door again, but it was still locked. He turned back to Rachel. "What's the big idea? Let me out of here."

Before she could say anything, Gaul turned on the ignition. Bucky fidgeted in his seat. "I don't know what your deal is, but I want you to let me out right now. I said I'd see you to your car, and I have. There's nothing more that I can do for you."

Rachel gave him a sly smile. "Oh, but there is. Much more. You seem nervous, Bucky. You don't have to be. I just thought I'd take you back to my place for a nightcap to thank you for your kindness. I figured Gaul, my driver, could bring you back here after. But if you don't want to go…" She lowered her eyes. "I'm sorry. I shouldn't have assumed that you'd want to. I could sure use the company on the way back." She pointed to the front. "Gaul's kinda stiff. Not much fun to talk to."

"Are you coming on to me?"

She ran a finger down his chest. "That depends. Would you like me to?"

He thought about it for a minute. "I have a girlfriend. I can't do this."

"I just need a little companionship tonight. Companionship doesn't have to translate into sex."

He sighed. "Let me just tell someone inside that I'm going. I'll be back."

He moved to open the door, but Rachel grabbed his arm and snuggled up close to him. "They'll be fine. You won't be gone for long. Don't go. I've been so lonely. I bet you have too."

Bucky knew that he shouldn't have left without telling anyone, but he thought she was me. Part of him felt sorry for her. He knew what had happened to Rory and was familiar with my reputation in town after that, how I'd isolated myself inside the mansion. He was indeed lonely, and so was she. He saw nothing wrong with keeping her company for a little while. He gave her a nod. "Okay, as long as I'm not gone for too long."

"We can go now, Gaul," Rachel said.

They drove for several minutes in silence until they got close enough that the mansion was visible on top of the hill. Bucky, who was looking out the window, turned to face Rachel.

"I can't believe I'm going to the Wickcliff mansion. There're a lot of stories about that place."

"What stories?"

"Are you kidding? You live there, you outta know. Is it really haunted?"

She chuckled. "That's preposterous. There are no such things as ghosts."

He ignored her comment. "They were all whack jobs, so the legend goes, especially the daughter. You know the freak. What was her name? Rachel, that was it."

She glared at him with contempt in her eyes. "She wasn't a freak. She was born with a disease, a deformity. It wasn't her fault."

He put his hand up. "Sorry. I didn't mean to make you defensive.

It's just I heard that she was locked away like some animal and that she went nuts."

"It wasn't her fault, her family made her that way!"

He pushed himself away. "Jeez. I guess I hit a nerve." He turned back to look out the window.

"I'm sorry," she said, trying to calm herself. When he turned to look at her, she forced a smile. "I didn't mean to snap like that. It just all sounds so horrible."

The car stopped, and Gaul put it in park.

"Well I guess we're here," Bucky said. "I'll help you inside."

She stared into his eyes for a moment and as she did, the hunger pains intensified. She writhed in pain.

Bucky sat back from her. "Oh my God. I'm taking you to the hospital."

She didn't respond, but peered into his eyes, as her hunger grew deeper. "Hold me. Please. I'm so afraid."

Bucky complied apprehensively. Rachel opened her mouth. Her teeth jutted out and transformed into sharp, razor-like fangs like those of a wild animal. She sunk her teeth deep into his neck, and he shouted out in pain.

Chapter 11

I watched, horrified and stunned as I witnessed her take a gash out of his neck. Up until now, I was convinced that she wouldn't go through with it. She seemed so fragile, so delicate, and because she never had a normal life, somewhat naive. I didn't want to believe she was capable of attacking someone like a wild beast, but it was happening right in front of me.

He pushed her away with all his strength and put his hand on his neck. He looked at his hand. It was covered in blood. More blood poured from his neck.

"What the fuck did you do to me?"

Rachel opened her mouth and let Bucky see her teeth for the first time. He was horrified, his face full of fear. "What the hell are you?"

She didn't answer. She got closer to him. He tried to open the door, but it was locked. He squirmed. "Stay away from me!"

She pounced on him like a wild animal, going for his throat. Blood spattered the interior. I shut my eyes and covered my ears, unable to stand the sound of his shrill screams. I couldn't watch what she was doing to him. I could still hear the sounds of her biting him, sucking his blood, although they were muffled by his shrieks.

Within moments, Bucky fell silent. I looked at her again. His lifeless body lay slumped down in the seat next to her. He was covered in blood. It looked like his throat had been torn out. She seemed to be in a trance, staring at him in shock and then down at her hands.

"What have I done? Someone, please help me."

She flinched when Gaul opened the door. "You did what you had to do to survive, Rachel. How do you feel?"

She held out her bloodstained hands. "How do you think? I don't remember anything. I lost all control of myself."

"I meant has the pain subsided?"

She put her head down. "Yes."

"I suspected as much. Your color looks better already. Soon you'll look just as you did when you first came back. I want you to go upstairs and get out of those bloodstained clothes. I'll dispose of them and take care of cleaning the car and disposing of the body."

She began to cry. "I'm a monster. I can't go on killing. I'd rather die all over again."

He took her hand. "Don't you ever say that. Greater torture awaits you in the dark realm than anything you can inflict on anyone else. You have no choice. Now go. I have work to do here."

Rachel got out of the car and raced up the path that led to the front door. For the first time since she'd been back, she wished she wasn't. She hated her brother for bringing her back like this, knowing that she'd be some immoral, vile creature. Blinded by tears of rage and fear, all she thought about was what would happen to her if the people of Sleepy Meadows ever discovered what happened to Bucky.

* * * *

I turned back to Rory in the spirit realm. "She's a monster. Rachel's not human."

Rory approached me. "I didn't think Rachel was like the rest. I didn't know her, but based on the stories, it didn't seem as though she was like Jeremy or Harold."

I cringed. "That's not what I meant. I could see that she didn't want to do it, but she tore a boy's throat out. She had these razor sharp teeth, and she kept attacking him. He was screaming." I put my head in my hands. "She couldn't control herself. Gaul says that she needs blood to survive because I was dead when she inhabited me. It was horrible to watch."

He held me close. "I know how hard it is for you to see these things, but we need you to keep going."

I looked into his eyes. "I don't know if I can. You don't know what it's like. I've found out things about my family that no one should ever know. I've watched a woman who looks exactly like me murder an innocent man in cold blood. I don't know if I can take this."

Rory took in a deep breath. "I got a message from Damon while you were focused on the mortal realm. His abilities are telling him that Jeremy's about to make his next move. We need you, Shell."

I looked into my husband's kind eyes, knowing that the last thing he wanted to do was put me in a situation that caused me any discomfort, but I could see in his eyes just how desperate he and Damon were for my help.

"I'm afraid of what I'll see next."

He touched my face, and our eyes met. "I'm right here. Nothing's going to happen to you while I'm here, okay?" He kissed me softly and smiled.

"I'm so sorry that everyone thinks you committed suicide because Ethan and I lied to the police. I never meant…"

Rory put his index finger to my lips. "Don't worry about that now. It's over. We can't change the past."

"But I do worry about it. I love you, and I would never do anything to hurt you."

"I know that, darling, and I love you. What happened to us in our previous lives was Jeremy's fault, not yours or mine. Justice will be served. That's why I need you to tell me what you're seeing. We have to know every move he makes. Knowing what Jeremy's plans are can only give Damon the upper hand when he confronts him."

I exhaled slowly and went over to the window. In the spirit realm, it was still dark, but as the vision of what was occurring in the mortal realm came into focus, I saw that it was daylight there.

* * * *

I found myself inside the police station. Graham Withers was at his desk doing some paperwork. He stood up, opened his file cabinet and put the file he'd been looking at away. Before he could sit back down, he heard the front door of the station burst open. It was Shirley Loring, Bucky's mother.

"I need to see Sheriff Withers immediately," she said, standing at Raymond's desk.

"I'll see if he's available," Raymond said.

"That wasn't a request. This is an emergency."

Graham went to the door of his office and peered out into the waiting area. He saw her standing there. "It's okay, Ray. Shirley, what's wrong?"

She faced him with bloodshot eyes. "Can we talk in private?"

He gestured for her to come forward. She entered his office, and he closed the door behind her. He motioned to the chair across from his desk. "Have a seat." They both sat down. "What's happened?"

"It's Bucky. He's disappeared. I need you to help Hal and I find him. Please say you will. If something's happened to him…"

He put his hand up. "Slow down. Take a deep breath and tell me why you think he's disappeared."

She nodded slowly. "He was at the bar covering for Hal and I last night. In the middle of his shift, he left. I thought it was strange that he'd do that without letting someone know. Some of the patrons said they saw him leaving with Shelly Wickcliff and that she didn't look well. They said she was practically hanging on him as they walked out the door. She could barely stand up."

He tilted his head. "Shelly was at The Hook last night? Doesn't seem like the kinda place she'd hang out. No offense, Shirley."

"None taken. She doesn't hang out there. That's what's made her being there so strange. Bucky's car was still in the parking lot this morning. He never came back for it. We've tried calling him, and he doesn't answer. This doesn't make sense. He's never just vanished before."

He nodded. "I see. You know, Bucky's a nice looking young man, and Shelly's an attractive woman. She's probably been lonely and…well, you see where I'm going with this."

She wiped her eyes and shook her head. "I know what you're thinking, and you're wrong. You don't know the whole story."

He folded his hands and leaned forward. "I'm listening."

"He was supposed to go fishing at Misty Lake this morning with Ralph Chambers and didn't show up. Ralph called the house this morning wondering if we'd seen him. Hal went over to his apartment, and he wasn't there either."

"Of course he wasn't. He probably went home with Shelly and lost track of time."

She leaned forward in her chair. "That doesn't make me feel any better. He doesn't even know her that well. Besides, he's dating Brynn Wexler. He's not that kind of young man." She sighed. "Even if he did go home with her, I don't like the idea of my son hanging around the Wickcliff place."

He raised an eyebrow. "I can't blame you there. Reed's been doing odd jobs up there, and I don't like the idea of him being there either."

She got up. "I know my son. Regardless of whatever was going on, he would've called to cancel with Ralph." She sighed. "We even called the Wexler house, and he's not with Brynn either. Hal and I have both left messages for him, and he's not calling back. I don't know what else to do."

He got up. "Now Shirley, let's not get too excited."

She stepped back. "I'm telling you that something's happened." She started to cry harder and her face reddened. "You're a parent. What would you do if you thought Reed was in trouble?"

He nodded. "Fair enough. I'd do the same thing you're doing. Officially, I have to wait 48 hours before I can file a report and by then I'm sure he'll be in touch with you."

Shirley turned around to walk out. "Fine, I'll go." She opened the door and turned back around. "But if I don't hear from him, I'm coming right back here, and you'd better pray that nothing's happened to him while you're dragging your feet." She walked out and slammed the door behind her.

Graham picked up his hat from the desk. He supposed that it wouldn't hurt to talk to Rachel, thinking she was me to find out if she knew where Bucky had gone after he left her. He walked into the waiting area.

Raymond sat up straight at his desk. "Where ya goin', sheriff?"

"I need to go up to the Wickcliffs. Hold down the fort."

"Does this have anything to do with Shirley? She seemed pretty upset when she left."

"I don't know, Ray. I'll be back in a little while." He went outside and got into his police car. I decided to follow him. I knew that he would probably encounter Jeremy there, and if he did, I might be clued in on what he was planning to do next.

On the way up to the house, Graham thought about what Shirley said about not wanting her son hanging around the grounds. It reminded him of the visit Kasey paid him when he found out that Reed was hanging around with Pit and lurking around the grounds in the middle of the night. He figured that I may know something about Reed's reasons for being there, as he knew Reed had supposedly seen me the day I disappeared. However, he wasn't going to get anything out of Rachel. He was concerned that he hadn't heard from Reed since the day my dad died, and even that meeting in the hospital was accidental. He didn't understand why his son had been ignoring him.

A short time later, he arrived at the mansion and rang the bell. Rachel opened the door and greeted him with a smile.

"Hello, Sheriff Withers. This is a surprise."

Graham took off his hat. "Hello, Shelly. I was wondering if I could talk to you."

"Of course, come in." She stepped aside and motioned for him to enter.

Graham stepped into the foyer. "I'm glad to see you looking so well. The last time I was up here, I thought that something may have happened to you. Your family was very worried about you."

"I'm sorry to have put you through the trouble, but as I explained at my father's funeral, I just had to get away for a few days."

He put his hand up. "No need to explain. I'm just glad it all worked out. I wanted to talk to you about something else." Graham went into the parlor, and Rachel followed. "May we sit?"

Rachel motioned to the sofa. "Please."

He sat down. "I was sorry to hear about Jeffrey."

"Thank you, sheriff, but I don't think you came all this way just to say that. What is it?"

"I got a visit from Shirley Loring this morning. She was looking for her son, Bucky."

Rachel's throat tightened, but she remained cool and collected. "I see. How can I help?"

"Several patrons said that they saw him leaving with you. Is that true?"

Rachel gave him a nod. "That's partly true. I wasn't feeling well, and he helped me to my car."

"And then what happened?"

Rachel shrugged. "Nothing happened. I left him in the parking lot, and my driver, Gaul, brought me back here."

His eyes narrowed. "So you haven't seen him since last night?"

"No, I'm afraid not."

Graham stood up. "I have another question. Have you heard from Reed?"

Her brow furrowed. "Why no. Why would I?"

Graham put his hat back on. "He was up here doing some work for your family the night that your father had his heart attack, or so I hear."

"Really? Well, I wasn't here."

Graham shifted his stance. "I know you weren't when I arrived, but he said that he saw you before that before you left."

"Now that you mention it, I did see him briefly. It was such a brief encounter, and I was in such a hurry that I forgot all about it."

She hadn't known that Jeremy lied to Ethan about being aware of my whereabouts or that Graham knew about it. Now she felt backed into a corner. She tried to determine if he believed her, but she couldn't tell. If he didn't, she wasn't sure how she'd get out of it.

Before she could say anything else, the door to the parlor opened and in walked Jeremy. He stood there for a moment gazing at Graham and Rachel, not knowing what to say.

Graham was stunned. Now he knew for sure that Rachel was lying to him. If she'd lied about Reed's whereabouts, his instincts told him that she was lying about Bucky too.

"Reed, what are you doing here?"

Jeremy walked towards him, meeting eyes with him.

A look of bewilderment washed over Graham's face, as he realized for the first time that there was something different about his son. Instinctively, he put his hand on his holster and glanced at Rachel.

"I thought you said you hadn't seen Reed. Why did you feel the need to lie to me?"

Her head lowered. "I don't know what to tell you."

"Tell him the truth," Jeremy said. "There's no reason to deny it any longer. Soon everyone will know, dear sister."

Graham turned back to Jeremy. "Sister? What are you talking about?"

"If I told you, I'd have to kill you." Jeremy snickered, looking over at Rachel. She stood with a stoic expression on her face. "Come now. Where's your sense of humor? I thought that was funny."

"Is this some kind of joke?" Graham said. "I may have a missing person on my hands. I don't have time for games, Reed."

"Please, Sheriff Withers," Jeremy said, "just look at the painting above the mantel. It'll explain everything." He pointed to the painting of himself on the wall.

"I don't understand any of this. Why are you calling me Sheriff Withers?"

"The painting will tell you all you need to know. I'm not Reed." He pointed to Rachel. "And she isn't Shelly."

Graham froze. "What are you talking about?" He turned to Rachel, who had a foul look on her face. "What do you know about this?"

"She'll tell you nothing," Jeremy said, pointing to the painting of himself above the mantel. "Now I command you to look!"

Graham felt compelled to look. Jeremy was getting inside his head, just as he'd done mine and Reed's.

Jeremy walked up to the large painting on the wall. He turned around and faced Graham again. "This painting hangs in its rightful place now. Do you know who that man is?"

Graham didn't say anything. He had a vacant stare in his eyes.

"I asked you a question," Jeremy said. "Do you know whose portrait this is?"

Graham glanced at the handsome blond man in the painting with the intense green eyes, chiseled features, and then gazed at Jeremy. Graham shook his head and stepped back. "This can't be happening."

Jeremy pushed his chest out. "But it is. Reed Withers is gone. Only Jeremy Wickcliff remains."

Graham grabbed his gun and pointed it at him. Rachel gasped. "I don't know how the hell this happened, but I want you to tell me where my son is right now."

The Possession

"Put the gun down!" Jeremy said, putting his hand up. "You can't shoot me. If you do, your precious Reed dies."

"I would listen to what he says," Rachel said, whispering softly into Graham's ear from behind. "He holds all the cards." She took the gun out of his hand when he began to lower it.

Jeremy got closer to him, not taking his eyes off him.

"Are you going to kill me?" Graham asked.

"Of course not. I need your help, Sheriff Withers, and you're going to help me, aren't you?"

"Help?"

Graham didn't understand what was happening to him, but Jeremy had put him under one of his spells. He was frozen in place, unable to move. The blood rushed to his face turning his cheeks bright red. He heard Jeremy's voice echoing in his head, just as I had for so many years. He put his hands on the sides of his head, attempting to shut out his voice. I knew better than anyone how fruitless that was.

"Leave me alone!" Graham said.

"If you want your son to live, you'll do as I tell you." Jeremy pulled up his sleeve to reveal Reed's black flesh.

Graham looked away, once again not able to move. "What's happening to my son?"

"My spirit's dying in this body," Jeremy said. "If I die, he dies. Is that what you want?"

Graham faced him again. "Let my son go!"

"Watch how you speak to me. I'm warning you."

I knew from talking to Reed that he was all Graham had and how desperate he'd be to get him back safely.

"I just want my son back," Graham said. "I'll do anything."

Jeremy grinned. "I was hoping you'd say that because I want to be reunited with my son too. That's where you come in." He looked up at his painting and then back at Graham. "I need to find my son if I'm going to stay alive. I need to inhabit someone of my bloodline. If I find him, my spirit can move into his body. That means I can let Reed go."

Graham was horrified, but he had no choice but to listen.

"Who's your son?"

"Kasey Menze. I need you to go to him and lure him here so that I can make the transfer. I don't have much time."

Graham's eyes widened. "Kasey's your son? How is that possible?"

"It doesn't matter. I don't have the time to tell you my whole life story. You have one chance. You can either decide to help me, or you and your son both die. What'll it be?"

"If she's your sister, what's happened to Shelly?" He paused. "She's dead, isn't she? Kasey was right."

"You'll tell no one of our true identities. We need people to believe we're Reed and Shelly for a little while longer. Have you made your decision?"

"I'll help you," Graham said, devoid of any feeling. "I'll find Kasey and bring him to you."

Jeremy grinned. "Excellent."

The hold Jeremy had on him seemed to let up, and Graham breathed in deeply. I followed him out and watched him drive away. The farther he got from the house, the more Jeremy's spell over him seemed to lift. He pulled over to the side of the road and became ill. As he caught his breath and made it back to the car, he wondered how he could sacrifice Kasey to get Reed back. He'd dedicated his life to helping others. It wasn't in his nature to harm them, but he wasn't sure how he'd be able to get Reed back otherwise.

"I'm not going to let that Wickcliff bastard get away with what he's done to you, son. I swear that to God."

Chapter 12

A moment later, I was back at the house, watching Rachel pour herself a drink in the parlor. Jeremy was there too, smiling smugly.

"I think that went rather splendidly, don't you? Graham Withers is completely powerless to resist me. Soon my son will arrive, and I can put the next phase of our plan in motion." He turned to look at her and noticed the scowl on her face. "What is it? I thought you'd be pleased."

Rachel took a sip. "Pleased? I'm more miserable now than I ever was. I didn't even think that could be possible."

"Why would you say that?"

She locked eyes with him. Her voice was full of resentment. "I know what I am, Jeremy."

"I don't understand. What you are?"

"Don't play naïve with me. You know what I'm talking about."

"Oh, that?" Jeremy chuckled. "A minor price to pay for being able to live again, don't you think?"

Rachel scoffed. "Minor? I tore some poor kid's throat out last night. Gaul had to dispose of the body. Do you think that's minor? I don't find it the least bit humorous. You've turned me into a monster."

"You, my dear sister, are alive because of me, and you best not forget that."

She downed the rest of her drink. "I suppose you want me to thank you? I don't owe you anything after what you've done to me, especially gratitude. I don't know how much longer I can go on like this. The sheriff knows Bucky's missing. That's why he was here. People saw me leaving with him. They're going to connect the dots."

"Graham Withers is a fool, much like his father was. He's

inconsequential. He's no match for me. Besides, he's under my power now. He'll do nothing to you. You're safe here with me, and I won't allow anyone to harm you."

Her face fell. "I thought things were going to be different this time. I'm just as grotesque as I was before. Only this time on the inside. You said you loved me. If you do, how could you bring me back just so that I suffer?"

"You want to talk about suffering? You've forgotten how spirits are subject to endless torture in the dark realm. What you must do now to survive is nothing compared to what you'd be subjected to there."

"I don't care what you say. I'd rather be dead."

He shook his head. "You wouldn't say that if you remembered what I've saved you from."

"I'm not like you or Father. I've never done anything to intentionally hurt someone until last night. I didn't deserve to be sentenced to the dark forever."

"Your fate was determined long ago. It didn't matter what you did or didn't do in your life. The result was always going to be the same. But I changed things. I rescued you from that fate."

"What are you talking about?"

"It's not important. All you need to remember is that you're a Wickcliff, Rachel. The evil's inside you whether you know it or not."

She began to walk away. "Stop it, Jeremy!"

He grabbed her arm and turned her around, so she was facing him again. "Wasn't there a part of you that loved what you did last night? Didn't you love having someone's life in your hands?"

She writhed in his grasp. "I said stop it!"

He didn't let go. "Did he beg for his life? Did you relish it when he asked you to stop?"

"I thought you were everything. I looked up to you. I wanted to be like you. Now I realize that you're just a monster, more hideous on the inside than I ever was on the outside."

"No, my dear, I'm a Wickcliff, and we do what we need to do to survive, regardless of the sacrifice or the price. Once Kasey's brought here, the next phase of our plan will be completed, and our family will rise again."

"It's not my plan," she said, breaking away. "I don't want any part of this. Do you hear me?"

"It's too late now. There's no going back for you. You're a cold, heartless murderer. There's no coming back from that."

She burst into tears. "You're demented. I'll never forgive you for what you did to me, never. One day I'll make you regret you ever brought me back." She ran from the room.

Jeremy shrugged it off. It didn't matter to him if Rachel didn't understand her destiny right now. He was convinced that in time, she would. He had to focus on his plans for Kasey and not be worried about his sister's qualms.

I just hoped that Graham was able to remain strong and not play into Jeremy's hands. He needed to do the right thing and tell Kasey the truth.

* * * *

I heard Rory call my name, and I turned to him. I scoured the room, looking for Reed and Damon, realizing that we were alone.

"Where's Reed?" I asked. "What's happened to him?"

"He's fine. He's with Damon."

"Graham Withers knows the truth about Jeremy and Rachel."

Rory ran his hands through his hair. "Is he alright?"

I nodded. "I think so. Jeremy tried to put him under his power, but I think he was able to resist once he left the mansion, or at least that's what it seems like. Maybe that's what we should've done. We wouldn't be in this spot now if we hadn't stayed in this Godforsaken house."

"That's in the past, and we can't go back. We need to focus on the now. What does Jeremy want with Graham?"

"He's using him to get to Kasey. He's moving forward with his plan to inhabit the man he thinks is his son. I'm trying to warn Kasey, and he's shutting me out. I only hope that Graham can do it for me."

Rory's eyes drifted to the side. "And I suppose he agreed to let Reed go if Graham brought Kasey to him?"

Reed appeared in the doorway. "I heard my name. What's going on here?"

I walked over to him. "Reed, why don't you sit down? I need to talk to you."

He glared at me. "I don't want to sit down. I can tell that something's wrong. What happened?"

Damon appeared behind him. "I wanted to check in to see what else you've learned in the mortal realm. Do you know the next phase of Jeremy's plan?"

"Graham Withers found out who Jeremy was," Rory said, "and he's using him to get to Kasey."

Damon's eyes lowered. "I see. Kasey's in grave danger."

Reed turned to him. "Kasey? What about my dad? Jeremy could kill him."

I moved closer to Reed giving him a serious look. "We're not going to let that happen."

He scoffed and moved away from me. "What are you going to do about it? You haven't been able to do shit so far."

"Hey, that's enough," Rory said, pushing Reed back. "Don't talk to my wife like that."

Reed glared at us. "No, it's not nearly enough. I've had it with trusting all of you. You can't do anything to help me get my life back, and I know it, so why don't you stop jerking me around?" He went into the foyer and headed for the front door.

"Reed, wait," Damon said, moving towards him. "You shouldn't go out there alone."

Reed faced him and put his hand on the doorknob. "I'm through listening to you. I'll find my way back to the mortal realm. I'm not going to stand around here while my dad gets killed."

He opened the door and ran out of the house.

Damon turned to Rory quickly. "I need you to come with me. We need to find him before he gets into trouble."

I closed my eyes. "Wait. I can see where Reed's going just as clearly as I could if he were in the mortal realm. I can see through his eyes."

"Tell us, Shell," Rory said. "What is it that you see?"

As I followed Reed, I could feel that fear and panic had completely taken over any sense of logic he'd possessed. He worried for himself and his father, and I worried that the fear could destroy him.

Reed wandered around the grounds of the estate. He was unable to see everything that was ahead of him at first. His vision was blurred, and although everything appeared familiar, his sense of direction was off. This heightened his anxiety.

"There's gotta be a way out of here."

As he got farther from the house and closer to the cemetery gates, he felt an energy pulling him toward the cemetery. He was looking for a way out, but he didn't know where to look or what he was looking for. He thought that the pull he felt toward the cemetery was the clue to a way out. After awhile, his vision became clearer. The trees, shrubs, grass, all of his surroundings had come into focus.

Although it was dark, the moon was full and shone brightly enough to illuminate his path. He saw the gate that led to the cemetery. Getting closer, he realized that the tall, black, wrought iron gate, full of rust and corrosion after years of being out in the elements, was the same as it was in the mortal realm. He touched the gate, peering inside the cemetery. Thinking there was nothing there, he took his hand back and began to walk away.

He took a few steps and stopped cold when he heard someone whispering his name from behind him. He turned back around to face the gate again.

"Who's there?" He stood there convinced he'd heard a voice. It filled him with fear and uncertainty. He didn't know what was out here and realized he'd made a mistake by leaving the safety of the house. He started back when he heard the whispers again. This time, the voice was clearer.

"Come to us," the voice said.

Reed faced the gate once more. "Who's there? I know someone is. I hear you."

The voice became louder and for the first time, both he and I realized that there was more than one voice calling out to him.

"We're beyond the gate," a second voice said.

"Who are you?" Reed asked.

"We'll tell you if you come to us." It was the voice of a third unseen force.

"I don't know who you are, but if you don't tell me, I'm going to go back to the house."

"Do you want to go home, Mr. Withers?" The first voice said.

Reed's eyes widened. "Excuse me?"

"You heard us," the second voice said. As the voices got stronger, I could tell that this voice belonged to a woman. "We can see to it that you get home."

"How do you know my name?" Reed asked. "And how can you make sure I get home?" There was silence. Reed grabbed a hold of the gate. "Tell me!"

The voices cackled.

"Don't laugh at me! Tell me what you know, dammit!"

"We'll answer all your questions in good time, Mr. Withers," the woman said. "It doesn't matter what the others have told you. They're lying to you. We're the only ones that can help you get back to the mortal realm."

"I want to know how. If you want me to trust you, you'll have to give me more than that."

"Damon and Rory told you about the Wickcliff ancestors, Mr. Withers," the first voice said. It was a man. "That's who we are. We have powers beyond your wildest dreams."

"Come in and we'll tell you whatever you want to know," the woman said.

Reed stood there debating whether he should comply. He didn't know much about the ancestors of the Wickcliff family, but they were offering him a chance to get home. That wasn't something that Rory and Damon could guarantee.

The cemetery gate creaked when Reed opened it. Apprehensively, he walked up the path that led deeper into the cemetery, and, with each step he took, the voices grew even stronger and clearer. He realized he was approaching the family mausoleum. They called his name repeatedly, which made him cover his ears with his hands.

"Where are you?" he asked. "I can't find you."

"Get to the cemetery now," I said, breaking my concentration and turning to Rory. "The ancestors are trying to lure Reed to them."

"Let's go," Damon said. "We don't have a moment to lose."

I turned my attention back to Reed, who was continuing to be enticed by the ancestors.

"Look ahead of you, Mr. Withers," the woman said. "We're inside

The Possession

the mausoleum."

"We're waiting for you," the third voice said. It was also the voice of a man.

Reed found the narrow path that led to the mausoleum and followed it. When he reached the mausoleum, he stood silently, gazing at the gray stone structure with two columns in front. It was covered with vines and moss, abandoned by time and a prisoner to the elements.

It was obvious from his demeanor that he was hesitant to enter, but he was desperate. I'd hoped that Rory and Damon could find him before he went inside, but as he lay his hand on the doorknob, it was clear that they weren't going to be in time to stop him.

"Please let this be my way home." He opened the door slowly and coughed when he breathed in the musty, dank air. "Hello? I'm here. Where are you?"

He strained his eyes to adjust to the dark. Just enough light shone through the cracked, stained glass window for him to see. In the middle of the room, stood a tall cenotaph.

"What is that thing?" Reed asked.

"It's our home now," a voice said, filling the room.

Reed jumped back, startled by the sudden sound that echoed. It was one of the voices that had lured him inside.

"Our souls are trapped here," the female voice said. "It's where we were doomed to spend all eternity."

"Why?"

"It doesn't matter any longer," the second man said. "Because you're going to free us."

Damon had told us that the ancestors could be let out, and with him not guarding the cemetery gate at the moment, they were trying to take advantage of Reed's desperation and naiveté. Where were Damon and Rory? Why hadn't they arrived?

"I'm not going to do anything to help you until you start answering some questions," Reed said.

"You aren't in a position to bargain with us," the woman said. "If you want to go home, you'll start doing what you're told."

"At least tell me who you are," Reed said.

"My name's Mag," the woman said.

"I'm Har," the first man said.

"I'm Err," the second man said. "We're the ancestors of the Wickcliff family."

"Tell me how you can help me get home."

"First you give us what we want," Mag said, "and then you'll get what you want."

Reed pointed to the cenotaph. "You didn't answer my question before. What's that?"

"It's a cenotaph," Har said. "Usually, cenotaphs are empty, more like monuments than tombs, but in this case, we were cursed, and our souls have become trapped."

"What did you do to get trapped there?"

"It doesn't matter," Mag said. "It's beyond your comprehension. We have the ability to take on new lives, new bodies, but we needed a mortal with connections to the mortal realm to find us. You're still a mortal, even though you're here. You're here because Jeremy possessed you, not because you died. You aren't a spirit like us."

Reed turned to face the door and began to walk away. "I think there's been some misunderstanding. I can't help you. Have a nice life...afterlife... whatever." As he approached the door, he heard the wind howl. The door slammed shut, and the room went darker.

Outside, Damon and Rory arrived. Rory ran up to the door and tugged on it with all his strength. "The damn thing's locked up tight." He groaned. "It won't even budge."

Damon's face was forlorn. "The ancestors have trapped Reed inside. They're using their powers to keep everyone else out. I'm afraid we're too late."

Inside, Reed whipped back around to face the cenotaph. The ground underneath him started to shake. He lost his balance, stumbled forward, and held on to the cenotaph for support. "What the hell's going on?"

A blue light shot up from the top of the cenotaph illuminating it. For the first time, he could see that there were skeletons carved into the stone.

He backed up toward the door again as the room continued to shake. There was a crash behind him, and he turned to look. The movement made a coffin shake loose from one of the tombs. The coffin had fallen

The Possession

to the ground. The lid was ajar, causing the skeletal corpse to tumble out.

He screamed and turned back around to face the cenotaph. Screams filled the air. They weren't his. They were the cries of the ancestors who had lured him there. Suddenly, the room stopped shaking.

He ran to the door and pushed with all his strength, but it wouldn't budge. "Someone help me. Please let me out!"

"Reed," Rory said. "Damon and I are here. Hang tight. We're going to get you out of there."

The air was filled with the sound of crumbling stone, causing Reed to face the cenotaph again. The skeletons on the cenotaph began to take on a life of their own. The figures broke apart from the structure, writhing, shifting their bodies until they were free from the cenotaph.

Reed screamed.

"What the hell's happening in there?" Rory asked.

Reed turned back to the door, tugging on it harder. "They're coming. Please, God, help me."

Slowly, each of the three skeletons approached and stood before him. One of them had pieces of rotted flesh clinging to its bones while the other two had none left at all. Each stood there, their hollow-eyed sockets piercing through him. He felt a dead chill in the air, and darkness had surrounded him.

He turned back to the door, pounding on it frantically. "Rory, get me out!"

Har reached out and put his bony hand on Reed's back. Reed shrieked and pressed himself up against the door. Har opened his mouth to speak, and a maggot crawled out. Reed could barely speak, but managed to get a whisper out.

"Stay away from me. I can't help you."

"All those years of waiting for someone to find us," Har said, enthusiastically. "And now we're free."

"It took the warm touch of a living soul to bring us back," Err said.

Reed's eyes broadened as Mag approached him too. All of them surrounded him. "Look, you got what you wanted. I still don't understand how I let you out, but I did it. Either you keep your end of the bargain and help me get home or let me out of here at the very least."

Mag touched his face with her bony hand. "Such a handsome,

young, virile man. I could have fun with you."

Reed recoiled, repulsed. "Please, I'm running out of time." He held out his arm, which was now almost completely black. "My body's dying with Jeremy's spirit inside it. If I don't get back soon, it'll be too late."

Har put his hand up. "In life, I was Harold Wickcliff, Jeremy's father. We've seen everything that's happened in the mortal realm. He took over your body as part of a plan to bring us back to life. Why would we want to stop him?"

"If he could bring you back, what did you need me for?"

"We already told you," Mag said. "Jeremy has a great deal of power, but he doesn't know that only the warm touch of a mortal hand would end our curse. Only you could free us. We should thank you, Mr. Withers."

Reed wanted desperately to run, but he was trapped.

"We had a deal. You promised to get me home."

"Whatever they promised you," Damon said from outside, "don't listen to them."

"You're too late, Shields," Har said. "We're free, and there's nothing you can do about it."

"And as far as our deal," Err said, "deals are meant to be broken."

"But you promised," Reed said, his voice filled with desperation. "Please, I'm running out of time."

Mag gave him a vicious grin. "We do agree on one thing, Mr. Withers. You are indeed out of time. Jeremy has your body, and we now have your soul."

They surrounded Reed and held his arms, making way so that he had a clear view of the cenotaph again. Backed up against the door, he watched in horror as a black, formless entity rose from its top. It morphed into a skeletal face. It had red, glowing eyes and looked massive enough to swallow him whole.

He opened his mouth to scream, but he never had a chance to let it out. He'd come face-to-face with pure evil right before it absorbed his soul.

Chapter 13

After what I'd seen in my vision, I rushed out to meet Damon and Rory outside of the mausoleum. They turned to greet me, and I noticed that all of the color had gone out of Damon's already pale face.

"I should've known," Damon said. "The ancestors feed on the energy and souls of the living. Reed was able to get to them because I wasn't standing guard. How could I have been so careless?"

"That doesn't matter now," Rory said. "We have to get Reed out of there."

"I saw the whole thing," I said. "They held Reed down while some black mass came out of the cenotaph. It completely engulfed him." I no sooner got the words out before I started to feel faint.

Rory noticed that I'd become disoriented. "What's wrong?"

"It's all unclear," I said, putting my hand on my forehead. "I'm dizzy. Everything's fuzzy."

My knees buckled, and I almost collapsed. Rory held me up and called for Damon to help. Damon rushed over and grabbed one of my arms.

"You're alright now."

I exhaled deeply. "Thank you. I don't know what happened. I just felt dizzy all of the sudden."

"You're not used to this realm yet," Damon said. "You haven't been anywhere but inside the house. It might look the same as the mortal realm, but it's not. It'll take time for your senses to adjust."

"Are you going to be okay?" Rory asked.

I waved my hand. "I'll be fine. We need to focus on getting Reed out of there."

"I want you to go back to the house where you'll be safe," Rory said. "The ancestors are loose, and they'll be coming out. It's not safe here."

"Rory's right," Damon said. "You should go."

I threw my hands up. "I'm not leaving him. It can't get any worse. What can they do to me? I'm already dead. It's my fault that Reed's here in the first place. I'm the one that pulled him into this realm. He wouldn't have even been here if it weren't for me."

"He wouldn't be here if it weren't for Jeremy you mean," Rory said, adamantly. "This isn't your fault. You need to stop beating yourself up about things you can't control."

I scoffed. "I haven't had control over much lately. I'm sick of letting the Wickcliffs beat me. It ends right now." I started towards the door to the mausoleum.

"Why must you be so stubborn?" Damon said. "You don't know how to handle them. I do."

"Don't start acting like you care about me, Damon. You may be my biological father, but Jeffrey Hawkins is and always will be my real father."

His eyes lowered. "I see you've discovered the truth."

"You aren't going to deny it?"

"What purpose would that serve?" He met eyes with me again. "I'm your father, and while I may not know you, that gives me the right to care."

Before anyone could say anything else, the sound of malicious cackling filled the air. I jumped, and Rory reached out to calm me.

Damon put his arm out to keep us back. "Get back to the gate, quickly, we must keep them trapped inside the confines of the mausoleum."

"I'm not leaving Reed," I said.

Damon grabbed my arm, pulling me toward the gate. "It's too late for him. I can feel it. We're too late. That's why they're laughing at us."

We got outside the gate, and as Damon reached out to close it, we heard a zapping sound, like electricity. A blue light surrounded the gate.

I stared at in awe. "What is that?"

Damon turned to me. "It's the force field that keeps the ancestors inside the cemetery in this realm. They may have gotten out of the cenotaph, but we can't allow them to get out of the mausoleum."

"How does it work?"

Rory spoke up. "We use our energy and willpower bestowed upon us by the spirits in this realm to keep them at bay. Damon and I do this together. We let our guard down for a minute and look what happened." We heard a shriek and saw Reed in the distance running towards the gate.

"Rory, shut it now!" Damon said.

Rory complied and shut the gate just as Reed got to it.

"What are you doing?" I said turning to Rory. "How can you be sure they've gotten to him?"

"I see it in his eyes," Damon said. "They're blank, emotionless. His soul belongs to the Wickcliffs now. Heaven help us."

Reed touched the gate. "Don't listen to them. They don't know what they're saying. Please, Shelly, open the gate. They're coming for me. Let me out before it's too late."

I reached for the gate, but Damon grabbed my wrist. "Don't touch it. I'm telling you it's too late. He's trying to trick you into letting the ancestors out."

"That's not true," Reed said. "He's crazy. I'm scared. They're coming. We have to hurry. They did try to steal my soul, but it didn't work. I have to get out of here before they try again."

I glared at Damon and Rory. "Don't you hear him begging for help? Do something."

Damon put his hands on my arms. "I know you're angry with me for not telling you that I'm your father, but you have to trust me. I'm telling you the truth. We must leave him here."

"He's the one that's lying," Reed said, grabbing hold of the bars of the gate. "He doesn't want me to get home. That's why I felt like I had to come to the ancestors for help in the first place."

I turned back around to face Reed, searching his eyes for any sign of life.

"It's your fault I'm here," Reed said, gazing straight at me. "You have to help me."

"You're right. I'm sorry." I lowered my head. I couldn't face him any longer.

Rory lifted my head with his hand. "Don't listen to him. You know that Reed might have been angry, but deep down he didn't blame you for any of this. He told you so. If this were the Reed we knew, he wouldn't be saying these things to you."

Damon cried out in frustration, looking up at the sky for answers. "Why did this have to happen? This boy was innocent. He didn't ask for this."

"Get me out of here now!" Reed said.

"They're right," I said, turning my back on him. "I know Reed would never blame me for what's happened. He was my friend." I kept my back to him as he continued to cry out.

Rory took my hand in his. "There's nothing more we can do here. Come on. Let's go back to the house."

"If only he'd waited for me to try to exorcise Jeremy," Damon said. "Why did he have to be so damn impatient?"

We began to walk away and stopped when we heard a new, deeper, voice behind us. I recognized it from my visions. We turned to see Reed standing there smiling. His voice had changed. It was more ominous and sounded devoid of all emotion.

"You'll never get away with this, Shields! You're going to all crumble until there's nothing left of you!"

I turned, but Rory held onto me. "Don't listen to him. It's the ancestors speaking through him. We need to get you out of here."

Reed's face had become twisted, distorted.

"You can't keep us here forever. The real Mr. Withers released us from the cenotaph. We possess him now. It's only a matter of time before we escape the cemetery too, and when we do, all the souls in this realm and any other will be at our mercy. Jeremy's in the mortal realm right now preparing for our return. Your little force field is no match for his power."

"We'll see about that," Damon said. "My will's stronger than any evil you or Jeremy possess."

"Shelly," Reed said, with a malicious grin on his face, "your son will be ours someday as well. Freddy's a Wickcliff, and our blood runs through his veins. He's meant to be with us, and he will be. Don't ever forget that."

I clenched my fists and gritted my teeth. "Stay away from my son or—"

Unintelligible, guttural noises came out of Reed's mouth, as he got angrier. He balled his fists and looked up at the sky as a turbulent storm formed above him. A bolt of lightning struck as he yelled and screamed indecipherable words.

"They're just trying to goad you," Damon said, gazing into my eyes.

"What if Freddy is in danger?"

"They're trapped here. Freddy's safe in the mortal realm."

"He's right," Rory said, putting his arm around me. "Come on. Let's go."

We began walking towards the house, unable to shut out the evil inside of Reed howling and screaming to get out.

"The Wickcliff's anger," Damon said, "their power, has become fiercer inside of Reed because acquiring his soul has made them stronger."

As we walked, my mind wandered. How much longer could Damon and Rory keep the ancestors contained within the cemetery in the spirit realm? What would happen if they escaped? I pushed those thoughts from my mind. I made a choice at that moment. I would do whatever it took to get back to the mortal realm to protect my son. There's nothing that can come between a mother's love for her child, not even death. I would find a way. I'd pay any price. Nothing was going to keep me from my son in this realm or any other.

Chapter 14

We didn't get more than a few feet away from the cemetery gate before I stopped, feeling overwhelmed with guilt. I'd brought Reed into the spirit realm when I'd brought him out of Jeremy's painting. It had been my inability to get us out of the attic before Jeremy and Rachel had taken hold in the mortal realm that caused Reed to be so impatient and run from the house alone, fearing for his life. I wished we could've met Damon sooner. Maybe he could've helped us before Reed became so desperate and hopeless that he felt like he had no other choice but to turn to the ancestors for help.

I then thought about Freddy. Most everyone in the mortal realm thought Rachel was me. I couldn't bear to think of what could happen to him if Rachel got near him. After seeing what she'd done to Bucky, I didn't want her within 100 feet of my child.

I wished that Hilda would tell Mom that Rachel wasn't me, but I was afraid she wasn't going to. She feared that the knowledge of what happened to me would distract Mom from her mission of helping to bring down Jeremy and Rachel. At least if Mom knew the truth, she could protect Freddy. If anything happened to my son, I'd have no one to blame but myself. My only hope at keeping him safe was to find a way back to the mortal realm. Damon and Rory would try to stop me. That much I was sure of.

I wanted my return to the mortal realm to be a second chance to be a part of my son's life. My biggest regret was that because of what Jeremy had done to me, I could never be the kind of mother to my son that I wanted to be. Having been aware that Jeremy caused me to be mentally unstable, I convinced myself that Freddy was better off without me. I loved him, and I'd do anything to ensure his safety, even if it meant sacrificing my existence.

Rory touched my cheek, and I was disrupted from my thoughts. "The ancestors are gone for now, but they're not going to give up." His eyes inspected mine. "I know what you're thinking. Reed's the one who made the choice to run off. He knew that it was dangerous out here. We all tried to warn him. You aren't responsible for any of this."

I shook my head. "You're wrong. I should've tried harder to get us out of the attic. In fact, I shouldn't have pulled him through that damn painting. I was trying to come to terms with my death, and I was vulnerable and alone. All I could think about when I heard his voice calling out to me was how wonderful it would be to have some company. I was selfish. Maybe I should've just left him there."

"You couldn't have known what would happen," Damon said. "You gave Reed many great things by pulling him out of that painting. Your friendship for one."

I put my head down. "He is my friend. That's why this bothers me so much." I made eye contact with them again. "I refuse to believe that there's nothing we can do."

Rory put his arm around me. "We'll talk about it after you've had a chance to rest."

I pulled away. "I don't need to rest. I'm not a child. You don't have to treat me like one."

"I'm not. I just don't think that this is the time or the place to discuss it any further."

"Listen to Rory," Damon said. "You've seen how the ancestors will use trickery, deceit, guilt, whatever they need to to get out. It isn't safe here."

I put my hands on my hips. "Do you think I'm stupid or naïve? That I can't take care of myself?"

"He didn't say that," Rory said. "We need to stick together, and that means that no one stays out here alone."

I nodded, and we all walked back to the house in silence. Once we were back in the parlor, I broke the silence.

"It isn't what just happened to Reed that's bothering me. It's seeing and feeling everyone else's pain. Seeing what's happened in the mortal realm has been terrible. I watched Jeremy kill my father. I've watched my family fall apart, and I can't do anything about it. Jeremy and Rachel have caused nothing but chaos. What's the point of being a spirit if you can't do anything to change all of the suffering?"

Rory took my hand and led me over to the couch. "You said before that you wouldn't let Jeremy and the Wickcliffs defeat you anymore. Don't you realize that if you keep beating yourself up for things that you can't control, that's what you're letting them do?"

Damon sat down next to us and nodded. "Rory's right. What's done is done. All we can do now is deal with the fallout and do our best to minimize the damage."

I turned towards Damon. "How?"

"Rory and I will continue to guard the gate, just as we always have. We have to make sure that the ancestors don't escape the cemetery. It's going to be more difficult now that they've absorbed Reed's soul. They're stronger now than they were. At least now there's no rush in trying to get Jeremy out of Reed's body. Even if Jeremy were to die, even if Reed had a body to go back to, it doesn't matter because he no longer has a soul."

I scoffed. "Well, I'm glad to hear that you have it all figured out. It only took poor Reed losing everything to make your life easier."

Damon lowered his eyes. "I didn't mean it that way. I wasn't trying to be cruel. I was just stating a fact. The longer Jeremy remains in Reed's body, the better for our cause."

"He's not going to be deterred from getting to Kasey." I got up. "I've got to stop him. I can't let Kasey experience the same fate Reed did."

Rory stood up too. "You can't save the world, if you can't grasp that, your spirit will never find peace."

I chuckled and then sneered. "Peace? My father's dead, and there's an evil spirit inhabiting my body who's a murderer. My mother lied to me my whole life. I've left my son an orphan...should I go on? I'm afraid there's going to be no peace for me, but I will use the eternity I'm stuck here to make sure the Wickcliffs pay."

Rory put his head down. "I'm ashamed to bear their name."

My face softened. "Darling, I didn't mean you. You know I don't think you're like them."

Damon stood next to me and put his hand on my arm tenderly. When I looked at him, I noticed him clearly for the first time. I could see myself in his features. He had an oval face with a fair complexion. Although he was bald, his eyebrows were dark, and I imagined his hair must've been as dark as mine was.

I could see the compassion in his eyes when he looked at me. "I haven't known you that long, and yet I feel like I've known you all my life. I can see you're in pain, and I'm sorry that I couldn't be there for you to protect you, as a father should. I'm glad Jeffrey could be there for you. When you talk about him, I can tell that you loved him very much."

"He was my father in every way." I paused. "Did you love my mother?"

Damon nodded. "Very much. Caroline and I are from different worlds. All she ever wanted was a normal life. Although she has powers, she always wanted to be like everyone else. I couldn't give that sense of normalcy to her. I had another destiny."

"The one that led you here?"

He gave me a nod. "My ability to use my mind to transcend the realms was too valuable a gift to waste. Through my meditations, I'm able to make my spirit body go anywhere. I was chosen to be the guardian of this gate by my predecessor, and it's a responsibility I take very seriously. In many ways, it's become my whole life. I don't have one of my own, especially when it comes to things like love."

"I understand. I don't hold it against you that you weren't there." I looked at Rory. "I had a happy life, for awhile at least."

"Don't worry," Rory said, a firm and fierce determination in his voice. "Jeremy will pay for what he's done to us. The ancestors will remain caged, and Jeremy will go back to the dark."

He straightened his back and stood tall, handsome. His dark eyes sparkled with confidence. Listening to him reminded me of why I fell in love with him. He was strong, virile, and passionate about his beliefs, but he was also loving, compassionate, and kind.

He knew who he was, what he wanted, and how he was going to attain it. It made me think of how much different our lives would've been if not for Jeremy.

Still distraught, I exhaled and headed towards the foyer. Rory followed me and grabbed my arm from behind, turning me back to face him.

"Where are you going?"

"I know how confident you are, and I know that you believe what you're saying, but neither you nor Damon can guarantee that you'll be able to stop the ancestors. I need to go back to the gate so that I can confront them."

"We've been able to keep them at bay this long," Damon said. "Reed just happened to get past us. It's not going to happen again."

I broke away from Rory and stared into his eyes. "I just want to make everything okay again. I know you and Damon don't believe it was my fault, but I can't shake the guilt."

"What happened to Reed happened to him because it was his fate," Damon said. "The universe doesn't make mistakes."

I grimaced. "You're saying that no matter what happens to us it's meant to be? I don't believe that. I don't believe that my destiny was to be tortured by Jeremy to the point that I committed suicide. I don't believe that it was meant for my son to be an orphan, and I sure as hell don't believe that fate or God or whatever let me die was just so that Jeremy and the rest of the Wickcliffs could live."

Damon managed a small smile. "There's so much you don't understand. Sometimes bad things happen. It's just the way life works. It was meant for Jeremy to come back. He was becoming too powerful in the ghost realm, but as a mortal, he's vulnerable. He can finally be neutralized. Because he's returned, Lucy's been given a chance to live again. He stole her life just as he did yours and Reed's, just indirectly. Your actions resulted in something positive. Focus on the good things."

I took a step back. "Maybe I could if it were just me who was sacrificed, but there are others involved here. Reed was innocent, and so was Rory." I met my husbands' gaze. "You wouldn't be here either if it weren't for me."

Rory shook his head. "That's not true. Jeremy got to me through you. It was through my spilled blood that he became strong enough to put the rest of his plan in motion. He used you, yes, but that doesn't make you weak, and it doesn't make it your fault. I died because we didn't understand Jeremy's power and even if I'd known about what Jeremy was doing to you, I wouldn't have been able to stop him then."

"But now you can?"

"Our wills have to remain stronger than Jeremy's power."

"If we're going to stand a chance," Damon said, "we need to know his every move. We can't have any surprises. That's why we need you to continue to tell us what's happening in the mortal realm. We need you to go back."

I scratched the top of my head and thought for a moment. "It's exhausting, and a lot of what I see upsets me, but I'll continue until this is over."

"What you're seeing is essential to our success," Rory said. "Which makes me wonder how Lucy's return is going to factor into Jeremy's plan."

"He wants to pretend that he doesn't love her anymore," I said. "But I know he does. I can feel it when I'm with him and when I think about them."

"Then it's time for you to go," Damon said. "We're wasting valuable time here."

I turned to face the window, wrapping my arms around me. I shut my eyes, took a breath, and focused my energy on Jeremy.

* * * *

When Jeremy came into focus, he was in his car, driving to Lover's Bluff. He wanted to get out of the house and get some air, and soon found himself drawn to the place where he'd died. He parked the car at the top of the cliff, got out, and peered out at the ocean below. The sound of the crashing waves on the rocks was deafening.

As I watched him, I came to a realization. As evil and vile as Jeremy was, and as much as I resented him for the hell he put my family and me through, I had to admit that I saw a human side to him, a side that was in pain because of the rejections he'd experienced.

He'd been thinking about Rachel and how excited he'd been to have her back. She hadn't known that she'd have to kill for survival and when she found out, she was incredulous. He worried that she'd never forgive him.

Then he thought about Lucy and how much he'd loved her. He felt betrayed by her not once, but twice. He'd resented her when he found out she'd kept his son from him and then when she orchestrated the events that led to his death. He wished he could hate her because then her betrayal wouldn't hurt him so much, but he couldn't.

"Why did you have to betray me, Lucy?" Jeremy said. "We could've been happy. You, me, and our son. You had to take it all away from us."

He groaned again and rubbed his arm. When he pulled up his sleeve, his flesh was even darker than it appeared before. Reed's body was decaying rapidly. It made him think about how he'd put Graham under his control, willing Graham to bring Kasey to him.

There was a rustling in the bushes behind him, and he turned, realizing that he wasn't alone. It was too dark to see who had made the noise; all he could see was the dark outline of a figure. It wasn't until she spoke his name that he knew who it was.

As Lucy approached him, the moonlight lit up the features of her face. He noticed that she looked just the same as she did when she'd died. Her eyes were just as blue; her skin looked just as smooth. He stood there mesmerized by her beauty, just as he'd been when they were first married. Seeing Lucy standing before him made him almost want to smile, but he held back.

"Why do you haunt me?"

"Haunt you?" She got closer and touched his hand. "Do I feel like a spirit to you? You aren't the only one who can return during Midnight's Edge."

Her touch made him want to take her in his arms and kiss her. He wanted to forgive her for everything, to tell her he still loved her, but his resentment for what she'd done was just as strong as his love for her and his emotions confused him.

"I should've known that you'd try that. Underestimating you was what got me killed in the first place. I'd never be stupid or naïve enough to underestimate you again."

"I know what you did to that boy. Reed, isn't it? What you did was cruel, although not surprising."

He smirked. "Hilda told you I gather?"

She shook her head. "She didn't have to. I saw it."

He laughed. "I get it. That's why you've come back. You think you're going to stop me, don't you? No one's going to stop me from bringing my family back, especially not you. We deserve to live."

"Not at the expense of the innocent. You had your time to live. You have no right to take another life so that you can have another chance."

"Are you really going to stand there and talk to me about rights? You had no right to take my life, but yet you did it. You caused the accident that killed us both. Since it was planned, maybe I shouldn't say accident. It was more like murder."

"What I did was for the good of humanity, what you've done is for your selfish gain. It isn't the same."

He grabbed her arm. "It's exactly the same. You justify your actions because you can't admit that what you did was wrong. Admit it. You're a murderer."

She pulled away. "Don't you ever grab me like that again. Your touch sickens me. Just being around you turns my stomach."

He scoffed. "I can't believe I ever loved you, a woman that caused my death. I gave you everything. I wanted to so desperately. But you gave me nothing but pain and sorrow. You lied to me. You took my life. You took my son away from me. I'm going to get it all back, and then I'm going to make you suffer."

She sneered. "I wouldn't count on it."

"Wipe that smug look off your face."

"If I'm smug, it's only because I know I'm stronger than you. I'm not going to let you hurt anyone in this town, especially my son. You're a monster, and that's why I decided to keep him from you in the first place."

"He's my son too! You had no right to take him away from me. He carries my blood in his veins and soon he'll know it."

"You'll never be able to poison his mind as you've done with so many others. The moment he sees you, he'll see what everyone else sees, that you're nothing but a soulless, vile monster."

The words stung him. There was a part of him that wanted to believe she still loved him and that she understood why he had to bring his family back.

"I'll ask you one time. Be my wife again. I know you loved me once, you can love me again. We can be so happy together."

She laughed. "I loved you because I was young and naïve. I didn't know any better. I was blinded by lust, unable to see you for who you were. I'll never love or trust you again."

"Don't do this, Lucy. When my ancestors return, there will only be two sides, those who are with us and those who are against us. I can't protect you if you choose not to stand with us."

Her eyes pierced through him. "I'll never join forces with you. I curse the day I met you."

"How can you say that? We wouldn't have Kasey if it weren't for our time together."

She paused. "Kasey?"

"That's right. Despite your best efforts to keep him away from me, I know who he is. You and those useless old bitches you call friends weren't successful. If you don't stand by my side, you'll fall with all the others. After what you've done to me, I shouldn't even offer you the chance for immunity. I guess I'm just a sentimental fool."

She chuckled. "Well, at least you got the second part right."

"I'm not amused."

"My sisters and I went to great lengths to bring me back, and it won't be for naught. You'll be destroyed. Be prepared for the fight of your life, or afterlife." She turned to walk away, and he followed her.

"I'm not going to be the one who's destroyed. Kasey will come to me, and when he does, he'll realize that he has no choice but to join me. My spirit will be able to leave this wretched, decaying body for a strong, virile one."

She whipped back around to face him. "Kasey will never help you!"

"We'll see, Lucy. My son will make it possible for me to live and to fulfill my family's legacy. I'll be able to destroy you, the pathetic wench that bore him."

"We'll see which one of us is the last one standing, Jeremy. You forget that I'm not without my own powers."

In the sky, there was a flash of lightning. The thunder snapped, making Jeremy jump back. Temporarily distracted, he searched the area around him. Lucy had vanished.

Jeremy felt angrier than ever. His pain over her betrayal soon turned to rage. She not only turned down his offer of reconciliation, but she'd vowed to bring him down for the second time. He wouldn't let it happen again. He wanted to hurt her. He wanted to make her suffer. He knew that the best way to do that was to start with her friends. He vowed to kill them all. He knew how much it would hurt her if he saved her for last so she could watch her friends fall one by one.

Gracey would be the first to go.

Chapter 15

Gracey had been Lucy's midwife, one of only a handful of people that knew that Lucy was pregnant. Not only did she assist in the birth and keep it quiet, but she'd also raised Kasey as her own. Returning the Wickcliffs to the mortal realm was only part of Jeremy's motivation for returning to life. The other reason was vengeance. Out of all the witches, he hated Gracey the most. Not only did she attempt to help Lucy destroy him, but she was also the only one of them who had helped keep his son away from him. It was time he made good on his promise to make her pay.

I watched Jeremy get into his car, and as he headed to her house, I turned my attention to Gracey, who was there alone. I called out to her, attempting to warn her that Jeremy was on the way, but she hadn't heard me. I watched in anxious anticipation as I saw her sitting there in the kitchen, fearful of what was in store for her.

I turned my attention back to the outside. It was dark and quiet on her street, allowing Jeremy to sneak around inconspicuously. He went around to the back door of the house, looking for signs that anyone else might be there with her. He noticed that Hilda's caravan wasn't outside and that Gracey appeared to be alone.

He knocked on the back door and waited patiently for her to answer. I tried calling out to her again to tell her not to open the door, but it was to no avail.

Gracey put her hand on the chain lock. "Who's there?"

"Kasey," Jeremy said, muffling his voice.

"Kasey? It doesn't sound like you," she said undoing the lock. "Are you okay?"

The Possession

The door burst open, knocking her back. She dropped her cane and fell to the floor. She gasped, and then looked up at him, hatred in her eyes. She groaned from the pain in her bad leg.

"I know you aren't Reed Withers. I knew it would only be a matter of time before you'd come looking for me. I've been expecting you, Jeremy Wickcliff."

He chuckled. "Have you now? Here I am in the flesh so to speak."

She reached for her cane. "Stay where you are."

He stepped on it and kicked it away out of her reach. Still on the floor, she pushed herself further away from him.

"What do you want?"

"I want you to shut the hell up. The sound of your voice makes me ill. Besides, you should keep it down. Should anyone discover me here with you, I'd have to do away with them too. You wouldn't want their blood on your hands. That can get awfully messy." He looked around the room. "Where's that old bitch, Hilda?"

"She's going to be back any moment. If you know what's good for you, you won't be here."

He examined her face. "You're lying. I can tell. You can't manipulate a master manipulator." He sighed and placed his hands on his hips. "You all think you're so smart, don't you? You think you have my plans for my son all figured out and that you'll be able to intercede. You're pathetic."

She pointed to the door. "Get out of here. I'm not without powers, and you know it. Don't make me use them."

"You're useless without those bitches you call family."

She glared at him. "That isn't true."

"Oh no? Boo!" She flinched, and Jeremy laughed at her.

"If you kill me, you'll just make them angrier."

"I suppose you think that because Lucy's returned, you're all invincible? That's right, I've already had the displeasure of seeing the wife who betrayed me and she's just as disillusioned as the rest of you are. I've come back stronger and more powerful than ever before. I'm young and virile. You're all weak and fragile."

She took notice of the blackened skin on his hand. "You don't look so strong and virile to me. I know what happens when a spirit inhabits the body of a living, breathing mortal. You're a foreign visitor. You don't belong here. The body destroys itself to force the foreign spirit out."

He put his hand behind his back. "This is only temporary. Once Kasey's brought to me and I have my son, I can transfer my life force into his body, and I'll continue to live on. What happens to this body is of no consequence to me."

She tried to get up, but she'd injured her bad leg in the fall. All she could do was scoot farther away from him so that her back was against the kitchen cupboards. She realized that Jeremy was mistaken about Kasey's identity, but decided to say nothing.

"Stay away from my son or I'll destroy you myself!"

He approached her and crouched down, getting in her face. "Oh my dear Gracey, that's where you're wrong. Kasey's my son, and you helped keep him away from me. You helped Lucy deprive my son of his birthright and for that, you must die."

"If you truly loved your son, you would understand why we did what we did. Do you believe that he should've turned out like you? Cruel, ruthless, unfeeling?"

Jeremy stood up, towering over her. "The people in this town made my family that way. With their envy, with their jealousy. They resented us for our wealth and for the fact that we were respected, and they tried to destroy us. My father was murdered. Even as old as you are, I'm sure you haven't forgotten that."

"That's rubbish. What happened to Harold was an accident."

He groaned. "You're a hypocrite. You witches are always criticizing our family for being dishonest when you're the ones that are the most dishonest. Maybe I should kill you slowly, destroy your other leg. You should suffer before you die as you made me suffer. I'm not going to make this easy for you."

"One thing I'm not is dishonest. I've lived my life with pride and honor, and I have no regrets. I'm not afraid of you. If I'm to die tonight, I'll do it with integrity. I'll never give up on trying to stop you. Even from the spirit realm."

His eyes pierced through her. "I've had it with you old woman."

"So kill me. Kill me like you killed Jeffrey Hawkins. You're a murderer. A spineless, gutless coward! Jeffrey didn't have powers. I do. I can fight back."

"I'd like to see you try."

She gazed up towards the ceiling. "Hear me! I call upon all the forces of nature to be at my disposal tonight."

He folded his arms and rolled his eyes. "This should be interesting. I could use a good laugh."

She stared at him. "There's an evil presence here tonight that must be extinguished. With all that I am and all that I have, I demand that this demon from the darkness be vanquished and forced back to the pits of darkness and despair."

Jeremy's eyes broadened when he heard thunder in the distance. "Quite an impressive parlor trick. I'm afraid I don't have time for any more. My son should be at my house by now. I can't be entertained by you all evening."

She didn't acknowledge him. "There's a young man, Reed Withers, in another realm. He shouldn't be there. He hasn't crossed over. He's been possessed. Jeremy Wickcliff's a force against nature, and he must be stopped. Allow the innocent soul that's been displaced from his life to return and drive this soulless monster out."

It was grueling watching this exchange for Gracey wasn't aware that Reed's soul was now in the possession of the Wickcliff ancestors. That didn't seem to matter though because whatever she was doing appeared to be working. I watched as Jeremy groaned and grabbed his side, crying out in pain.

She gazed at him with fierce determination. "It's over for you, Jeremy, let go. Let that boy back in."

He clenched his teeth. "Never! Now you die old woman."

"You can't fight it. Your soul's floating away. You can feel it. I see it in your face."

He grabbed the sides of his head. "No!" He looked at her blankly and then collapsed to the floor, where he remained motionless.

She touched her chest, got back to her feet slowly, and approached him. "Reed, is it you? Are you alright?"

"Yes. What happened?"

"I'll explain everything to you later. Can you stand?"

"No."

"Let me help you up."

She reached down to grab his hand.

Jeremy noticed that her cane was within reach from where he'd kicked it. With his free hand, he grabbed the cane and hit her on one of her kneecaps. She cried out in pain and collapsed again.

She rubbed her leg, not taking her eyes off of him. "You won't get away with this!"

"And who will stop me?" He leaped to his feet. "You obviously can't."

"Lucy and my sisters, they'll stop you."

"It's over." Jeremy clenched his fist. "You just demonstrated that you're a bigger threat than I anticipated. You just signed your death warrant."

Gracey put her hand up. "I command you to stop."

The last display of power she exhibited had left her weak, and her words had no effect.

"You made the biggest mistake of your pathetic life when you crossed me. It's time to exact my revenge and time for you to take your punishment."

She tried to back up from him, but there was nowhere for her to go. Her shattered kneecap limited her mobility even further. He raised her cane up above his head and hit her so hard and fast that she didn't even see it coming. She screamed. He heard her dog bark and turned to see Scruffy running into the kitchen. She snapped at him and began biting his pant leg.

Gracey whimpered. "Scruffy, no."

He kicked Scruffy off with one fell swoop. She hit the wall and fell to the floor motionless. Gracey wailed, screaming out her dog's name. Then she glared at Jeremy with loathing. Her cupboards opened and closed rapidly. Plates and saucers flew out towards him, crashing against him and at the wall behind him.

The veins in his head protruded. "That's it? That's all you've got left?"

He hit her again with the cane, and her face hit the hard tile. She whimpered with pain and touched her head. Blood trickled from her forehead, staining the tile red. She was beginning to lose consciousness. As she looked up at him, he squatted down beside her. He clenched his fist in her face.

"Had enough, Gracey?"

"It must make you feel good to kill a defenseless old lady. What a big man you are."

"You're a hell of a lot more than that, and we both know it."

Her breathing intensified. "You're a coward. This isn't the end."

"Oh yes, it is." He closed his eyes and focused on the darkest energies dwelling in the center of his being. He opened them again and looked into her desperate eyes. "You'll start to feel a tightening around your heart."

Her eyes widened, and pain covered her face. She opened her mouth wide, took in a swift breath, and then gritted her teeth. It reminded me of the same thing he'd done to Dad. I could barely stand to watch it again.

"And then you won't be able to breathe."

She tried to breathe in, but she couldn't. She grabbed her neck and choked.

"Try to breathe, Gracey. You can't, can you? Are you afraid? You should be."

She choked slowly, and he watched patiently as she took her last breath. Her body went limp at last. Her eyes stared lifeless into the unknown distance, her mouth agape.

He stood up again, and broke her cane in half, throwing it to the floor beside her. "It's about time. I thought you'd never die. I have to give you credit, though. You put up a good fight. You're not as pathetic as I thought you were." He strutted towards the door and turned to take one last look at her body on the floor. "One down and three to go." He stepped out of the house and shut the door behind him. "It'll be different this time. I'll see each one fall."

The vision of Jeremy disappeared, and I opened my eyes. I was in the parlor again. Rory and Damon were sitting on the sofa and got up when they noticed I was struggling to breathe.

"You saw something," Damon said, his eyes full of concern. "What was it?"

"Gracey's dead," I said, almost unable to say it. "Jeremy killed her just like he did my father. I couldn't stop him this time either. All I could do was watch. I feel so useless."

Damon rubbed his chin. I could tell that he was distraught at the news too. "It's not that you're useless. If you couldn't save her, it means that it was her fate, just as it was Jeffrey's. They're both meant to be part of the spirit world now." He turned to Rory. "He's getting stronger. He should be getting weaker as the mortal body dies. He's got one hell of a strong will if he can hold on this long."

Rory had his arm around me. "What now?"

Damon looked at me. "You need to go back and tell us what happens next."

I stepped back from Rory. "No more."

"I know it's difficult, Shelly, you have to stay strong," Damon said.

I put my hands on my face. I was burning up. "If we can't stop him, what's the point in knowing what he's going to do? It's causing me nothing but misery to see all the terrible things he's done."

"But we can stop him," Damon said. "At the right time."

"Which will be when? How many more people have to die?"

He softened his tone. "I'm asking you to trust me. Can you do that?"

His voice and the message in his eyes soothed me. His demeanor comforted me, and I realized the answer was yes. I nodded and turned away once more, ready for whatever I was about to face next in the mortal realm.

* * * *

The next person I saw was Hilda. I found her in the meadows, the place she always went when she felt the need to be alone. She'd come here to meditate and prepare for the battle with Jeremy. Lightning struck in the distance, causing her to flinch. Her instincts told her that it wasn't any normal lightning strike. Something was amiss.

Hilda's thoughts were disrupted when she heard Lucy call out to her. She turned around and saw that Lucy wore a morose expression.

"What's wrong?"

Lucy moved towards her slowly. "I ran into Jeremy at Lover's Bluff a little while ago."

"Why would he want to go back to the place he died? I suppose he went there to remember the past and his motivations for fighting us now. I'm sure that it wasn't a pleasant conversation."

"He truly believes that he's going to be successful in bringing the Wickcliff ancestors back. He asked me to join him so that he could protect me from their wrath."

Hilda chuckled and shook her head. "He never gives up, does he? Even after all these years and after all you went through, he still believes you belong together. The gall of that man."

"I'm afraid that I antagonized him. I told him that we wouldn't stop until he was defeated. There's no telling what he's going to do now that I've rejected him again."

"I did the same thing during my little visit. It's hard not to when he stands there so smugly." Hilda put her hands on her hips. "I know what you're worried about. You're thinking about your sons, aren't you?"

Lucy nodded. "You could always read my mind. Jeremy thinks that Kasey's his son, which puts Kasey in danger, and if he finds out about Jason, that puts him in danger too. I couldn't stand it if he got his hands on either one of my sons, especially Jason. He's the one that's Jeremy's son. If Jeremy were to find him, he wouldn't stop until he poisoned Jason against me. The whole town will be in peril if Jason and Jeremy cross paths. Jeremy didn't look well. It's obvious he's running out of time to make the transfer. He wouldn't waste any time at all."

"I haven't heard Jason's name mentioned in many years. We always said we wouldn't mention him for his sake."

"I have to now. I feel like he's close. I think he's here." Lucy shivered and rubbed her arms. "Have you spoken to Roxanne lately? She'd most likely know where he is."

Hilda sighed. "I'm sorry to have to be the one to tell you, but she passed away."

Lucy looked down. "I'm sorry to hear that."

"She kept the promise that she made to us when I gave Jason to her as a baby. She kept him away from the Wickcliff influence. I believe she was a good mother to him. She did her best to give him a decent upbringing amongst the gypsies."

Lucy looked back up. Her eyes filled with tears. "I wanted nothing more than to be a mother to my sons. I was so afraid that Jeremy's influence would destroy them both that I thought it best to keep my distance. Then I lost my life. I have so much time to make up for."

"You said you feel like Jason's close. Do you know where he is exactly?"

Lucy closed her eyes. When she opened them a moment later, she shook her head. "No. I don't have a sense of the exact location, but I need to find him right away."

"I should go with you. I could help you look."

Lucy put her hand up. "No. I have to do this alone. I need some one-on-one time with my son. I have to explain to him why I had to give him up. I have to make him understand and warn him about his father."

Hilda shivered, and through her psychic abilities, she saw the same vision I'd seen a few moments before, Gracey on the floor with Jeremy hovering over her.

Hilda looked at Lucy intently. "Gracey's in trouble. I think Jeremy's gone after her."

Lucy put her hand to her cheek. "If he has, it's my fault. I pushed him too far at the bluff. I could see he was furious. If he's gone after Gracey, it'll have been to get revenge on me. You go to her, make sure she's all right. I need to find my son and explain to him what's happening." Hilda started to leave, but Lucy called after her. "Be careful."

The expression on Lucy's face worried Hilda. She'd seen the same one on Lucy's face the night she'd died. I followed Hilda as she raced to Gracey's house. She didn't want to believe that her dearest friend could be hurt or worse, but her instincts told her that Gracey was already gone. She knew it in her head, but her heart wouldn't accept it.

Chapter 16

I found myself back outside Gracey's house and was surprised when I saw Kasey at her front door. How did he know to come here? Gracey had just died; he couldn't have found out about it already. He knocked, and of course, there was no answer, and then he tried all the windows, but they were locked too. He started to panic.

"Mom, please open the door! I need to talk to you!"

He gasped when he saw Gracey's face appear in the window to the right of the doorway. I saw it too, and I didn't understand how. I had an uneasy feeling that something wasn't right.

At first, she was smiling, but then her face turned into a skull. He screamed, and the next thing I knew, I was in his bedroom watching him sit up in bed, drenched in sweat. I hadn't realized it, but I'd inserted myself into Kasey's dream. It was another one of my new abilities that I didn't fully understand, but I couldn't think about that now. Kasey was about to find out his mother was dead, and I just wanted to be there to support him.

Kasey wiped his brow. "It was just a dream. Mom's fine."

He turned on the light by the bed. He'd tried to convince himself of that fact, but he knew he couldn't sleep until he knew for sure. Despite his proclamation that it was just a dream, he knew it could be one of his visions. He picked up his phone and dialed her. He figured that she'd yell at him for waking her up in the middle of the night and then they could both go back to sleep.

He called five different times, and she never answered. He decided that he'd have to check on her. It was then that he began to worry. It wasn't like her not to answer the phone regardless of the hour.

Kasey got dressed and went out into the night. The wind was relentless. It was cold this time of year, but he was so worried about Gracey that the temperature didn't faze him. I followed him to her house, and as soon as he pulled into the driveway, he knew something was wrong. There wasn't one light on, and Gracey always kept the porch light on as well as nightlights on throughout the house.

He went up to the back door and found it slightly ajar. The house was still and quiet. He opened the door slowly. "Mom?"

It was dark inside, but he saw Scruffy limping over to him. He bent down to pet her.

"Scruffy, what happened to you? You okay?" Scruffy licked his hand. "Where's Mom? Huh, girl?"

He felt something wet on her and realized it was blood. His heart began to race, and he stood up and turned on the light. The whole kitchen was in disarray. Scruffy limped away and moved towards the corner of the kitchen.

As he looked ahead, his whole world was shattered. He saw Gracey's body leaning up against the cabinets, bent over. He noticed the blood on the side of her face, her eyes wide open, cold and lifeless. He ran to her and got down on the floor, checking for a pulse. Finding none, he took her into his arms. It was clear to him that she'd already been dead for awhile, as the blood had begun to dry, and it was too late to revive her. The grief overcame him. He wasn't thinking about anything at that moment other than his need to feel close to her. He began to sob as he buried her face into his chest.

"Oh my God! No!" He looked at her, her eyes vacant, her pupils dilated. He rocked her and continued to sob. "Why did this have to happen?"

As he held her, it reminded him of when he was little, and how she'd comfort him when something went wrong. The difference was that now, instead of being comforted by her warmth, he felt nothing but death. She'd already gone cold.

He sat there crying for several more minutes, attempting to get a grip on what happened. His mom was his rock, and the idea of his life without her in it devastated him.

After he'd composed himself, he called an ambulance and sat there thinking about what could've possibly happened. He wondered why the door was ajar, why Scruffy was limping, and why there was such a mess.

"Jeremy. He did this."

His mind raced as he pictured her all alone, suffering, calling out for help with nobody to hear her. He prayed that it hadn't happened that way and that she didn't suffer.

I was glad that Kasey's version of the events spared him from seeing what happened. Soon Hilda appeared at the door and came hobbling in.

"Kasey, what are you doing here?" She put her hand over her mouth when she saw Gracey.

He faced her, stood up, and turned her away from his mother. "Don't look at her."

Hilda embraced him, sobbing. "I knew that something was wrong. I didn't want to accept that I was right."

He broke the embrace and looked into her eyes. "How did you know?"

"Your mother and I share an unusual bond, a special connection. We always know when the other is in danger. I felt it, but by then it was already too late."

He wiped his tears. "I can't believe this is happening. I always knew this day would come, but I'd secretly hoped that Mom would go on forever."

She nodded. "Me too. Do you know what happened?"

"I don't want to believe that someone would hurt Mom on purpose, but the door was ajar, her cane's snapped in half, Scruffy's hurt. Look at this place. It's a mess. I think Jeremy did this."

Hilda approached Gracey's body. "I knew it was only a matter of time before he'd come looking for us. I failed to protect her. I thought we had more time before he made a move. It's my fault your mother's dead." She started to weep harder.

Kasey grimaced. "You heard what she said about Jeremy. She was so afraid. You knew that he'd try to do this to her, and you didn't do anything to stop him."

"We were trying."

He threw his hands up. "Oh, well, that just makes it all okay. My mother's dead, but I should take comfort in the fact that you tried?"

She exhaled. "I don't blame you for being angry. Your anger can't compare to the anger I feel toward myself."

He shook his head. "How noble."

She sobbed uncontrollably. He realized how much his words had hurt her. "I'm sorry, Hilda. I'm just hurting so much right now. I know you did all you could. I'm just as angry with myself. I made a vow to Mom that I'd protect her. I let her down."

"No, you didn't. Your mother was the most incredible person I've ever known. She was so proud to call you her son. You could never let her down."

He ran his hands through his hair. "I guess I'm still trying to wrap my brain around the idea of someone returning from the dead. It just doesn't make sense."

"Evil never dies, Kasey. The dead returned to walk the earth once many moons ago, and now, it's happening again."

"Jeremy's going to wish that he'd stayed dead after I'm through with him."

Kasey's grief turned to rage, consumed with thoughts of killing Jeremy with his bare hands. "If I didn't care so much about Reed, I'd kill that bastard. To think he was right outside the house the other night. If I'd had realized then, if I'd paid more attention, Mom would still be alive."

"You can't blame yourself. You had no way of knowing."

Hilda and Kasey embraced again. Moments later, Kasey pulled away. "I want to help avenge Mom and get Reed back."

"I know what you're thinking, and you can forget it," Hilda said.

"I can let him use me. The son of a bitch will come looking for me anyway."

Hilda shook her head. "No. I can't allow that."

"You don't have a choice."

"If anything were to happen to you, I don't know how I would explain it to your mother."

Kasey appeared confused. "Huh? Mom's gone. There are no explanations needed."

Hilda sighed. "There's something you don't know. Lucy returned at the last Midnight's Edge to help us defeat Jeremy. Although, without Gracey, I'm not even sure that's possible now."

His eyes widened in shock. "When were you planning to tell me this? Where is she?"

"That doesn't matter right now. What matters is that you cannot, under any circumstances, confront Jeremy alone. It's not safe. Do you understand?"

He balled his fists. "I'm not going to let Jeremy get away with what he's done to Mom or my friend. What would happen if he tried to possess me?"

Hilda didn't say anything.

"I want the truth. I think you owe me that much."

"Since you aren't his blood, his spirit would continue to weaken, and he'd be sent back to the dark from where he came."

He managed a small smile. "What are we waiting for?"

"There are dangers to you. As his spirit dies, the mortal body dies as well. You run the risk of not being able to get back."

He thought about Ethan, the only good thing he felt like he had left now that Gracey was gone. He didn't want to lose what they'd rekindled but knew that they could never be happy as long as Jeremy was still around.

"It's a risk I'm willing to take. You stay and wait for the ambulance. I've gotta get out of here."

He started to leave, but she grabbed his arm. "I don't think you heard me. You could lose your life, Kasey. You could lose your soul."

"I heard you. If that's what it takes, so be it. I'm going to avenge my mother's death. I'm going to make that son of a bitch suffer worse than he made her suffer."

A sinking feeling overtook me. Kasey knew now what Jeremy had done. I'd seen what Jeremy had done to my father and Gracey. I'd seen how the ancestors tricked Reed into giving up his soul. The Wickcliffs were unbelievably ruthless and powerful. In knowing Kasey as I did, he wasn't going to stop until he got revenge for what happened to his mother even though it could jeopardize his very existence.

* * * *

"Kasey knows that Gracey's dead," I said, returning to Damon and Rory. "He's planning to go to Jeremy and pretend to be his son so that he can trick him into inhabiting the wrong body. What are we going to do to stop it?"

"Perhaps nothing," Damon said.

I could feel the astonishment in my face. "Excuse me?"

"Perhaps the best course of action is to do nothing at all."

"How can you say that after everything I've told you about what Jeremy's done? If he's allowed to roam free and bring back the ancestors, who knows how many other innocent people will be hurt."

"He isn't going to be roaming free, Shell," Rory said. "We won't allow that."

"Are you trying to tell me that you're all for standing by and doing nothing while Jeremy takes over Kasey's body and life?"

"It's only a temporary situation," Damon said. "If he inhabits the body of another one not of his bloodline, he'll be weaker and more vulnerable than ever. He'll die, and Kasey will get his life back. The witches may not be strong enough to eliminate him on their own. It may be our only hope to get rid of him."

I shook my head. "Reed didn't get his life back. There's no guarantee that Kasey will either. What if his body dies or even worse, what if the ancestors trick him into giving up his soul as they did Reed?"

"That's not going to happen," Rory said. "Jeremy's barely holding on now in Reed's body. He can't withstand another non-bloodline transfer."

"He was strong enough to kill Gracey. He can't be that weak."

"That took a great deal of strength," Damon said. "It's accelerated the process of his destruction. I know what I'm talking about. I promise you. Once Jeremy's inside Kasey, I have a ritual I can use to vanquish him. With the witches help, we can do it if we all work together."

"Will they be able to do it without Gracey?" I asked.

"Gracey's spirit will always be with them," Damon said. "Just because her physical body's died doesn't mean she won't live on. The spirit never dies."

I sighed. "The more terrible things I see, the more hopeless the situation seems."

Rory smiled at me. "We're here together, aren't we? Did you ever think that would happen?" He touched my face tenderly. "Don't give up hope. Even when things seem the bleakest, it isn't the time to give up."

"Please go back to the mortal realm and tell us what you see," Damon said. "If Kasey's going to go through with the transfer, we need to know the precise moment it happens."

* * * *

Back in the mortal realm, it wasn't Kasey that I was drawn to, it was Lucy's other son, Jason. He didn't know his true identity, but I knew that it was only a matter of time before he found out. Lucy was going to find him. I wondered how he'd react when he found out who he really was.

I found him and Rebecca at the Moonlight Inn sipping champagne, toasting the job that Ethan offered him. Rebecca put down her glass and put her arms around him.

"I guess since you got the job, you're going to stay in Sleepy Meadows?"

He shrugged and smiled. "You're stuck with me."

She squeezed him. "Oh, how terrible. I don't know if I'll be able to stand it."

"You only have yourself to blame." He cupped her face and kissed her gently. "If it weren't for you putting a good word in for me with Ethan, I wouldn't have this job in the first place."

"Don't sell yourself short. You're extremely talented in a lot of ways."

He chuckled. "Really? How so?"

"Why don't you let me congratulate you properly so you can demonstrate?"

He swept her off her feet and laid her down on the bed. He glanced into her eyes, and her heart melted. Her body tingled with desire. He began to kiss her neck, and just as he undid her blouse, they were interrupted by a pounding at the door.

"Ignore it," she said, trying to catch her breath. "They'll go away."

He began to kiss her again, but the person at the door persisted. "Becca, its Brynn! Please open the door. I need to talk to you right now! It's an emergency."

Rebecca sat up and buttoned her blouse. "What's my sister doing here?"

Jason sat back and shrugged. "How am I supposed to know?"

"She sounds upset. Can you give me a moment, please?"

He sighed. "Sure."

"I'm sorry."

"I know we haven't known each other that long, but I think we've got something real here. Are you ashamed of me? Is that why you don't want me to meet your sister?"

"Of course not. How can you even think that? It's just that I can't let Brynn find me here with one man while I'm still married to another. She's just a teenager, and very impressionable. Even though it's over with Pit, it doesn't set a good example."

He gestured with a nod. "I'll give you some space."

She gave him a peck on the cheek. "You're wonderful. I'll make it up to you, I promise."

He headed to the bathroom. Rebecca got up, went to the door, and opened it. Brynn's freckled face was flushed. Her eyes were red and puffy, matching the color of her hair that hung in her face.

"Thank God you're here," she said, pushing her way past Rebecca and entering the room. "I didn't know where else to go."

Rebecca shut the door and rotated around, putting her hands on her hips. "Sweetie, what's wrong?"

"It's Bucky. He's disappeared."

"What do you mean disappeared?"

Brynn sat down on the bed. "Just what I said. He's gone. No one knows where he is or what's happened to him."

Rebecca sat down and put her hand on Brynn's. "Did you guys have a fight?"

Brynn shook her head. "No. We haven't exactly gotten along well lately, but that's not the point."

"When was the last time you saw him?"

"It's been two days." Brynn clasped her sister's hand tighter. "I'm scared, Becca."

"What makes you think he's disappeared?"

Brynn wiped her eyes with the back of her free hand. "He isn't answering his phone. He always answers his phone when he sees it's me calling."

Rebecca shrugged. "Maybe he just needed a break. You said you weren't getting along. He probably just needs some space."

Brynn shook her head adamantly. "It gets worse. He was supposed to meet his friend Ralph for a fishing trip this morning at Misty Lake. When he didn't show, Ralph called his parents. They haven't seen him either, so they called me hoping that I'd heard from him. That's when I realized he's missing."

"He probably just got tied up with one of his odd jobs. Maybe he had to go out of town for a couple days."

"No! You're not listening. He would've told someone. His folks said he just disappeared from their bar the other night. He was helping out serving drinks and left in the middle of his shift. People saw him leave with Shelly Wickcliff."

The mention of my name made Rebecca think about how I, or Rachel rather, had shown up at my father's wake, and how odd and strange she'd acted. Few people knew that Rachel wasn't me. She thought it odd that I'd show up at The Hook and leave with her sister's boyfriend, a boy several years younger, but she didn't let on.

"There has to be some explanation for that."

"Shirley went to Sheriff Withers, but she said she didn't think he took her seriously. I want to see him myself, but I'm afraid he'll just look at me like some hysterical kid. Will you come with me?"

Rebecca glanced toward the bathroom where Jason was hiding. "I don't—"

"Please, Becca? I can't do this alone."

Rebecca saw the desperation in her sister's eyes, so she agreed. She told Brynn to wait for her outside. Hearing that she'd gone, Jason came out of the bathroom.

"I have to go," Rebecca said.

"I heard. It's okay."

She kissed him. "I'll be back as soon as I can." She grabbed her coat and headed out the door.

* * * *

I followed the Wexler sisters to the police station where they asked to see Graham. Raymond said that he'd be right with them, but they were kept waiting for a while. When Graham finally emerged, he appeared pale and sweaty.

I'd wondered why he hadn't gone to Kasey to tell him of Jeremy's plan, and now I understood. He was trying to get up the courage. He'd been a nervous wreck, which explained his appearance. He'd tried to get in touch with Kasey, but he hadn't called back. After he'd placed the call, he'd heard from the coroner's office what had happened to Gracey, and decided that now wasn't the time to confront Kasey with Jeremy's plan.

Rebecca noticed right away that Graham wasn't well. "Are you sick? You look ill."

He pulled a handkerchief from his pocket and wiped his forehead. "I'm fine, just tired. I'm sorry to keep you two waiting."

He stepped aside and allowed them to enter his office. He sat down at his desk and motioned to the chairs across from it. The two sisters sat.

"I know why you're here," he said, turning to Brynn. "I can only tell you what I've told Shirley. Your boyfriend isn't missing until he hasn't been seen for 48 hours."

"That doesn't help us," Brynn said. "You could, at least, question Shelly Wickcliff. A ton of people saw them leaving together."

"I have. She claims that all he did was help her to her car and that she left him in the parking lot."

Brynn brushed a piece of hair from her face. "Do you believe her?"

Graham felt sick inside. He thought about how he'd come to the house to question me only to realize that Jeremy had possessed his son and that Jeremy's sister had possessed me. He knew they were unnatural, not human. He couldn't admit the truth to anyone. If anyone were to find out what he knew, he could jeopardize his only chance at getting Reed back. He had to lie.

"I don't have any reason not to."

Rebecca cleared her throat. "I'm not saying that Shelly wasn't telling you the truth, but she acted very peculiarly at Jeffrey's wake."

Graham folded his hands and placed them on the desk. "In what way?"

"She was cold, distant as if she were a million miles away. Her family was scared to death when they couldn't reach her after Jeffrey's heart attack. She didn't even seem to care that she'd caused them so much worry."

"Well, she just lost her father," he said. "I can understand her being standoffish. We all handle grief in our own way."

Rebecca shrugged. "I suppose so, but she didn't seem to be handling it at all. It was almost as if Jeffrey were a stranger to her. She showed little emotion for someone who supposedly loved her father so much. Now all of the sudden she's hanging out at The Hook? She hardly ever left the Wickcliff mansion before."

Graham sighed. "I admit that it's a tad peculiar that he left in the middle of his shift and that nobody's heard from him. However, as of now, I have no reason to doubt Shelly's story, and there's no evidence to suggest that he's disappeared. There are 24 hours left in the 48-hour window. If Shirley and Hal haven't heard from him by this time tomorrow, she can come in and file a report. I'll launch an investigation."

Brynn stood up and pounded on the desk. "That's all? That's all you're going to do?"

Rebecca rose and put her hand on Brynn's back. "Come on, sit down."

Brynn pushed Rebecca's hand away. "That's not good enough."

Graham put his hands up. "I'm sorry that you're upset, but I've got to follow standard procedure."

"I'm surprised at you Graham," Rebecca said. "I can understand the procedure, but we've come to you with a legitimate concern and it doesn't seem like you're the slightest bit interested in helping us. Do you even care?"

He scoffed not meeting eyes with them. "Of course I care, but as I told you, I can't bend the rules for you or anyone else. Shirley has to wait another 24 hours."

Rebecca noticed him glancing at the clock nervously. "What's wrong with you tonight? You seem so distracted."

He exhaled swiftly and met her stare. "I've told you I'm fine. Now it's getting late. You two should be getting home. Bucky will probably be in touch by the morning, and there won't even need to be a report filed." He knew full well that wasn't true.

Rebecca got up and motioned to the door. "Let's go, Brynn."

After Brynn had walked out of the room, Graham stopped Rebecca.

"Rebecca, wait. You know Kasey Menze pretty well. You grew up together, didn't you?"

Rebecca raised an eyebrow, not understanding what Kasey had to do with what they were talking about. "Uh-huh."

"What's your opinion of him?"

"He's a wonderful person. He's been a true friend and always there when I needed him."

"That's what I thought you'd say." His eyes drifted away, and she noticed.

"Why do you ask? Is Kasey in some sort of trouble?"

"Not if I can help it."

She tilted her head to the side. "What does that mean?"

He shook his head and waved his hand. "Nothing…nothing at all."

After Rebecca left, Graham sat down at his desk, overwhelmed by lying to her, having to work with Jeremy, and the possibility of putting Kasey in harm's way. All of that coupled with Bucky's disappearance and the peril that his son was in was becoming too much for Graham to handle. While Jeremy and Rachel hadn't admitted it, he knew it wasn't a coincidence that the last person to see Bucky had been Rachel. He couldn't tell Brynn or Rebecca, but he believed that Bucky may be hurt or worse. He looked up towards his ceiling; his hands clasped together.

"Dear God, help me. Please help me."

Chapter 17

As I shifted my focus away from Graham, I tried to connect with Kasey, but I saw Jason instead. I was realizing more and more that I don't always have control over where I go or who I see. When I'm pulled somewhere I don't intentionally want to go; it means that there's something that I'm meant to see.

Since Rebecca was with Brynn, Jason decided to get some air, and I found him at Lover's Bluff. This was my first time seeing him in awhile that he wasn't with Rebecca. When he's with her, his thoughts are clouded, he's preoccupied with the fact he's falling in love with her and forgets what his motivations were for coming to Sleepy Meadows. Without Rebecca around I could read his thoughts clearly for the first time.

As I watched him, I realized that he knew more about his past than he'd let on to the stranger that had given him a ride, to Rebecca, or anyone else he'd encountered so far. He'd come to Sleepy Meadows to ingratiate himself with my family and was using Rebecca to do that. He knew that she was attracted to him, and she'd mentioned knowing my family, so he thought he could use her as a link to get closer to them. He hadn't planned on developing genuine feelings for her.

Jason stood there on the bluff looking out at the water, letting his mind drift into the past. He hadn't known much about his family, that much was true, but as I watched his memories flash before me like a movie, I knew my instincts about him were right. I was reluctant to trust him, sure that there was a deeper, darker motive for his coming here, and I wasn't wrong to feel that.

The only family that he had growing up was a group of traveling gypsies. He'd never had a permanent home as they were always moving from place to place. He felt unloved because his mother gave him away at birth and until he met Rebecca, he never thought he truly could love or be loved in return.

The closest thing he had to a mother was a gypsy named Roxanne Beckett. She was part of the gypsy coven, but she was always more attentive to him than the rest. She took him under her wing. Six months ago, she'd died and made a deathbed confession that shook Jason to the core.

He'd entered her caravan on that day knowing she didn't have much time left, even though he didn't want to accept it. He approached her bed and took her hand in his.

"Is there anything I can get you, Rox?"

"There isn't much time now," Roxanne said, in a low, raspy voice. "I need you to listen."

He shook his head. "Don't talk like that. You're going to get well."

She waved her free hand. "Come closer. There's something you must know."

He leaned in. "I'm listening."

She wheezed. "If I'm ever going to be able to rest, I need to tell you the truth about your parents."

"You always said I was better off not knowing."

"I wanted to protect you. I was wrong. Everyone deserves to know where they come from. Your mother was a friend. I promised her I'd never tell you. I'm afraid I must break that promise now."

"Who are they, Rox?"

"Your mother was the most loving and giving woman; your father was the most spiteful and hateful man."

"Was?"

"They're both gone. They have been for a long time now."

"I see." He bowed his head, extremely disappointed, and silently mourning the fact that he'd never get the opportunity to confront them about why they never wanted him. "How did I end up here?"

"Your mother wanted to protect you while she still could. Had she kept you, your father's influence would've destroyed you as it did him, as it did your mother."

"I don't understand."

"Your father was evil personified."

His forehead furrowed. "Evil? You mean he wasn't a nice guy?"

"It was much more than that. He was cruel, unfeeling. He was disturbed."

"You mean he was nuts?"

"Certifiable."

Jason let go of her hand. "Don't you think you should've told me that? If my father was a wacko, I think I had the right to know. It's genetic, isn't it?"

"If you only knew." Roxanne began to weep.

"So tell me. How did they die? Who were they?"

"Jeremy and Lucy Wickcliff were their names. They died in an accident. Only it wasn't."

"What do you mean?"

Roxanne moaned. "She had to stop him before he hurt anyone else."

"Are you saying that my mother killed my father?"

"She didn't have a choice. She went to the witches for help, Carol Hawkins, Gracey Menze."

Jason didn't think at the time that she'd made much sense. She lost consciousness never to regain it again. She mumbled a few choice words throughout the night: evil, Hawkins, feud, Sleepy Meadows. She muttered the same words repeatedly until her last breath.

He did some research and found that Sleepy Meadows was 250 miles away. He'd come here with a million questions and not many answers. He'd come to learn what these women, Hawkins, and Menze, had to do with what happened to his parents. Originally, his only goal was to find out what they knew. He'd planned to get revenge on them if he found out they had anything to do with the death of his parents.

Meeting Rebecca had changed his plans. She saw the good in him that he'd tried to relinquish long ago. He'd become so angry and jaded in his youth because of the rejection he felt that revenge was all he could think about before meeting her. Now, he knew that he had to make a choice between vengeance and perhaps his last chance at true love.

"I know you're confused, Jason," Lucy said, from behind him, jolting him out of his thoughts, "but I can explain everything."

He turned around and faced his mother. His eyes widened with bewilderment. "I've seen your picture. I know who you are. How can you be here?"

Lucy stepped forward. "You know I'm your mother?"

He stepped back. "Don't come near me, you're dead! Rox told me so."

Lucy got close enough to touch his hand. "I'm not, not anymore. Feel the warmth of my touch. I know this is a lot to take in, but I'm alive again."

He pulled away. "I told you to stay away from me!"

She put her hands up. "I'm not going to hurt you, Jason. I'm here to help you."

"I don't need your help, whatever you are. I can take care of myself."

"I don't expect you to understand how I've come back. It's a long story, and maybe I'll be able to explain it to you someday. But I need you to understand this. You do need my help. Your father's alive too. He's come back to find you, and if he does, he'll destroy you."

"You expect me to believe that both of you have come back?" He put his hands on both sides of his head. "I must be hallucinating."

"This isn't a hallucination or a dream. He needs to inhabit the body of someone of his bloodline if he's to continue to survive in the mortal world. If he finds out who you are, he'll take over your body and your life. He's a monster. You have to be prepared to fight him, and you have to let me help you do that."

He scoffed. "You're insane. My father's alive and wants to take over my body? Yeah right." He turned to walk away.

"I know this sounds crazy," she said, following behind him, "but it's true I swear it."

He whipped around. "Why should I believe you? I don't even know you. You're just the woman who gave me away."

"I did that for your sake, so your father couldn't get to you."

"I should've been given the opportunity to know my father. That's my choice. You didn't even give me the chance to know him. You had no right to do that."

"I know you're upset, but Jeremy doesn't care about you. You're a means to an end, and that's all."

He huffed. "And you do care? You weren't there either. There were times when the urge to be cruel, unfeeling, and relentless was so overwhelming that I thought of killing myself so that I wouldn't give into the urge to hurt someone else. Do you have any idea what that feels like?" He paused. "I bet you do. Rox told me about how you arranged the accident that caused my father's death. You sound like you're the evil one to me."

"You don't understand. I saved countless lives by taking his and I won't apologize for it. You felt the way you did because your father's legacy lives inside of you. There's nothing that we can do to change that. We can only neutralize it with the good that you possess. The part of you that's me."

"It's a bit late to be matronly. I've always been on my own. I'm a loner. I can take care of myself."

"I'm afraid you don't stand a chance against him by yourself." She paused and held out her arms. "Come here. Let me hold you this once, please."

He didn't want to admit it, but he longed to be comforted by her. It had been his dream to meet his mother, one he never thought would come true. He felt the warmth that radiated from her. He didn't understand everything he'd heard or seen, but he relented and let Lucy take him into her arms.

"My son, my beautiful boy." She caressed the back of his head. "Jeremy's never going to harm you as long as there's breath in my body. That's my vow to you."

* * * *

I returned to the spirit realm, rested for a while, and then filled Damon and Rory in on the latest developments with Jason and Lucy. By the time I went back to the mortal realm, it was a new day. Seeing Lucy reunite with Jason made me think about how much I missed my family. I was comforted by the fact that I'd reunited with Rory, but it didn't change the fact that I longed for Mom, Gram, and Ethan. I focused my attention on Mom's house.

Ethan entered the kitchen and found Mom sitting at the table crying.

He stood next to her.

"Mom, what's wrong?"

She looked up at him. "It's Gracey. She's dead. Hilda just called. She wanted to call last night, but it was the middle of the night by the time Gracey was found. She wasn't in any shape to talk. She's devastated."

He exhaled. "I'm sorry, Mom. I know she was a good friend of yours. Do you know what happened?"

She shook her head. "Hilda didn't want to discuss it over the phone. I'll see her later."

He ran his hands through his hair. "Are you going to be okay if I head out for a bit?"

"You're going to see Kasey, I suppose?"

"I have to. He's gotta be a wreck."

She stood up. "I don't think you going to see Kasey is a good idea."

He went to the door and grabbed his coat. "Kasey helped me keep it together when Dad died, and now I'm going to be there to support him. I don't have time to argue with you."

* * * *

I followed my brother to Kasey's trailer. When he got there, he went up to the door and knocked.

Kasey answered the door looking haggard. His eyes were bloodshot from the lack of sleep and tears. Without speaking, Kasey let him in, and they hugged.

"Why didn't you call me, Kase?"

Kasey shrugged. "It was a mix of shock and not wanting to accept it I guess. I had a lot to think about. I didn't want to see or talk to anyone last night."

Ethan touched Kasey's arm tenderly. "I'm so sorry."

"I was finally starting to have hope again, you know? You came back, we were together, and now I've lost Mom. I'm scared."

"Scared of what?"

Kasey exhaled. "Of not being able to cope with the loss mostly, but I'm afraid I'll never be happy."

"You will. We both will, together."

"When?" Kasey's tough facade crumbled and his voice broke. "I just don't know if I can believe that. I don't know if I can have faith in anything anymore."

"Do you still have faith in us?"

Kasey touched Ethan's face. "I want to…so much."

"I did it, Kase. I told my Mom about us."

"You did?" He managed a small smile through the tears. "Really?"

Ethan returned the smile. "Really."

"So does this mean…?"

Ethan nodded. "I'm staying in Sleepy Meadows, and I want to give us a shot if you'll still have me."

Kasey's heart sank. Under any other circumstances, he'd be elated. Ethan returning and them being together was his dream come true. However, now he'd decided to confront Jeremy and let him possess his body in an attempt to rid him of the mortal world. He'd just got what he'd always wanted, but if he made one wrong move, he knew he could lose it all. He pushed the thoughts away, trying to enjoy the moment.

He embraced Ethan again. "You know I will." He stepped back after a moment. "Mom always told me that you'd be back and that we'd be together. She said it was written in the stars."

"She was a wise woman. She knew before I did."

"I love you, Ethan. I never stopped."

"I love you too, Kase, I always have, even though I had trouble coming to terms with it. I'm sorry I denied it for so long."

"You coming here and telling me that was the only thing that could make me smile today." He paused. "It hurts so much to know that she's gone forever. How am I going to deal with this? I wish I knew."

Ethan squeezed his arms. "By letting me be there for you. I'm home now, and I swear to you I'll never let you down again."

Kasey buried his head in Ethan's chest and wept. Ethan stroked his hair and put his other arm around Kasey's neck.

"I've got you. Let it all out."

After a moment, Kasey composed himself. "I didn't mean to unload on you like that. I know you're still in mourning yourself."

"We can help each other through this. We're going to make it this time. I swear." He took Kasey's hand. "Come on, you need to get some sleep. I know you're exhausted."

"Will you stay?"

"Of course I will."

They laid down on Kasey's bed. Kasey put his head on Ethan's chest. "This is nice."

"I have to ask. What happened to your mom?"

"Hilda's convinced that Jeremy Wickcliff killed her, and to tell you the truth, I believe it too."

Ethan sat up. "Did you say Jeremy Wickcliff?"

"I know what you're thinking, and it's an unbelievable story, but Mom thought he was alive, and Hilda confirmed it."

"Dad said the same thing right before he died. It didn't make sense then, but now I don't know what to think."

Kasey sat up too. "You know about him? It's the only explanation. Look at everything that's been happening. Your dad dying, my mom, I don't think those are coincidences. Jeremy's responsible. He's possessed Reed. That's how he was able to return. There's so much I still don't understand about it."

Ethan's eyes widened. "This is all too impossible to believe." He groaned. "My God. Reed was with Dad when he died. I left him alone with him. If this is true, I handed Dad right over to him." He shook his head. "I don't believe this."

Kasey caressed his arm. "You couldn't have known. It's not your fault."

It wasn't long before Kasey fell asleep. Ethan laid there with him, unable to relax. All he could think about was how he was responsible for Dad's death. Of course, it wasn't true, but he blamed himself for things he couldn't control, just as I did.

Before long, there was a knock on the door. Ethan answered it to find Hilda standing there with a platter in her hand.

"May I help you?" Ethan said, studying her face. "Wait a minute. Hilda? It's me, Ethan Hawkins."

She smiled. "Oh my, Ethan. I'm sorry I didn't recognize you at first. You've grown into quite the handsome young man. Your mother mentioned that, but I thought she was just biased as mothers tend to be."

He blushed. "Thank you. Won't you come in?"

She entered, and he shut the door behind her. "I brought Kasey some food. I figured the poor dear hasn't eaten, and I couldn't sleep anyway so…"

"I'm sure he'll appreciate it. Are you alright? Mom mentioned that you were very upset."

She shrugged. "Not really, but I'm doing the best I can."

"I'm glad you're here. I'd like to talk to you. Kasey said that you told him that Jeremy Wickcliff's back and that you think that he killed Gracey. Is that true?"

Her eyes filled with panic, fear, and rage all at once. "Yes."

"How is that possible?"

"It's a very long and complicated story, but I swear to you it's the truth."

"I believe you. If Jeremy's back, he's obviously up in the Wickcliff house. I've got to get my sister out of there."

Her expression turned grim. "I'm afraid it's too late."

"I don't understand."

Hilda sighed. "There's no easy way for me to say this. I haven't even told your mother yet. I can't keep the truth from the family forever. Soon everyone will know. I went to the Wickcliff's to confront Jeremy, and when I was there, I ran into the woman that's passing herself off as Shelly. Jeremy's used dark arts to return his sister Rachel's spirit using your sister's body."

Chapter 18

My heart became heavy. The truth about what had happened to me was finally revealed. It needed to be done, but it broke my heart to think about my family having to mourn my death when Dad's loss was still so fresh.

Ethan expression became grim. "Is this some sick joke?"

Hilda touched his arm softly. "I know that you think me mad, and I don't blame you, but it's the truth. Jeremy plans to return each of his family members from the grave one by one."

Ethan thought about encountering Rachel at Dad's wake. He couldn't put his finger on it, but he'd known there was something different about me. Rachel had been strong and confident that day, a sharp contrast to the state I was in at the end of my life. He didn't want to believe it, but it made sense.

"If that's true and Shelly's Rachel, then where's my sister?"

Her face fell. "For Rachel to live, Shelly's spirit had to vacate her body."

My brother's face went red. "You can't mean…" He shook his head. "That isn't true. It can't be."

She touched his arm once again. "Oh, honey, you know in your heart that I'm right."

He began to tear up. "You have to be mistaken."

"I wish I were, but I'm not."

His grief turned to rage. He saw nothing but red. "Dad was the first to discover the truth. Jeremy killed him to keep him quiet. I know that now. He killed my father, sister, and Kasey's mother. That bastard's dead. If it's the last thing I ever do, Jeremy Wickcliff will be sent back to hell."

Ethan headed for the door, and Hilda followed him.

"Where are you going, Ethan?"

He looked back at the bedroom thinking of Kasey. "I have to talk to my mother."

"I haven't told her about Shelly. I was waiting for the right time, and there never seemed to be one. Perhaps it would be better coming from you."

"I'll take care of telling Mom. Can you stay with Kasey? I told him I'd be here when he woke up. Just tell him that I'll be back."

Hilda gave him a nod, and he dashed out the door. She wondered if she'd made the right decision in telling him about me. There were so many secrets; it was time to let them all out.

* * * *

I followed Ethan back to Mom's house. I wanted to be with him when he told Mom about my fate. I couldn't do anything to comfort them, but I still wanted to be there. He was in tears the entire way, and it made me feel horrible. I wished I could tell him how sorry I was for what I'd done.

When he entered the house, he found Mom lying on the kitchen floor unconscious. He ran to her, crouched down, and supported her head with his hand.

"Mom, can you hear me?"

Mom moaned softly and slowly opened her eyes. "What happened?"

"I was hoping you could tell me. Can you get up?"

"I think so." She stood with Ethan's help, and she rubbed the back of her head. "I'm starting to remember something. I heard a noise like someone was entering the house and then everything went black. My head hurts. I think I was hit with something."

"Where's Gram?"

"She isn't here. It's just Freddy and me." She paused, and her eyes became wide with panic. "Freddy. Make sure he's alright."

Ethan ran into the living room yelling Freddy's name. Getting no answer, he went upstairs. Freddy still didn't answer.

After he searched the entire house, he went back in the kitchen.

"He's not here."

Mom pointed down to the linoleum floor. There were large footprints.

Ethan thought about the conversation he'd had with Rachel at Dad's wake. She'd seemed eager to have Freddy come home with her and he'd shut her down. Now he was convinced that she'd made it happen.

I swallowed hard. Because I'd been with Ethan and Kasey, I didn't realize that the Wickcliff's had gotten to Freddy. The footprints on the floor were large enough to be Gaul's. It was obvious that he was the one who'd taken him. I was terrified that my son was with those monsters. What if Rachel did to him what she'd done to Bucky? I could barely think straight. I was consumed with fear for his safety.

Ethan's expression was grim.

"We need to call the police," Mom said.

"You don't need to do that. I know where he is. He's at the Wickcliff's."

Mom was confused. "Shelly wouldn't take him in such a brutal manner. She'd have no need to."

"That's not Shelly up there in the mansion. You want to believe it is, but it's not. Hilda told me she went up to the Wickcliffs to confront Jeremy and while she was there, she came across who she thought was Shelly at first. She admitted that she was Jeremy's sister, Rachel."

Mom's face went white. "No! It's not true." She began to shake.

"I know he's come back, Mom. You needn't deny it any longer. He killed Gracey. Hilda's sure of that. I'm not sure why you felt the need to lie about it, but I know the truth. I need you to start being honest."

She clenched her fists. "I wasn't lying when I told you your father was confused. I was in denial. I didn't want to accept that Jeremy was back then. Now I have no choice."

"Mom, Shelly's dead."

"I don't want to hear it."

Tears streamed down his face. "It's true, and I think you've known in your heart. Dad told us so, we just didn't want to believe it. As much as I wish to God it wasn't true, it is. Jeremy's behind Shelly's death, just like Dad's and just like Gracey's."

She shook her head back and forth, crying. "I don't believe you. We saw her at your father's wake."

"Who we saw was Rachel. You saw how different she acted. How nonchalant she appeared when she knew she worried us sick. It's because she was different." He wiped his eyes. "I can't pretend to understand all of this, but he used her body to bring back his sister."

She let out a wail. "My baby! My little girl!"

"I know. I know." He took her in his arms. "It's going to be alright."

She stiffened and pushed away from him. "I know it is because I've got to be strong. I've got to avenge your sister and your father. Jeremy's going to pay. Whatever he encountered in the dark is nothing compared to what I'm going to do to him."

"We have to get Freddy away from Jeremy and Rachel."

She looked away. "How could I let this happen?"

"It's not your fault. You couldn't control it."

He headed for the door. She followed him. "Where are you going?"

"To get Freddy out of there. I couldn't save Shelly from that prison, but I can save her son."

She grabbed his arm. "I don't want you going up to that house. You don't know what you're up against. You don't know the power Jeremy has. I've already lost your father and your sister. I can't lose you too."

"If I don't go, Freddy's life could be at stake. They can't get away with what they've done to our family."

"Freddy's not in danger, and the Wickcliff's aren't going to get away with anything. I'm going to protect us from now on. Everything's under control."

He examined her strange expression. He didn't know about Mom's powers or her past with Jeremy. "What aren't you telling me, Mom? You made a similar comment a minute ago, and I thought it was just grief talking."

"You've just got to trust me, Ethan."

"That isn't enough." He stepped out on the porch.

"Please, don't go."

He didn't look back. "I love you, Mom."

He stepped off the porch and she called after him. He didn't turn around.

Rachel's audacity didn't cease to amaze me. She'd already taken over my body and my life. Now she was going after my son. My family in the mortal realm meant well, but I had no guarantee that they'd be able to do anything to protect him. It was up to me to protect my son.

* * * *

I turned my attention back to the house. I needed to make sure my son was safe. As I thought about Rachel, I found her admiring herself in the mirror in her bedroom and talking to Gaul.

"I can't believe I let you talk me into bringing that kid here. I can't be anyone's mother. I'm not the mother type." She turned to face him. "What I am is a monster."

"You aren't a monster. You had to do what you did to Bucky to survive. We went over this already. It may have been the first time, but it won't be the last. You'll learn to adjust to it."

"I'll never get used to it. I don't trust myself around that kid. He shouldn't be here."

"People need to believe you're Shelly. If you ignore Freddy, you'll raise suspicions."

She shrugged. "The real Shelly ignored him, didn't she?"

That comment infuriated me. It wasn't true. If it weren't for Jeremy making me so unstable, I would've had my son with me. It was his fault. It had nothing to do with me not loving my son. With every word she spoke, my rage increased. I wanted to see her destroyed.

"Besides," Rachel said. "That old crone Hilda knows who Jeremy and I are. Soon others will too."

"It doesn't matter," Gaul said. "You know that Jeremy wants Freddy here. He's a Wickcliff—he's part of this family. He wants all of you together. Once Jeremy sets his mind on something you know we have no choice but to obey his wishes."

"Like hell. You may not, but I refuse to let him control me."

She walked over to the closet and pulled out a suitcase, headed towards the bed, and slammed it down on the mattress.

He stared at her. "What are you doing?"

She looked up at him and opened the suitcase. "I need to get away from here. Away from this house. It holds too many bad memories for me. If I'm going to start over, I need to go somewhere where no one knows who I am or should I say what I am."

"You can't leave here. You don't know anything about the world. You wouldn't last five minutes on your own."

She laughed and began grabbing clothing from her drawers. "I'm a lot more resourceful than you give me credit for. You know damn well that if you could leave, you would."

He came over to the bed and put his large hand on her suitcase to stop her. "Leaving here isn't going to change what you are. No matter where you go, you can't escape it."

She put her hands on her hips defiantly. "Once word gets out about who we are, the people of this town will come after us. They'll try to destroy us just like they did before."

"Not if we get to them first."

"What are you saying?"

"You make them afraid of you. If they fear you, they won't come near you. Use Freddy as your shield. No one would hurt a child."

"I don't want him around. I don't want to be his mother any more than Shelly did."

"You don't have to be. Use him. Pretend you care about him as part of your family. Appease Jeremy for now until we're ready to make a move. If you stick with me, we can overthrow Jeremy, and we can rule this town, just the two of us."

This had been the first time that I'd heard Gaul say anything against Jeremy. Jeremy had thought that Gaul was nothing but an emotionless slave, a being that had no choice but to obey his every whim. It was clear that this wasn't the case. It had been his love for Rachel that allowed him to resist Jeremy's will. I could feel his hatred for Jeremy growing ever stronger, and it felt good to know that there was a possibility that he could be betrayed by someone in his inner circle.

Rachel's eyes widened. "How can you say that? You're supposed to be his servant."

"Servant to the family, yes. If you're the only one left standing, then I only answer to you."

She peered into his black eyes. She was searching for answers, but there was nothing, as always. "Do you think it'll work, Gaul? If I can free myself of Jeremy, everything may be different."

He touched her face with his coarse hands. "I know it will. Remember, you hold all the cards."

* * * *

When I focused my energy back on my brother, I expected by now that he'd be halfway to the mansion. Instead, I found him in the driveway in front of our Mom's house still. Just as he'd gotten to his car, Pit had pulled up in his truck and stopped him.

Pit wasn't aware that anyone knew that I'd died and that Rachel had come back in my place. He'd kept that secret because he'd feared for his life, but as I saw him standing there shifting his stance nervously, I could tell that he was genuinely sorry about the part he played in helping Jeremy cover up my death and for keeping quiet about Rachel's return. He seemed gruff and hard on the outside, but I felt a sense of loneliness inside him. He wasn't a bad man. He'd taken Rebecca's leaving him harder than he let on, and I felt sorry for him.

"What do you want?" Ethan said, putting his hands on his hips.

"We've never been best friends, Ethan, but can you just give me two seconds? I need to talk to you."

"That's an understatement. We've never had much use for each other. I don't mean to be rude, but if you'll excuse me, I'm in a hurry."

Ethan started to get in his car, but Pit grabbed his arm.

Ethan glared down at Pit's hand, and Pit let go. "This'll only take a minute."

Ethan tried to push his way past. "I'm sorry. I don't have time for this."

"Meeting your boy toy?"

"Not that it's any of your business, but I need to get to my nephew."

"What I need to tell you concerns your nephew. I know what happened to your sister."

His eyes narrowed. "How do you know that something's happened to her? Only a few of us know."

"I'm one of them. We can't talk here. Let's go somewhere."

Although Ethan was worried about Freddy being with Rachel, he was desperate to find out what happened to me. If Pit did know something, he couldn't pass up the opportunity to find out what it was.

Ethan didn't know just how dangerous Rachel could be. He had no idea that she was responsible for Bucky's disappearance or that she was a cold-blooded killer. Had he known, he would've made getting Freddy away from her more of an immediate priority, but at least I knew that Rachel and Gaul had no immediate plans to hurt my son. I followed him and Pit to The Hook. Once they got there, they sat at the bar and Pit got himself a beer, which he downed in a few gulps.

"If Jeremy finds out I'm talking to you, I'm dead." He looked around. "Maybe this wasn't such a good idea. He could have spies everywhere."

He started to get up, but Ethan pushed him down. "He's not going to find out. Just tell me what happened. How do you know about his return and what's happened to my sister?"

"I've been doing some odd jobs for the Wickcliffs for the past year or so. You know minor repairs on the house, that sort of thing. I got to know Gaul, that servant of theirs."

Ethan nodded. "I remember Gaul. He's been working there for years, used to scare the hell out of Shelly."

"He's the one that found Shelly's body. He said that no one could find out about her death. They wanted people to think she was still alive."

"So Jeremy could use her to bring back his sister. Sick fuck."

Pit shrugged. "I guess that's what he was planning all along." He shivered. "I saw him take over Reed's body. Gaul had called us both there. I've never seen such freaky shit in all my life."

"Pit, what happened to my sister? I know a healthy young woman wouldn't just die of natural causes. Did Jeremy kill her?"

He shook his head. "He said he messed with her head. Drove her crazy. He made her hang herself."

Ethan's expression fell. He bowed his head and put his face in his hands.

"I'll never forget what she looked like," Pit said. "She was just hanging there. Her face was blue, her eyes…I still have nightmares."

Ethan looked up at him. "Please stop. I can't take it." He took in a deep breath. "Who else saw her?"

"Reed did, but by the time Jeremy was done with him, he was in control and Reed couldn't tell anyone."

Ethan shook his head. "My God, Shelly, how could you do this?"

I wanted more than anything to tell my brother that I was sorry, that I'd fought Jeremy for as long as I could, and that I loved him. Knowing that I'd inflicted more pain on my family in addition to what they were already going through killed me inside.

Pit leaned in and softened his voice. "I'm sorry. I know this is tough."

Ethan pulled away and stood up. "I appreciate you coming clean, but it's too little, too late. When I look at you, all I see is someone who helped cover up my sister's death. We've gone through hell, and you helped contribute to that."

Pit stood up too. "Don't you think I know that? I've been racked with guilt. I haven't eaten, haven't slept. I had to come clean. I didn't have a choice. My life's in danger. I knew who Jeremy was. If I didn't go along with him, he would've killed me. He still might."

Ethan started for the door. "I gotta go."

Pit stopped him. "Ethan? I hope you nail the bastard."

Chapter 19

I was about to turn my attention to Rory and fill him in on what I'd seen so far when I got an overwhelming sensation that I needed to remain in the mortal realm. I wasn't sure where it was coming from, but by now I'd learned to trust my instincts and go with them instead of questioning them. I took a deep breath and cleared my head of everything, not sure where I was going to be led next.

When my vision became clear, I found myself back outside Kasey's trailer. Hilda had stayed with him while Ethan went to talk to Mom. Lucy had shown up in the time I was focused on my family.

"Is Kasey alright?" Lucy asked.

"He's asleep. The poor thing was exhausted after what happened to Gracey last night."

"You don't have to stay, Hilda. The time's come for me to tell my son who I am and I'd prefer to do it alone. He needs to realize how much danger he could potentially be in and that he needs to let me protect him."

Hilda nodded. "I understand. Just be aware that Kasey probably won't warm up to the idea of you being his mother. I don't know him all that well, but he and Gracey loved each other immensely. I don't want you to be hurt if he's aloof towards you."

"I wouldn't blame him if he were. That's not important now. All that's important is that I'm able to keep him safe."

Hilda patted her arm. "I suppose I should check in on Carol. Ethan went over to the house to see her. I told him that Shelly's dead. It was one of the hardest things I've had to do. He was going to tell Carol. She doesn't believe that I still care for her or her family after being away for so many years, but I do. I need her to see that."

Lucy smiled. "She will. We're a family, regardless of the time and space that separated us. I think Carol realizes that, and she'll realize how much you care."

Inside the house, Kasey awoke from his nap and became concerned that Ethan wasn't there beside him. He went outside and called for him, but he soon realized that he'd left.

I could feel the pain that radiated from him. He felt lost without Gracey and was having trouble wrapping his head around the fact that she was gone. The only thing that gave him a little bit of happiness was the fact that Ethan was back in his life.

A warm breeze touched his cheek, and he smiled. He thought it was Gracey's way of telling him it was okay to be happy, and I felt that it was.

He gazed into the distance and saw Lucy standing on the floor of the framework of the house he was working on. Because Lucy appeared as she had when she'd died, she was no older than Kasey was.

He ran over to the structure and stepped up on the floor. Lucy had her back to him and turned to face him when she heard him approaching. She smiled at him.

"Hello, Kasey."

He stared at her, clearly not knowing who she was. "I'm sorry, do I know you? What are you doing on my property?"

She put her hands up. "I know you don't recognize me, but I can explain everything. My name's Lucy."

His eyes brightened. "You're my…"

"Your mother, that's right. I gather Gracey and Hilda spoke of me?" She stepped closer to him. "I know you've got to be confused and that you must have a lot of questions, but I'm here. I'm alive and in physical form. I came back to protect you."

"From Jeremy?"

She nodded. "He thinks you're the Wickcliff heir. He's going to come after you and you need to be prepared."

He backed up. "I don't believe you're here. You can't be. This must be another one of my visions."

She extended her hand. "Take my hand, son. I'll prove it to you."

He stared at her, not accepting her hand. "I'm not your son. Don't call me that. I had a mother, and now she's dead."

Lucy gave him a closed smile. "I understand how you must feel. Gracey was a wonderful mother to you because I couldn't be. I'm sure of that. I loved her too, you know. In spirit, she was my sister, and I'm going to miss her too. She helped return me to the mortal world." She held out her hand again. "Go on, take it."

He didn't say anything and took her hand, meeting eyes with her. "It's warm. You are alive. I don't understand how it can be, or why you're no older than me."

She took her hand back. "It's a lot to try and explain." She reached out and touched his face. "My strong, handsome, admirable son. You've turned out just as I prayed you would after I gave you to Gracey to raise."

"She told me why you gave me away. I spent my whole childhood wondering why my mother didn't want me. Then when I found out you'd died, it felt even worse because I thought I'd never get the chance to ask you why."

Lucy began to tear up. "I know how you must've felt. What I did I did out of love and a desire to protect you. You aren't Jeremy's son. I was in love with another man."

"My father, Damon?"

"You know of him?"

"Mom…Gracey told me about him."

"It's alright. You can call Gracey mom. That's what she was to you after all. I cared for your father very much. I still do. He's a shaman, a man of another world. We couldn't be together. I was pregnant with you when I met Jeremy, but he didn't know it. He swept me off my feet, and we were married shortly after that. He's a vengeful, jealous man. He would've killed us both if he learned that I had a child with another man."

He felt a sudden surge of anger. "I guess I should thank you because you gave me a mother that was strong, loving, and independent."

"Yes, Gracey was all of those things."

He turned away. "I'd like you to go now."

She inched towards him. "I was weak. I admit it. First, I lied to your real father. He didn't know about you. Then I never told Jeremy about you. It was the only way I knew to keep you safe. I felt even more trapped once I no longer had my son to hold onto. I felt so alone, and I felt like I had no option but to stay with Jeremy. I honestly had nowhere else to go, so when Jeremy came back from his trip abroad, my sham of a marriage continued. I became pregnant again, and this time, the baby was his. A son I told him died."

He turned around to face her again. "I have a brother?" His tone softened slightly. "Is he alive?"

She nodded. "And he's here in Sleepy Meadows."

He ran his hands through his hair. "I can't believe what I'm hearing. Who is he?"

"His name's Jason Beckett, and if Jeremy finds out he exists, Jason will be in just as much danger as you are. I've come back to protect you both."

They heard a car coming up the path to Kasey's trailer. It was Graham's police car. Lucy looked at the car, closed her eyes and raised one hand.

"What are you doing?" Kasey said.

She kept her eyes closed. "I can feel that the sheriff's under Jeremy's control." She turned and focused on Kasey again. "Jeremy thinks you're his son and has sent the sheriff here to bring you to him. Don't trust him."

He turned to face Graham, who was now walking up the path towards him. He turned back around quickly to where Lucy had been standing, but she'd vanished.

Graham approached him noticing the bewildered look on Kasey's face. "I was just passing by and saw your bike on the edge of the path. Since you were home, I thought I'd stop in and check on you. How are you holding up?"

"I'm fine under the circumstances."

"I was sorry to hear about your mom. She was a good woman."

Kasey stepped off the platform and walked over to where Graham stood. "I believe you mean that, but I also know the real reason you're here."

Graham cocked his head. "What do you mean?"

The Possession

"Don't bother denying it. You're here because Jeremy asked you to come, didn't he?"

Graham bowed his head and took his hat off. "I won't deny it. I don't know how you know that, but it doesn't matter." He looked Kasey in the eye. "I wasn't going to lure you to him, Kasey, I swear it. I couldn't do it. I came here to warn you that you're in danger. I don't know what he is, but whatever it is, he's not human. He's inside my boy. I know how crazy that sounds, but it's true."

Kasey felt Graham's pain. "I know that, and I believe you. I'm going to go with you."

Graham's eyes widened, and he shook his head. "You can't do that. You go there, and he'll kill you. He'll do it so he can live."

"He doesn't know I'm not his son. If he tries to possess me, he'll die. Maybe you'll get the real Reed back. I'll do it for Mom, Ethan's dad, and for anyone else the Wickcliffs ever hurt. I'm not going to let Jeremy get away with the havoc he plans to unleash on this town."

Graham gave him a half smile. "You're a virtuous man, Kasey Menze. Your mother would be proud. I'll do whatever I can to protect you."

Kasey still wasn't listening to me. I tried to tell him that it was already too late for Reed and that jeopardizing his life wouldn't change that. It was clear that the visions I'd shown him of my death were too emotional for him. He couldn't handle seeing someone he loved in such a state, so he found a way to shut me out.

"I've got a lot to live for," Kasey said. "Ethan and I are back together again, and I'm going to fight for everything I've got. I'm not going to let him beat me."

"Let who beat you?" Ethan said, walking up behind Graham. "Good evening, sheriff."

"Hello, Ethan," Graham said. He looked nervously at his watch. "I need to get back to the station. We'll talk later, right, Kasey?"

"Yeah, we will. I'll see you soon."

Graham left in a hurry without saying another word.

Ethan's eyes narrowed. "What's he so uptight about? He looked like he was going to jump right out of his skin."

"Forget about him," Kasey said. "Where did you go?"

Ethan explained what Hilda had told him about me and how hard it was to break the news to Mom. He told Kasey about Pit and what he said about how I'd died, and about how Freddy was taken from Mom's house. Pit had stopped him from coming up here to get Freddy. Kasey didn't tell him that he'd already known I was gone. He was afraid of how Ethan would react to the fact he'd kept such a secret.

"I have to get Freddy out of that house," Ethan said. "After what Jeremy's done to my dad and your mom, I don't trust that Freddy's safe there. I just stopped by to tell you I wouldn't be back tonight."

"It's more dangerous if you try to get him out of there. Listen, Ethan, I'd leave Freddy there."

I wasn't surprised that Kasey had said that. If Ethan showed up to take Freddy away, it would tip Jeremy and Rachel off that my family had discovered much more than Jeremy thought and Kasey couldn't afford them tipping their hand.

"Why would it be better to keep Freddy there? Didn't you hear anything I just said?"

"They won't harm a child, especially one that represents the Wickcliff future. Isn't that what Jeremy's trying to do? Bring his family back? We don't want to make them suspicious. If they know that you know who they are, they'll be backed into a corner and get desperate. That's when Freddy really could get hurt."

"I suppose. God, if only I could've helped Shelly when I had the chance."

Kasey touched his arm. "I'm sorry about Shelly, I am, but Jeremy's going to pay for it. I promise you." He moved away from Ethan.

Ethan studied his face. "You don't seem very surprised to hear that Shelly's gone. I expected much more of a reaction. I know how much you cared about her."

Kasey sighed, still not wanting to admit his blame for covering the truth about my death. "I'm still numb over Mom. I guess the news about Shelly hasn't hit me yet."

"Are you sure that's it?"

Kasey ran his hands through his hair. "I'm dealing with a lot right now. My biological mother, Lucy's alive. She was here. She told me I have a brother."

"I don't know what to say. A few weeks ago, I would've called you crazy, but after everything that's happened, anything's possible around here."

"That's not all. My brother is Jeremy's son. Jeremy thinks I'm his son, but it's my brother."

Ethan sighed heavily. "Did she tell you who he is?"

"His name's Jason Beckett."

The color drained from Ethan's face. "Are you serious?"

He noticed Ethan's reaction. "Does his name mean something to you?"

Ethan didn't answer. He turned away from Kasey and began to run down the path. Finding out that Jason was a Wickcliff made him fear for Rebecca's safety.

Kasey shouted after him. "Where are you going?"

"I have to get to Becca. I'll explain later."

Kasey didn't tell him that he was planning on coming to this house to confront Jeremy. He wasn't sure what was going to happen, and he was too afraid if Ethan knew he'd try to talk him out of it.

Once Ethan's car was gone, Kasey locked up his house, got on his bike, and began his journey up here. He was confident that his plan to trick Jeremy into possessing him was going to be successful and then Sleepy Meadows would be rid of him.

Knowing Jeremy as I did, I wasn't so confident. He was stronger than people gave him credit for and he wasn't to be underestimated. I was afraid that Kasey was making a fatal mistake.

* * * *

Figuring that my brother was on his way to the Moonlight Inn, I went there and found Rebecca entering her room with a bag of groceries. Jason went in ahead of her.

"I got the veggies you wanted," she said, putting the bag on the table.

"I'll help you put them away," he said, not looking at her.

She examined him. "What's wrong with you today? You've seemed a million miles away all day long."

He still didn't meet eyes with her. "Nothing's wrong. I'm fine."

She shook her head. "No. You seemed fine before I went with my sister, but after I got back, your whole demeanor changed. Did something happen last night when I was at the police station?"

He finally made eye contact with her and kissed her softly. "I love you. I want you to know that."

She didn't respond and looked away from him.

"Does that make you uncomfortable, Becca?"

"I guess it does."

His eyes lowered. "I shouldn't have said it."

She touched his arm and made eye contact with him again. "No, it's okay. It's just that I haven't felt like this before. It's the way you touch me and the way you look at me. I genuinely want to believe it when you say it."

"I would never say it if I didn't mean it." He touched her face gently. "I love you, and I want to make love to you today, tomorrow and always." He reached behind her, pulled her closer to him, and kissed her again. "Becca, I want you so badly."

She led him to the bed, and they laid down. He put his hands on her face and with his eyes told her he loved her again.

"I love you too," she said, her eyes widening when she said it.

I could tell that she was just as genuinely surprised that she'd said it as he was hearing it. She hadn't intended to, it just slipped out, but it didn't mean that she didn't mean it. She did, and that's what concerned me. She was falling for this man who was a Wickcliff and she had no idea.

She began to unbutton her blouse.

He kissed her neck. "Becca? There's something I need to talk to you about, something is bothering me."

She peeled his shirt off, kissed his chest, and then felt his body pressed next to hers. She could barely think straight. "What is it?"

"I need you to know who I am before we take this any further."

She tried to look in his eyes, but they were off in a different direction. She propped herself up on her elbow. "Who you are? What does that mean?"

He put his hand over his face and rubbed his forehead. "I don't know where to start."

"Why not with what happened to you while I was gone? You seem…sad. You were fine earlier, weren't you?"

He turned to her. "I can't continue to go on this way. I can't fall in love with you until I know you can handle the truth about who I am."

She waited silently for him to go on. Before he could say anything else, they heard banging on the door that startled them both.

"Becca? It's Ethan! Are you in there? I need to talk to you!"

They sat up and got off the bed.

"I'll go into the other room," he said, "and let the two of you talk. It sounds important."

"Don't worry about him. I want you to tell me what you meant a moment ago."

The banging on the door persisted.

Jason sighed. "He's not going to go away. Just answer it."

She buttoned up her blouse and went to the door. "I'm coming, Ethan."

When Jason was out of sight, she opened the door. Ethan came in without being invited, and began scanning the room.

"Well hello to you too," she said, shutting the door. "Do you mind telling me what's the big emergency?"

He turned to her. "We need to talk. It's important."

She studied his face. "What's the matter? You look so serious."

"This is serious. I know it's going to sound crazy, but I need you to believe me. Jeremy Wickcliff's come back from the dead. He's responsible for everything that's happened here. He killed my dad and Kasey's mom."

Rebecca was bewildered. "Gracey's dead? Why didn't anyone tell me?"

"It just happened. I'm sorry. I've been preoccupied with Kasey."

"Of course. Poor Kasey." She paused. "Wait a minute. Did you say that Jeremy Wickcliff's back from the dead? This is no time to joke."

"I'm not kidding."

Her eyes narrowed. "You almost look like you're serious."

"As serious as the heart attack he caused my dad to have."

She shook her head. "Jeremy Wickcliff died when we were babies."

"He's back, Becca." He paused. "There's something else you don't know. He's killed Shelly and used her body to return his sister Rachel to life."

She put her hand on his head and then removed it. "You don't have a fever, but you're obviously delirious."

"My head's never been clearer than it is at this moment."

"We just saw Shelly at your dad's wake."

"That wasn't Shelly. That was Rachel." He gave her a look. "Don't look at me like that. I told you this sounds crazy, but it's not. I'm not."

She put her hand on his arm and squeezed. "I didn't say you were, honey. You've been through a lot with your dad dying and trying to keep the business afloat in the midst of family drama. I can understand why you'd be out of it."

"That's what I'm trying to tell you. My dad's death wasn't natural causes. Dad was the first one to suspect Jeremy was back. He thought Shelly was dead, and he was right. He tried to warn us, and it got him killed. Jeremy murdered him."

"So let's just say for argument sake that what you say is true. How could he accomplish all this?"

"He's obviously not human. He's got some sort of powers. I don't understand it all either, but he's done it somehow. He had no body, so he possessed Reed Withers."

Rebecca raised an eyebrow. "Possession? Oh, Ethan. I think we need to get you to the hospital, just to get checked out."

He grabbed her and shook her. "I'm your best friend. What I'm telling you is true. You have to believe me, please."

She writhed in his grasp. "Let me go."

He put his hands up. "I'm sorry. I didn't mean to hurt you."

"You're scaring me." She glanced at the door to the next room, hoping that Jason would come in.

"If you don't believe me, ask Pit. He's the one who told me about Shelly's death. He said Jeremy was inside her head, torturing her. That's why she shut herself off from the world. Jeremy was driving her insane. He made her hang herself. Jeremy murdered her."

She narrowed her eyes. "Pit told you that? I should've known. He's messing with you, the sick bastard."

Ethan was almost breathless now. "Under normal circumstances I'd agree with you, but there's more. Lucy Wickcliff, Jeremy's wife, is Kasey's mother, and she's alive too. You can ask Kasey. He told me himself."

"You truly believe these stories, don't you? Is that all?"

He shook his head. "No. Lucy has two sons, and that's why I'm here. You need to be warned."

"What does any of this have to do with me?"

Ethan softened his voice and touched her arms to brace her. "Kasey told me that Jason's Lucy's other son. Jeremy's his father. Jason Beckett is really Jason Wickcliff."

Rebecca stepped back. "Ethan, I'm really worried about you. These things you're saying just aren't reality."

"No. The lies that Jason's told you aren't reality. He's the son of a lying murderer, and I bet he knows it. Where is the son of a bitch anyway?"

Chapter 20

For the first time, Rebecca got the feeling that what Ethan said may be true. She thought about how upset Jason had been when she'd returned from being with Brynn. He'd wanted to tell her who he was before they were interrupted. Maybe he'd found out who he was, or maybe he knew all along, and that's why he'd acted so distant and nervous.

She went to the door leading to the other room and opened it. She found it empty and turned back to face Ethan.

"He's gone!" She noticed the open window. "He climbed out the window."

Ethan followed her and raised an eyebrow. "Jason was hiding in here? Why didn't you tell me?"

"We're keeping our relationship under wraps." She turned her head, unable to face him.

"You're sleeping with him?" When she gazed back at him, her guilty expression told him everything. "Becca, this man could be dangerous. He could be just like his father. You can't trust him."

"Even if it were true and I'm still not convinced it is, I'm a grown woman, and I can handle it myself. If he were dangerous, I'd know it."

"How do you know if he is or not? You barely know the man."

"I could say the same about you. You've only met him once. You don't know enough about him to know whether he's lying about who he is."

"He overheard us. Why do you think he climbed out the window? What more proof do you need that he is who I say he is? Why would he run otherwise? I would've taken you someplace else to talk about this if I knew he was here." He threw his hands up in the air. "Jesus, Becca."

"Don't talk to me like I'm some sort of idiot. You're the one that's come in here saying all these crazy things. I should be more worried about you than you are about me."

He sighed and dropped his shoulders. "I'm sorry. I don't mean to judge you, but I don't think it's wise for you to be with a man you hardly know anything about."

She crossed her arms. "That's none of your business."

He went into the other room and looked out the open window to the fire escape. "Do you have any idea where he might've gone?"

"I have no idea. After he heard you raving about him like a lunatic, it's no wonder why he took off. I don't blame him."

"I can't help it if I caught him in a lie. He's a liar, Becca. That's what the Wickcliffs do."

"Stop it, Ethan." She turned her back to him. "Just stop it."

He stepped in front of her and put his hands on her arms peering into her eyes. "We've known each other since we were kids. You know you can trust what I'm telling you. Who are you going to believe? Me or someone you just met? He could be dangerous, and I need to know every move he makes. Are you going to help me or not?"

* * * *

My brother seemed so angry at the Inn that I decided to follow him home after he left Rebecca. He wanted to check on Mom and Gram. Since Jeremy had already gone after Dad and me, Ethan figured that they could be next. He vowed to keep them safe no matter what, even if it meant sacrificing his well-being. When my brother's angry, he gets reckless, and that concerned me.

When he got there, he went into the house and found Mom in the kitchen with Hilda and Lucy. He'd never met Lucy, so he didn't recognize her when he saw her sitting at the table. "Mom, what's going on?" He gestured to Lucy. "Who's this?"

Lucy stood up, went over to him, and extended her hand. "Hello, Ethan. It's a pleasure."

Ethan shook her hand. "And you are?"

"I'm Lucy Wickcliff."

His eyes widened. "You are here. Kasey told me that he'd seen you, but seeing you here makes it real."

She nodded. "You know my son?"

Ethan rubbed the back of his neck. "We're...involved."

"I see."

"You don't look any older than us."

"I look as I did the day I crossed over. My spirit hasn't aged."

Ethan glanced at Mom. "Are you going to answer my question? What's going on? I want to understand how she got here. How is she alive?"

"We're having a brainstorming session," Mom said. "As far as the rest of it goes, it's too long a story to get into. What happened at the Wickcliff's?"

"I decided to leave Freddy there for now. Jeremy won't hurt him. He's family. I was afraid of tipping him off that we knew about Shelly if we went up there."

She nodded. "I told you to stay away. I'm glad you listened for once."

"Stop stalling. Answer my question."

"I can't. There's no time to explain."

"I've got time."

"I'm afraid we don't," Hilda said. "We're talking about what we need to do to get rid of Jeremy."

He looked at her. "No offense, but what do you think you're going to do about it?"

"We have the ability," Mom said. "There's a lot about us, about me that you don't know."

"You've got a dead woman in your kitchen. It doesn't take a rocket scientist to figure that out."

"When this is all over, we'll sit down, and I'll explain everything," Mom said. "Until then, just trust that everything's under control."

"His presence in this town means only one thing," Lucy said. "Everyone who doesn't have the name Wickcliff is in danger. I'm especially worried about the safety of my sons."

Ethan scoffed. "I'm worried about Kasey, but Jason? I don't trust him. I'd say good riddance."

"Ethan!" Mom said.

"I'm not going to hold back on how I feel. I believe him to be a liar. I think he's just using Becca although she can't see it. He's just like his father. I could see that there was something not right about him when we first met."

"I'm sorry you feel that way," Lucy said. "But I believe there's good in him."

Hilda stood up. "Jason's safe for the time being. Jeremy doesn't know he's his father. It's Kasey that's in the more immediate danger."

Ethan turned to her. "Why do you say that?"

"Jeremy thinks that Kasey's his son," Lucy said. "He's going to try to inhabit Kasey's body so that his spirit can continue to live on in the body of someone in his bloodline."

Ethan glared at Mom and Hilda. "Is that true?"

"I talked to Kasey," Hilda said. "He's convinced that he has to go through with it. He wants to rid the town of Jeremy to avenge the deaths of our loved ones. He's doing it for Gracey. I did my best to talk him out of it, but I'm afraid it didn't do much good."

Ethan's face went ashen. After all these years, he'd finally been able to admit how he felt about Kasey. The thought of losing him was more than he could stand.

"No way in hell is that going to happen. I won't allow it."

"How do you plan to stop him?" Mom said. "He's just as stubborn as Gracey was. If he's got his mind made up that he's going to confront Jeremy, he's going to do it whether you like it or not. Besides, I already told you that I didn't want you to get involved. I've already lost one child."

"I'll be damned if I stand idly by and watch the man I love risk his life. Kasey and I have waited too long to be together. We've both lost so much already. I'm not going to let this happen."

All three women stared at him not knowing what to say.

"Don't look at me that way. Any of you. This isn't over. Kasey and I are going to deal with this together, and when it's all said and done, we'll be together."

He turned to leave, but Mom stopped him. "Ethan, please don't go."

"I love you, Mom, but I'm sorry. I have to go. I have to find Kasey."

* * * *

I watched Ethan race to Kasey's house. He prayed the whole time that he wasn't too late to stop Kasey from confronting Jeremy. He noticed that Kasey's bike was gone when he got to the driveway. Figuring that Kasey was already on his way to the house, he decided that he'd just come up here. However, he stopped when he noticed a figure lurking around Kasey's property. He soon realized it wasn't just anyone. It was Jason. He pulled into the driveway, got out of the car, and called out Jason's name.

Jason turned and started to run, but Ethan went after him, tackling him to the ground.

Jason rolled onto his back and put his hands up. "Ethan, before you say anything—"

"Shut up. I don't want to hear one word that comes out of your filthy, lying mouth."

"I didn't mean any harm. I swear. I saw Lucy earlier, and she told me about Kasey. I wanted to meet my brother. Becca happened to mention where he lived."

"Yeah, sure. You and your sick, twisted old man aren't going to get away with this. Where's Kasey? Tell me or I'll beat it out of you."

Jason pushed him off and got up. "I think you're the one that's sick. I have no idea what you're talking about. Get away with what?"

Ethan stood up. "Don't play innocent with me. I knew there was something off about you from the minute I met you. You don't know who you're dealing with. I'd do anything to make sure that Kasey's safe."

"I don't know where Kasey is."

"I'm going to tell you one time and one time only. Stay away from Kasey and my family. And while you're at it, stay away from Becca too."

"Thanks to you, she won't want to have anything to do with me. You had no right to tell her who I am. I was going to tell her in my own time."

"When? After you had her totally snowed? She deserved to know the truth. She's been hurt and lied to enough in her life."

"I'd never do anything to hurt her. I love her."

"You don't know what love is you sick bastard."

Jason scoffed. "And you do? You stand there judging me as if you're all high and mighty. You're nothing but a queer!"

Ethan tackled Jason to the ground again punching him several times in the face. Rolling around on the ground, Jason overpowered him and responded in kind.

As I watched them fight, I saw another picture replace it. Fighting with Jason made Ethan remember the day, five years ago, when he'd come to the house to visit me. He'd heard my screams coming from the parlor. He burst in to see Rory and me struggling. I'd pulled a gun on Rory under Jeremy's instructions. Rory was only trying to get the gun away, but Ethan misunderstood and tried to defend me. He grabbed for the gun, pushing me away. Rory and he struggled, and that's how he got the scar on his face. The gun went off, and Rory was killed instantly.

As Ethan struggled with Jason now, the sound of the gunshot echoed in his head. He'd blacked out after the gun went off and awoke moments later, finding me holding the gun, sobbing hysterically, and cradling Rory's lifeless body in my arms. Ethan's mind had blocked out everything to protect himself. He assumed I did it, and I let him for the sake of his sanity.

He'd been afraid that no one would believe that it was an accident. He wiped the gun off and put it in Rory's hand. I was in no shape to disagree with him. We both agreed to keep it quiet. Now that he remembered, I doubted that he'd be able to handle the guilt.

Ethan and Jason were still wrestling on the ground. Jason hit him one more time. Ethan lost consciousness and Jason fled from the scene.

* * * *

There wasn't anything that I could do for Ethan, so I turned my attention to Kasey. He was in imminent danger. To make Jeremy believe that his attempt to put Graham under his power had been successful, Graham and Kasey decided they'd arrive at the mansion together. They planned to pretend that Graham lured Kasey there as Jeremy asked. They banked on the fact that Jeremy's plan to inhabit Kasey would fail, and they were hopeful that they could get Reed back. Neither of them was aware that Reed's fate had already been determined.

As Kasey stood outside looking up at the house, uncertain about what would happen when he got inside, he thought about how everything had changed for him since the last time he'd come here. He'd met his biological mother, lost his adoptive one, and reunited with Ethan. Some changes had been good, others devastating. Knowing that Ethan would be waiting for him when it was all over and Jeremy was dead was what gave him the courage to even think about stepping inside the house.

Graham stood next to him. "You don't have to do this, but I'm grateful that you're doing this for my son."

"I am doing this for Reed, but also for everyone else Jeremy's destroyed, or will destroy if he's allowed to roam free."

Graham nodded. "I know you're scared, not knowing what'll happen. I want you to know how much I admire your courage."

"I'm doing this for the all the people we lost because of him: Mom, Jeffrey, Shelly. He can't get away with what he's done."

Graham tilted his head towards the house. "I suppose we'd better go in. Let's get this over with."

They approached the doors, and after they'd knocked, Greta let them inside and told them to wait in the parlor. Kasey had been on the grounds recently, but he hadn't been inside. He stared up at the painting of Jeremy and saw the resemblance between him and Jason, his half-brother. They had the same eyes. While they'd never met, Kasey saw Jason at Dad's wake. As he stood there waiting for Jeremy, he wondered if he'd ever get the chance to meet his brother. He gestured to the painting and then looked at Graham.

"Have you ever seen this painting of him?"

Graham nodded and frowned. "He used it to try to hypnotize me or whatever you call it. I don't know what the hell he is or everything that's going on in this house."

Kasey glanced up at Jeremy's painting. "There are evil, supernatural forces in this house, that's what. I can feel that. What the Wickcliffs are defies any sense of logic." He paused, still looking at the painting. "His eyes are so intense."

Before Graham could reply, Gaul entered and asked them to follow him outside to the cemetery. Graham and Kasey exchanged glances because they hadn't anticipated this. Being inside the house was bad enough, but going to the dark, damp cemetery was even more intimidating.

I followed them outside and the closer Kasey got to the cemetery gate, the more physically ill he became. He began to sweat and felt nauseous. A foul smell filled the air that could only be described as death, which didn't help his queasy stomach. I felt it too. It was time for me to try and reach out to him again.

"Kasey, if you can hear me. I need you to listen. It's too late to bring Reed back. His soul's been taken by the ancestors here in the spirit realm. Even if Jeremy dies, there's no guarantee you'll get back. You're jeopardizing your life for no reason. Let my mom, Hilda, and Lucy take care of Jeremy."

He continued walking along the path to the overgrown cemetery. He hadn't heard me. He'd decided he didn't want to communicate with me and continued to shut me out. I knew that he probably wouldn't be receptive to my message, but I had to try.

When they reached the mausoleum door, Gaul opened it and let the men inside. Graham tried his best to hide his nervousness.

"Where's Jeremy? I called to tell him we were coming. I've brought Kasey as he asked. He's eager to help."

"He'll be here soon," Gaul said.

He proceeded to shut the door, leaving Graham and Kasey waiting inside together.

Kasey pointed to the cenotaph in the middle of the room. "What's this?"

"Jeremy said it holds the spirits of the Wickcliff ancestors."

In the spirit realm, the ancestors were free, and roamed the grounds of the cemetery but in the mortal realm, they couldn't be seen.

Kasey ran his hand over the stone, remembering what Gracey told him about Jeremy's plan to return his family to the mortal realm. She'd said that my family had been bitter enemies with the Wickcliffs for years, going back to Jeremy's father, Harold, and his grandfather, Pierre.

"Mom told me that the Wickcliffs tried to return years ago," Kasey said. "Do you remember anything about that?"

Graham shook his head. "I was too young to know about any of it. My father was the sheriff then. After he died, my mother never allowed the Wickcliff name to be spoken in her presence. I vaguely remember a time when there was a curfew on the town. No one was allowed out after dark. It had to do with the Wickcliffs I bet."

"I don't understand why the people of this town would keep the fact that the Wickcliffs have tried to return before a secret. There's something not right."

"Maybe they felt like if they denied it if they forgot about the Wickcliffs, they'd never be able to come back. If I'd known that they were a threat again, I could've protected my son."

"You couldn't have known. None of us did. The things that have happened in the past few days have been too incredible for anyone to predict. I'm going to do whatever I can to make sure we get Reed back, I promise."

Graham fixed his eyes on Kasey. "I can tell you care about my son. I'm grateful that he has a friend like you."

"He's a wonderful person."

Graham smiled. "He talked a lot about you. He liked you a lot. Now I can see why. I think he may have thought of you as more than a friend. I know my son's gay, and I don't care. I love him, and I want him back."

I could feel Kasey's emotions. He felt sorry for Graham because Reed was all he had. "We'll get him back."

"What if it's already too late?" Graham swallowed hard and looked away.

As a father, Graham's instincts were telling him that the son he knew was already gone. Damon and Rory had tried to get me to accept that, and although I'd begun to, there was still a small part of me that hoped they would be successful so that the real Reed could get home.

Chapter 21

While Kasey and Graham waited for Jeremy in the mausoleum, I got a strong inclination that I needed to check on Mom. At first, I thought maybe she'd been hurt, that the Wickcliffs had gotten to her, but as she came into focus, I realized she was fine. I found her in the meadows with Hilda and Lucy. They'd formed a circle and were calling out Gracey's name. Inside the circle laid Gracey's broken cane.

"You're now one of the spirits that we communicated with in life, my dear Gracey," Hilda said. "Share with us the knowledge that you've obtained in your new life. You have insights that we mere mortals can't understand. Help us."

"Gracey, if you know what Jeremy's planning," Lucy said, "you have to tell us."

Within moments, there was a gust of wind, and I could see Gracey's essence standing there in the center of their circle.

"It is I who need your help," Gracey said. "Kasey's in trouble. Jeremy's on his way to the Wickcliff mausoleum to possess him. I can see it. You have to stop him. Please, help my dear son. I'm trusting you with his life."

Gracey disappeared almost as quickly as she'd come. Lucy met eyes with the other two women. "We don't have any time to lose. We have to get there now. Take my hands, both of you. Hold on tight."

Mom and Hilda did as they were told and all three women vanished from my sight.

When the women reappeared, they did so outside the cemetery's wrought iron gate. They looked past the gate that surrounded the quarter acre cemetery that was large, the home of over fifty Wickcliff graves, and in the distance was the gray mausoleum surrounded by gnarly, ancient oak trees and vines, that looked as if they were about to engulf it. The entire cemetery was filled with the same gnarly trees, hovering over the headstones covered in brown and green moss.

Mom seemed stifled by the dense, rot-smelling air. She appeared pale and shaken. She got a sensitive glance from Hilda.

"Carol, are you alright?"

Mom nodded and took a deep breath. "I'll be fine. It's the air here. There's nothing more putrid. And, it's been a long time since I've used my powers. It takes a lot out of me. None of that matters now. We have to focus on Kasey."

Lucy pointed into the distance. Jeremy was headed toward the mausoleum. "There he is. I'll try to distract him."

They went into the cemetery, and Lucy caught up with him. "Jeremy, stop!"

He turned. "Well, well. Look who it is. I knew you'd show up here."

"Did you? Then I suppose you also know why I'm here."

"You aren't going to keep me from my son, not anymore." He turned to the mausoleum again where Mom and Hilda were trying to sneak in. "You two stop, or I'll strike you dead where you stand."

They stopped and turned to look at him. Jeremy chuckled and turned back to face Lucy. "Really, Lucy? Did you honestly think you could just sneak in here and take my son away from me for a second time? You had to have known it wouldn't be that easy. I'm hurt that you underestimated me so."

Lucy looked past him at Hilda and Mom. "Don't listen to him, get to Kasey. I'll protect you."

"Don't test my powers, ladies. Gracey tested me, and you see what happened to her. I have greater abilities than you'd even begin to understand. If you take even one single step, it'll be the last either of you takes."

"Are you going to kill me like you killed my daughter?" Mom said. "Or my husband, or Gracey, you bastard?"

"Oh, I didn't kill your daughter. I just gave her the push she needed to do it herself. She was so miserable after Rory died that she wanted to do it anyway. She just didn't have the nerve. I gave that to her. I have to say I did enjoy watching her panic as she asphyxiated to death. Watching Gracey choke was much more fun though because it took longer."

Mom darted towards him. "You sick son of a bitch!"

Lucy put her hand up. "Carol, no!"

Mom stopped in her tracks. "I can't listen to any more of this."

"He's just using what he did to them to try to goad you and distract you," Lucy said, pointing towards the mausoleum. "Go to Kasey."

"We can't leave you here," Hilda said. "We were separated from you once, and you lost your life. He was able to get to Gracey because we weren't with her. We're staying. There's strength in numbers."

"Oh how noble," Jeremy said. "But you're no match for me, none of you." He focused on Hilda. "Especially you, you pathetic old bitch."

"What happened to you?" Lucy said. "What happened to the man I fell in love with? There was good in you once."

"Goodness is for the weak," Jeremy said, locking eyes with her. "The last time I was weak, the last time I was in love, you murdered me. I gave you everything, and you made a fool out of me. Never again. Only the strong survive."

"You don't need me to make you look like a fool. You've done a good enough job of that on your own."

He narrowed his eyes at her. "I don't know why I'm saying this, but there's a part of me that will always love you. I'm going to give you one last chance. Walk out of here and never look back."

"What, so you can kill Carol and Hilda? Destroy my son? No chance in hell."

"He's our son, dammit! A fact that you so frequently forget."

Lucy shook her head. "I'm not going anywhere."

Jeremy exhaled. "Why do you make me hurt you? I don't want to do that despite everything you've done to me."

"You're the one who's going to be hurt."

He put his hands on his hips. "I suppose you've all forgotten what happened to you the last time we did battle? Not only were you not successful, but you almost died. This time, it'll be different. There will be no almost."

"It'll be different this time alright," Hilda said. "This time, you'll be destroyed."

Hilda, Lucy, and Mom breathed deeply and closed their eyes. They reached their arms to the sky, which became darker. Thunder rolled in the distance, and the wind picked up.

"Your parlor tricks aren't going to scare me or stop me," Jeremy said. "You don't have any power here."

"It's over for you, Jeremy," Lucy said. "Do you understand?"

"All I understand is that you're pathetic."

"We'll just see about that, won't we?" Lucy created what looked like a tornado with her bare hands. It came down out of the clouds. It was the most extraordinary thing I'd ever seen. She directed it over to a tree near where Jeremy stood, and it uprooted the tree from the ground.

He chuckled. "Is that all you've got?"

"Not quite." She jerked her hand and the tree came barreling toward him.

His expression changed to one of anger, and he put his hand up. "Back!" His command made the wind change direction, carrying the tree with it in Lucy's direction.

Mom was the first to realize what was happening. "Lucy, look out!"

Lucy didn't have time to react. The tree came down right on top of her crushing her underneath. Mom and Hilda yelled her name repeatedly, but there was no answer. They turned to face Jeremy, who grinned deviously.

"One down, two more to go."

Mom averted her stare to the iron fence that surrounded several graves. She stared intently as some of the wrought iron poles began to break free. Hilda watched the poles rise in the air and hover horizontally over Jeremy like arrows ready to shoot.

Jeremy stared at them with annoyance rather than fear. He stood in place, eyes open and commanded the arrows to change course, just as he did with the tree. This is what I'd feared. The witches weren't going to be strong enough to fight Jeremy. In their attempt to save Kasey, they were forced to do battle with him before they were prepared. Jeremy was making short order of the women, and it made me fear for Mom's life.

I watched helplessly as the arrows catapulted towards Hilda. One hit her in the arm, forcing her back, pinning her arm to the tree behind her.

Mom screamed and put her hands over her mouth.

"I'm alright," Hilda said, putting her hand up. "I'm just dazed."

Mom's facial expression turned to one of sheer horror. I saw that she was sinking into the mud, just as if it were quicksand. I wanted to reach out to her, help her, but I couldn't do anything.

Pinned to the tree about twenty feet from Mom, Hilda's arm throbbed in pain. She couldn't dislodge the rod from her arm to help. As I looked at her, I knew that she thought that Jeremy had been right. He had too much power inside the cemetery that held the souls of all the other Wickcliffs. The witches had no advantage here.

Hilda directed her attention from Mom to the tree that fell on top of Lucy. She was relieved when she saw Lucy wiggle and writhe her way free underneath it. I couldn't believe it, but then again, Lucy wasn't an ordinary mortal.

Lucy got sight of Hilda, and Hilda pointed towards Mom to show her what was happening. Lucy changed her focus to Jeremy, who watched as Mom sunk deeper and deeper into the muddy grave. The more Mom moved to release herself, the faster she sank.

Jeremy laughed. "I tried to warn you. Now you'll all die."

"No," Lucy said. "Not today."

Jeremy turned to her. "What's it going to take to get rid of you?"

"A lot more than what you're capable of." Lucy glanced up at the sky, and a bolt of lightning struck a tall obelisk headstone that towered behind Jeremy. He turned immediately and shrieked as it fell towards him. He jumped out of the way just in time as it crashed to the ground almost crushing him.

Lucy ran towards Mom pulling her out of the muddy pit. She and Mom were then able to get to Hilda and unpin her from the tree.

"You're bleeding," Lucy said, touching Hilda's arm gently. "We need to get you out of here."

Hilda groaned. "We all need to get out of here. He was right. We aren't strong enough to fight him here. This isn't over, but we need to come up with another plan."

"What about Kasey?" Mom asked. "We can't just leave him here. He needs our help."

Lucy met Mom's gaze. "You get Hilda out of here and make sure she's okay. I'll go to Kasey."

Hilda grabbed her arm. "We can't leave you alone."

"You have no choice. I'll be fine. I still have all my powers. I'm stronger than you think."

Jeremy, still stunned from Lucy's show of power, stumbled toward the mausoleum. He didn't want them to know it, but his strength was waning, that's why what he'd done to them wasn't fatal. He knew he had to get to Kasey immediately.

Hilda didn't want to leave Lucy, but Mom led her out. When they got to the gate, Hilda stopped and grabbed some dirt from the grounds. She reached into her pocket, got out a handkerchief, put the dirt inside, wrapping it up for safe keeping.

"What's that for?" Mom asked.

"We'll need this," Hilda said. "Let's go."

* * * *

Back in the cemetery, Lucy approached the mausoleum. When she tried to open the door, she got a shock that forced her backward. Jeremy had used the last of his power to keep her out. She tried the door again, and again she got another shock, this one greater than the last. She put her hand on her head, dizzied by the shocks. The longer she remained in the cemetery, the weaker she felt. Anger grew inside her, and she clenched her fists.

"Damn you, Jeremy! I know you can hear me. This isn't over." It had become dark by this time, and too hard for Lucy to see. She began to call out for help. "I need to help Kasey. Please, I can't let my son die. I'd give up my life for him if I had to. Just don't let him die."

Lucy put her head in her hands and didn't see the bright light that had appeared in front of her. It illuminated almost the entire cemetery.

"It's alright, Lucy," a man's voice said. "I'm here."

She glanced up, seeing the light. "Who is it?"

"I think you know."

"Vivek? Is it you?"

I didn't know who Vivek was, but through Lucy's memories, I began to realize. Vivek had been a father figure to her in her previous life.

"Come to me in the forest, Lucy. I know you don't want to leave Kasey, but I can help him and you."

She couldn't always trust her instincts where Jeremy was concerned. "How do I know that you're really here? Are you just another one of Jeremy's tricks?"

"This isn't a trick my dear friend. I'm here to help you. Come to me and I'll tell you how to save Kasey."

She didn't have a choice but trust that it was him. Her powers weren't working here. If she wanted to save Kasey, she had to get help and find her old mentor.

* * * *

So much had happened that I wanted to be able to tell Rory and Damon, but it was all happening so fast, I couldn't. I didn't want to leave Kasey's side, even though there was nothing I could do to help him. I was now inside the mausoleum, watching Jeremy staring Kasey down. Graham stood on the other side of the dimly lit room, out of the way.

"I'm sorry I'm so late," Jeremy said. "I was detained."

"I heard what sounded like a fight out there," Kasey said. "What happened?"

"Your mother and her bitch friends tried to stop me, but I've taken care of them."

Kasey's eyes shifted toward Graham briefly. He didn't want to let on to Jeremy that he was concerned. He knew that no help was going to arrive. He didn't have a choice but to go through with the transfer. He prayed that he'd be strong enough to get back once Jeremy was gone from his body.

"You killed them?"

Jeremy shook his head. "Unfortunately not. Their wills were strong. They were more resistant to me than I'd anticipated. None of that matters now, my son. We're finally together again, just as it was meant to be."

Kasey held back his anger and took in a slow deep breath. Graham couldn't take his eyes off Jeremy. All he could see was his son, a son who now looked like death itself. The black circles under his eyes had darkened. His skin was more pallid than before. The smell of rotting flesh surrounded the mausoleum almost suffocating Kasey and Graham.

This was the first time Kasey had seen Reed, knowing he was Jeremy. When he looked at Jeremy, all he could think about was how he'd killed Gracey. He wanted to tear Jeremy apart with his bare hands, but he couldn't. He had to get Jeremy to trust him if he were going to be destroyed.

"You look ill," Kasey said. "Are you alright?"

Jeremy wiped his brow, drenched in cold sweat. "I'll be fine in a few moments, son."

He put his hand on Kasey's cheek and stared into his eyes. The expression made Kasey sick, and he turned his cheek.

"Is there something wrong, Kasey?"

"No, not at all," Kasey said, forcing himself to look at him. It took every ounce of strength he had inside to pretend to be Jeremy's son. There was only one thing on his mind. He needed Jeremy to believe him. He needed Jeremy to believe that he was on board with his plan so that Jeremy would try to possess him and die. Kasey touched Jeremy's hand. "Father, I've wanted to meet you my whole life. I can't believe you're here."

Jeremy smiled. "If I'd known about you, that you were alive, I would've made sure you had everything." He gazed over at Graham and then back at Kasey. "Has Sheriff Withers told you why you're here?"

Kasey nodded. "I'll do anything I need to do so that the legacy of our family can live on."

"When do I get my son back?" Graham said, stepping forward, his voice shaking.

"In good time," Jeremy said, not taking his eyes off Kasey. "Now be quiet. Do you have any questions, Kasey?"

"No. I just want to get this over with. I want our family to live on. I'll give you everything I've got."

Jeremy looked at him with intensity. Kasey turned his head, but Jeremy moved his face to look at him.

"Don't be afraid, son. Once I'm fully alive again, you'll live in paradise until I can return you to this world in the body of another." He pointed to a tomb. "Lay down here."

Without a word, Kasey did as he was told.

"You won't feel any pain, Kasey. You may feel a warm sensation throughout your body. Take a deep breath. It'll all be over soon."

Graham approached them. "You promised to bring my boy back. I want him now."

Jeremy's head snapped towards him. "I need to transfer my life force first. Now stand back and stop distracting me or you'll join your son in the afterlife."

Graham stepped back. He gazed at Kasey not knowing what to do next. Jeremy turned Kasey's head towards him again.

"You must concentrate, son." He pressed his fingers against Kasey's temples. He began to hum and chant. "Ancestors from the dark, you are with me, inside of me, you surround me. It's our time. My son's here and I can move on."

His voice changed, and he spoke an indecipherable, guttural language that sounded like it came from the depths of hell. My spirit connected with Kasey's, and I could feel what he felt. It was an intense pressure inside his head, like a severe headache. Jeremy had told him it wouldn't be painful, but it was.

Kasey tried to release himself from Jeremy's grip. "No! I can't do this."

Jeremy glared down at him with intensity in his eyes. "Let go, my son. It's your destiny and mine."

Kasey struggled to break free, but the force was so strong he groaned in pain. Graham watched in horror, knowing that Kasey was losing control. He tried to move forward but felt as if there were a force stopping him. Whatever kept Kasey immobilized grew stronger. An internal struggle ensued inside of his mind. He saw different colors flashing in front of his eyes and began to feel weightless. The feeling was ethereal, foreign, and unknown. He didn't want to let go, but I could tell he was losing. I wondered if Jeremy would succeed after all.

Graham spoke up. "Stop this! You're killing him!"

"Let me in!" Jeremy peered into Kasey's eyes as if his were glued to Kasey's. "Stop resisting me. Let go."

Graham rushed forward. "I told you to stop! I can't let you do this. Forgive me, Reed. God forgive me."

Jeremy didn't look at him. "Quiet!"

Kasey couldn't break free from Jeremy's mental and physical grasp on him, and he felt as if he were losing consciousness.

Graham pulled out his gun and cocked it.

From the corner of his eye, Jeremy saw him. "Put that gun down or you'll never see your son again."

"You've done nothing but lie to me," Graham said. "My son's dead. I didn't want to admit it, but I can see that just by looking at you. There's no body for him to return to. I can't save him now, but I can save Kasey. I can make you pay for what you've done to my son."

Jeremy turned towards him. His face was red and veins protruded from his forehead. "You'll die, Withers!"

"Not me. You." Graham raised the gun and fired.

Chapter 22

The gunshot echoed inside my head and disrupted my thoughts. I was back with Rory in the spirit realm again. I faced him, shaking.

He could see the anguish on my face. "Tell me what's wrong."

"Everything. Ethan remembers how you died, that he shot you. The witches tried to fight Jeremy in the cemetery. They weren't strong enough. Whatever they did, nothing worked. Jeremy was stronger. He lured Kasey to the mausoleum. He's gotten to him. He's trying to take over Kasey's body. Graham Withers is there. There's been a gunshot. He's trying to kill Jeremy."

Rory ran his hands through his hair. "Good God. Okay. You go back to the mortal realm and keep an eye on them. I need to go to Damon. He needs to know what's happened."

Rory left the room, and I turned my back to face the window.

* * * *

Again in the mortal realm, I saw my brother, who had regained consciousness and was on his way to this house. He was angry that he'd let someone as unimportant to him as Jason keep him from getting to Kasey.

He'd raced up here so fast that he almost got into a few accidents. He ignored every traffic sign and light, although there weren't many in our small town. I was afraid of his mental state now that he remembered what happened to Rory, but he didn't seem concerned with that now. All he thought about was getting to Kasey before it was too late.

When he got here, he parked the car at the end of the driveway, sprinted up the path that led to the house, and banged on the door.

Greta answered it looking as perturbed as always. "May I help you?"

"Where's Kasey?"

She shrugged. "I don't know any Kasey."

Ethan grabbed a hold of her and shook her violently. "As God is my witness, you either tell me where Kasey is or I'll kill you where you stand."

Greta's eyes were wide with panic. "Mausoleum."

I followed Ethan to the mausoleum, and although he didn't feel the same shock Lucy had when he tried the mausoleum door, he still couldn't get in. Jeremy had made sure the door was locked. He tugged on the door with all his strength, but it wouldn't open. He heard screams coming from inside.

"Kasey! Are you in there?"

Graham heard him. "Ethan? It's Sheriff Withers. You need to get in here right now."

"I can't. It's locked." Ethan no sooner said it when he heard the snap of the door unlocking. He rushed inside to find Graham kneeling over Reed's body on the ground. Kasey was still on top of the tomb he'd been laid on. Ethan was relieved when he heard him groan. He rushed to his side and picked him up, holding him in his arms.

"Kase, can you hear me?" He shook him. "Kase, wake up."

Graham wept over Reed's body. "I was too late. I tried to save Kasey, but I was too late."

"Get away from him."

Graham shook his head. "This isn't Jeremy anymore. This is my son, what's left of him. He's barely breathing. It's only a matter of time now before it's the end." He sobbed.

"What the hell happened here?"

"I tried to save Kasey by shooting Jeremy. I knew I couldn't save my son, but I thought I could save him." He bowed his head.

Ethan heard Kasey gasp for air and turned his attention back to him. "Oh, thank God. Are you alright, Kase?"

Kasey opened his eyes and glanced up at Ethan. There was something in his stare that gave Ethan pause. Kasey's eyes and demeanor had changed in the most peculiar way. His entire aura had changed. My heart sank as I realized that Graham was right. He did indeed act too late. Kasey was gone, and in his place was Jeremy. The ritual to transfer his life force from Reed's body to Kasey's had been a success.

"What do we have here?" Jeremy said, pushing himself away from Ethan's embrace. "The knight in shining armor has come to the rescue. Only this time, it's too late." He sat up and got off the tomb.

Stunned, Ethan didn't know how to react. "No, please no."

"I think it's touching." Jeremy wiped the dirt off Kasey's jeans and feigned a sob.

Ethan's face reddened. "I know it's you, Wickcliff. What the hell have you done with Kasey, you son of a bitch?"

"He's gone. My son's allowed me to live once more."

Ethan laughed through the tears of rage that formed in his eyes. "Kasey isn't your son you stupid bastard!"

"It's too late to try to trick me, Hawkins. I know who my son is."

"You're an idiot. So many people are afraid of the big bad Jeremy Wickcliff, and it's all for nothing. You've been outsmarted."

Jeremy narrowed his eyes. "Who the hell are you to my son?"

"Kasey and I are together, and I love him. I'm going to get him back."

Jeremy laughed. "If you need to believe that, go right ahead."

"Laugh at me all you want. I know a lot more than you think. I know what'll happen to your spirit if you possess someone else not of your bloodline. You've done nothing but possess another stranger, just like Reed." He managed a small smile. "Think about it. If Kasey were your son, wouldn't you start feeling stronger by now?"

Jeremy straightened his back and narrowed his eyes. "I feel more alive than I have in a long time."

But he knew Ethan was right. He realized for the first time that he'd been duped. Sweat drained from his forehead, and he grabbed his stomach and doubled over. He gazed up at Ethan with eyes full of hate. "No. This can't be."

"It's true," Ethan said. "You might as well let Kasey go now since you're going to die anyway."

Jeremy found the strength to stand up straight. "If Kasey Menze isn't my son, who is?"

Ethan didn't answer. Instead, he glanced down at Graham, who was still holding Reed's decomposing body in his hands. He thought about that same thing happening to Kasey. He shut those thoughts out of his mind and met eyes with Jeremy again. "I'm not going to tell you anything."

Jeremy stumbled forward. "If you ever want to see your precious Kasey again you will." He raised his fist. "I have certain powers, Hawkins. I can use them to get you to tell me or maybe there's another way." He pulled out a pocketknife that was in Kasey's jeans. "A little knife can do a lot of damage if you know where to cut."

"You're bluffing, if anything happens to Kasey, you die too."

Jeremy groaned. "If I don't find my son, it's only a matter of time before I die anyway. Now that I know Kasey's not mine, just my wife's bastard kid, what happens to his body is of no consequence to me." He held the knife to his throat. "Kasey will bleed to death in mere minutes. The choice is yours."

"His name's Jason," Ethan blurted out. "He goes by Beckett."

I cringed. Now that Jeremy knew who his real son was, he'd become unstoppable. Ethan realized that too, but he loved Kasey so much that all he cared about was making sure his body stayed safe and that he didn't end up like Reed.

"Was that so hard?" Jeremy said, struggling to breathe. He drew closer to Ethan. "I need this host at least for the time being. You, on the other hand, are of no more use to me."

He hit Ethan in the face with the back of his arm, knocking him down.

Graham emerged from the corner with the gun in hand. He crept up on Jeremy to hit him over the head, but Jeremy turned and hit him with such force that Graham flew backward and hit his head on one of the tombs. Although Jeremy's spirit was weakening, Kasey's body was still strong.

Jeremy gazed at where Graham laid. "Ouch. That's gotta hurt." He grabbed Graham's gun and came toward Ethan.

Ethan was afraid to motion quickly, or fight him for fear of Kasey's body being injured, and tried another approach. "Kasey, I know you're in there. You have to fight him. We've waited so long to be together. We have a life now. You can't let him win."

"He's gone, you idiot." He stood over Ethan, the gun's trigger cocked. As he was about to fire, Jeremy suffered from another severe pain. He dropped the gun and turned to the door. "I don't have time to waste on you. I need to find my son." Then he escaped outside.

Ethan turned his attention to Graham. He was still alive. It looked like Reed was breathing too. I didn't understand that since he no longer had Jeremy's life force to keep him going and the ancestors had possession of his soul. I wasn't sure how it was possible. It didn't matter, though. As long as Reed was breathing, I had renewed hope that there was a chance for my friend to get his life back after all.

Graham moaned and rubbed the back of his head.

"Are you alright? You hit your head pretty hard."

"Don't worry about me," Graham said. "Just help Reed."

Ethan took out his phone and called an ambulance. Graham kept pressure on the wound where Reed had been hit in an attempt to stop the bleeding. "Please forgive me, son. I didn't think there was any hope for you. I was trying to save Kasey, and Jeremy got to him anyway."

I stayed with Ethan until I heard the sirens. The ambulance was arriving, but Ethan hadn't even heard it. All he could think about was Kasey and what he could do to bring him back.

* * * *

I tried to get a sense of where Jeremy was headed, but I couldn't seem to get a lock on him. Instead, I found myself at the hospital where Hilda lay in a hospital bed.

Mom entered the room. "How's your arm?"

"It's fine," Hilda said, studying Mom's face. "But you're not. Something's disturbing you."

Mom sighed. "I ran into Ethan out in the hallway. He's here with Graham and Reed. Jeremy no longer possesses him. His ritual to take over Kasey was successful. Reed's barely alive. He's been admitted."

Hilda sat up. "That bastard." She sighed. "We tried to stop him, and we weren't strong enough. We're to blame for what's happened."

"It's hard to see Ethan in so much pain. He's devastated."

"Where's Lucy?"

Mom shook her head. "I haven't seen her since she told us to leave the cemetery. Obviously, she wasn't successful in stopping Jeremy either. Ethan didn't see her at the mausoleum. He said there was no sign of her. I wonder if she went to find help."

"Maybe she went to find Damon."

"Damon can't help us. She doesn't even know where to look. He's spent years in seclusion."

"But if we can find him, he could help us. He's done battle with Jeremy before. He knows him better than anyone. Besides, he's Kasey's father, and he deserves to know what's happened to his son."

Hearing Hilda mention Damon reminded me of the secret that my mother kept about him being my biological father. It didn't matter to me that Kasey and I had a biological connection. In my heart, Kasey had always been my brother. I always loved him like one. My heart ached at the possibility he could end up like Reed.

Hilda touched her arm. "You know where Damon is, don't you? I can tell by the look in your eye when you said he was in seclusion."

"Yes, I know where he is. I promised I'd never see him again after what happened between us." She put her head down.

"Have you told Lucy that Damon's Shelly's biological father?"

Mom looked back up at her. "What would be the point in it? After she died, I spent a lot of time comforting him. One night our friendship went a step too far. That's all there is to it."

"That's a lie, and you know it. That's not all there was to it. You loved him just as much as she did."

"It didn't matter. I was with Jeffrey, and we already had Ethan. He forgave me and accepted Shelly as his own. Even if I would've wanted to make it work with Damon, he'd already chosen his mission. Now my son's in love with the son of the man who also fathered my daughter. I've really made a mess of things."

"It's not like Ethan and Kasey are related. Kasey and Shelly have the same father, but both Ethan and Kasey have two sets of different parents. It's okay for them to be in love."

Mom sat down at the end of Hilda's bed and began to tear up. "That's what bothers me the most. They are in love. Because I wasn't strong enough to stop Jeremy, my son might have to live the rest of his life without the man he loves just like I had to. I was wrong to try to keep them apart."

"It's okay, Carol. You can go ahead and cry if it makes you feel better, but it doesn't change anything. We need to find Damon."

Mom got up. "We can't."

"Where is he?"

Mom turned to her. "He's never left Sleepy Meadows. He's in an old monastery on the edge of town."

Hilda's eyes broadened. "He's been here the whole time?"

"He's been protecting us since our last battle with the Wickcliffs. He's been in seclusion so he can keep us all safe."

Hilda pushed her blanket aside. "Let's go. We need to get to him. He's the only one who can tell us how to save Kasey." She groaned as she got out of bed.

Mom reached to help. "Are you sure you can do this?"

"Absolutely."

Hilda asked Mom to grab her clothes from the closet. Mom helped her get into them. "What if the doctor won't let you go?"

Hilda scoffed. "No doctor in this hospital is going to get in my way."

* * * *

I tried once more to focus on Jeremy, and this time, I was able to connect with him. He'd found Jason down by the docks, and they were talking.

They hadn't seen that Rebecca was there as well, hiding behind some of my family's shipping crates. She'd come to clear her head, not realizing either would be there. She couldn't hear them, but she didn't care what it was they were saying. All she felt was the betrayal of another person she'd trusted. She'd been lied to and felt like a fool.

"You're Kasey, aren't you?" Jason said. "I saw you at Ethan's father's wake. I was wondering if we'd ever get the chance to meet. I went to your house to find you, but you weren't there. I know what Ethan's probably told you about me, but regardless of what it is, it's probably a lie."

Jeremy put up his hand. "Stop. I know this might be hard for you to understand. I may look like Kasey, I may sound like him, but I'm not."

Jason laughed. "Is that right? Who are you then?"

"I'm your father, Jeremy Wickcliff."

Jason stared at him for a moment and then backed up. "You're obviously just as crazy as that mother of ours."

Jeremy took a few steps forward. "Don't listen to a thing she says about me."

Jason backed up further. "Stay back."

Jeremy didn't listen and kept coming toward him. "If you're willing to believe your mother can return to life, why are you so convinced I can't? I'm your father, and I need your help."

Jason stopped. "Even if you were him, I wouldn't lift a finger to help you. You abandoned me."

"I didn't know about you. Your bitch of a mother told me that you'd died. She kept you from me. If I'd known better, I would've never left your side. I'm telling you the truth, son."

"I'm not your son. Everyone says you're crazy. Even if you are my father, I don't want to have anything to do with you. I thought I wanted to know more about my family, that's why I came here, but now that I have, I don't want to have anything to do with you or Lucy. You're both lying hypocrites."

"Don't say that. You don't mean it. I'm not crazy. Crazy's in the eye of the beholder. All I've ever wanted is for the legacy of our family to live on forever. That isn't so crazy, is it?"

Jason put his hands on his hips. "How did you even find me?"

"I found out your name from Ethan and Pit Bowen told me that you hang out often down here. I thought I'd take a shot."

It seemed to me that Jeremy was getting weaker, his breathing was much more labored. He looked like he could barely stand. It made me scared for Kasey. The weaker Kasey's body got with Jeremy inside, the less chance he had to return.

Jason noticed too. "Are you alright? You don't look so good."

"I was tricked into inhabiting this body by those damn witches. I thought Kasey was my son. I had no idea your mother had two sons. Kasey would be dead now if I didn't need this body. They were hoping I'd die. It's happening a lot sooner in Kasey's body than it did in Reed's.

It's because my spirit's weaker. I'm having trouble holding on."

"Forgive me if I'm not upset."

Jeremy grabbed Jason's arm. "I need to inhabit someone of my lineage to live on, preferably a male heir. You're the only one left. I need you so I can continue my journey."

Jason pulled away. "Like I said, you're crazy."

"It's my destiny to ensure that the Wickcliffs are allowed to return to the earth to live, to breathe, to regain the power and influence that we once possessed. You're part of that destiny now."

"So you'll live on in me and then what? What happens to me?"

"You'll rest for a while, my son."

"You mean I'll die?" He pushed Jeremy back. "I want you to stay the hell away from me. Do you understand me?"

He tried to walk away, but Jeremy grabbed him and gazed into his eyes intensely. "One never truly dies. It'll only be temporary. I'll find you a new host body once I'm strong enough. With my son by my side, our family will be unstoppable. We'll bring this town to its knees. We may even rule the world."

Jason's eyes widened. "I don't care what you say. I still think you're insane. Now let me go."

"Being insane implies that you don't know what you're doing. I know what I'm doing." He let Jason's arm go.

Jason rubbed his arm. "Screw you."

"You'd let the brother you never knew die? How sad."

"Forgive me. But if I had to choose between his life and mine, there's no comparison. Call me a selfish bastard."

Jeremy grinned. "You are my son. It's just such a shame that you don't realize that you don't have a choice. I'm not asking you."

Chapter 23

Rebecca bumped one of the crates that she'd been hiding behind, and it crashed to the dock. Jason and Jeremy saw her. She tried to run, but she tripped and hurt her ankle.

Jeremy went up to her, towering over her as she lay there writhing in pain. "It always pains me to have to harm such lovely young ladies. I hope you had fun playing spy because it's the last thing you'll ever do." He grabbed her arm and started pulling her up.

Jason put his hand up. "No! Let her go."

Rebecca having not heard the conversation was confused. "Kasey, what's wrong with you?"

Jeremy turned to Jason. "She knows too much of my plan. I can't have any interference."

"I don't know anything," Rebecca said. "Please, let me go."

Jeremy yanked on her arm. "Don't lie to me!"

"Please," Jason said, grabbing his other arm. "I'm asking you to let her go. If you are my father, if you want to make up for all the years we lost, you'll do this for me."

"It's all true, isn't it?" Rebecca said, glaring at Jeremy. "You are Jeremy Wickcliff. Ethan said you were inside Reed, but you're inside Kasey, aren't you? I thought Ethan was crazy."

"Quiet!" Jeremy said. "You're making me angry."

"Please," Jason said. "I love her. Don't hurt her."

Rebecca pushed away from them and then stared at Jason. "How dare you? How dare you pretend you love me? All you've done is lie to me. You knew you were a Wickcliff, didn't you? That's what you wanted to tell me before Ethan interrupted us, isn't it?"

"I do love you, Becca. I never lied about that."

"How does it feel to know that you made a fool out of me? Did you laugh at me behind my back after I told you how much I love you?"

"It wasn't like that at all."

"You can't even stop lying now." Tears of rage formed in her eyes.

"I've had enough of this senseless drivel," Jeremy said. "Because you're so lovely, I'll let you choose how you're going to die."

"Kasey's in there somewhere," Rebecca said. "He's not going to let you hurt me."

"Don't waste your final breath. Kasey's gone."

Jason stepped in front of her. "I'll do it. I won't fight you. You can use me, but only if you let Becca live. She can't do anything to stop you."

Jeremy tilted his head, amazed. "You'd do that for her? You love her that much?"

"I'd do anything for her."

Jeremy sighed and turned to her. "My son's very fond of you. He just gave you a reprieve. You owe him your life."

She glanced at Jason. "I owe no man anything. Especially a lying bastard like him."

Jeremy waved his hand to dismiss her. "You may go. Hurry before I change my mind."

"Regardless of what you think," Jason said. "I do love you, Becca."

"I hope you know what you're doing," she said. "There's no way out of this."

Jeremy put his arm around Jason. "Come, son. We can't do anything here. I have no power here."

"Where are we going?"

"You'll see." He glared at Rebecca. "If you try to follow us, I'll kill you. My son's pleas won't save you next time. Stay away."

Rebecca watched helplessly as they went off into the distance. Her ankle throbbed and her eyes stung from the tears. She wanted to call someone, anyone who could help. The sheriff. Or maybe Ethan. She didn't realize that both of them already knew about Kasey's possession. She checked her purse and realized she didn't have her phone inside. "Damn!"

As she went to her car, she thought about Jason and how much she loved him. She didn't want Jason's betrayal to turn her into an emotional train wreck as Pit had done to her for so many years. She wanted to believe he loved her. She believed the look in his eyes was sincere.

While Rebecca focused on her problems with Jason, I worried about both my brothers and how Jeremy's return had complicated both of their lives. It wasn't just that, I was worried about the fates of everyone else that lived in Sleepy Meadows. If Jeremy was strong enough to commit murder and to defeat three witches, there was no telling how much stronger he'd be now that he'd found Jason and he was willing to cooperate.

*****

I looked away from the mortal realm and found myself alone. I scanned the room and then went out to the doorway.

"Rory? Rory, where are you?"

He came down the hallway and took me by the hands. "I'm glad you're back. I'm sorry I didn't stay with you. I had to see Damon off."

We went over to the couch in the parlor and sat down. "Off?"

"He had to go back to the mortal realm. He can only stay here for so long. He can't remain away from his physical body for that long. If he doesn't go back for at least a little while, his mortal body will die."

"I see. There's so much I still don't understand."

He patted my hand. "It'll take time for it all to become clear. What's the latest in the mortal realm?"

"It's not good, Rory. Jeremy threatened to kill Kasey, so Ethan told him that Jason was his son."

Rory exhaled slowly. "You're right, that could be dangerous."

"It gets worse. Jeremy found Jason and talked him into letting him inhabit his body."

"How?"

"How else? He threatened Rebecca's life. He can intimidate anyone to do whatever he wants."

"Thanks for telling me. When Damon gets back, I'll make sure he knows."

"There's something else. Mom knows where Damon is. She and

Hilda are planning to go to the monastery to ask him to help Kasey."

"He's going to need to prepare himself for that. No one's seen him in the mortal realm for years except for a few nuns and a priest. Those that keep him in seclusion do so for a reason, and they don't like outsiders showing up."

"I'm going to go back. I just wanted you to know what was happening. Do you think that Damon can help us?"

Rory shrugged. "I wish I could tell you yes, but I can't lie to you. From what you've told me, Jeremy's becoming increasingly dangerous with Jason on his side. I don't know if anyone's going to be a match for him, even Damon."

"Well, at least you're honest." I rubbed his back. "I should be getting back."

Rory grabbed my hand and pulled me close. We kissed passionately. After a moment, I stopped him and looked into his sparkling eyes.

"I love you, my darling," he said. "As much as I hate what Jeremy did to you, it brought us together again."

"When you kiss me when you hold me, I believe that everything will be okay."

"As long as we're together, it will be."

* * * *

After Rory had left the room, I went back to the mortal realm, and since I'd figured that Jeremy would bring Jason back to the house, I went there. I found myself outside and instead of seeing Jeremy, I saw Gram. As I looked at her walking up the path to the house, I realized that she'd gone home. Finding no one there, she thought about what Mom had told her during one of their last conversations about bringing down Jeremy.

Gram had thought that maybe Mom would be here, but she was one-step behind. She hadn't realized that Mom had already been here and that she'd almost been killed. Things had been so chaotic that they hadn't spoken. When Gram got to the door, she was greeted by Greta again.

"You again. You have a bad habit of coming here in the middle of the night. It's one that you really must break. What do you want?"

"You know the drill by now," Gram said, pushing her way into the house. "I want to talk to Irma and don't give me any of that 'she isn't well' crap. I'm not in the mood."

Greta huffed. "Has anyone ever told you you're an extremely brash and rude woman? Quite frankly, I'm getting sick of you bursting into this house whenever you feel like it."

"Frankly, I could care less what you think, Greta. The Wickcliffs are messing with my family, and it's going to stop. Now, are you going to wake Irma up or do you want me to do it?"

"Ms. Ford…"

Gram stood defiantly. "I'm not leaving."

Greta complied and took her upstairs. Although Gram displayed a gruff exterior at the door, she was afraid as she ascended the staircase. There was a chill in the air that made her think that something terrible was about to happen. Death lurked in the vacant corridors. She almost thought about turning back.

When they reached Irma's door, Greta knocked. "Mrs. Wickcliff?" She opened the door. "Ms. Ford is here to see you again."

Gram entered the room. Irma turned on a light by the bed and appeared just as disheveled as before. It looked like a rat had made its nest in Irma's hair.

"Edie, it's you again. How many times in one week are you going to awaken an old lady out of a sound sleep?"

Gram approached the bed. "So you remember I was here before? That's something."

"Oh, I remember. I told you that I couldn't control Jeremy and that even if I could, I wouldn't. I threw you out. That means that I didn't want you to come back. Are you totally dense, woman?"

"You sound lucid tonight, Irma. You must be tired of the act."

"I don't know what you mean. Tell me what you want and get out. You're wasting my time."

"Do you remember our agreement from years ago, Irma?"

Irma sprung up in bed. "Why do you bring that up now?"

"Because you aren't holding up your end of the bargain. Why should the rest of us?"

Irma motioned to Greta, who was standing by the door. "Greta, help me into my wheelchair."

"But Mrs. Wickcliff, it's late."

"Now!"

Greta helped her into her chair and left.

"You have my attention, Edie."

"You have to remember how Harold used to delve into the occult and how Jeremy used to as well?"

"It's a part of my life I'd just as soon forget."

Gram snickered. "Most of the time, you do, or at least that's what you want people to believe. You don't fool me for a minute. You know exactly what's happening, don't you?"

Irma scowled. "You think this is funny? I know my mind's going. You don't have to throw it in my face during one of my brief periods of clarity. I'm not faking my memory loss regardless of what you think, and I don't care if you believe that or not. What about Harold and Jeremy?"

"You must remember how evil and cruel they were? How they used to torture people just for pleasure?"

Irma stuck out her chest. "I remember no such thing."

"Let me remind you. Remember the Simmons girl? How she disappeared suddenly and her mutilated body was found not too far from here? Word around town was that Jeremy was responsible."

Irma shook her head. "Sheriff Richard Withers never proved anything."

"But we all knew who did it. Before that, Delia Chambers disappeared right after Harold came to town. Things like that never happened here before the Wickcliffs arrived."

"Do you have nothing better to do than come to my home in the middle of the night and disparage my family's good name? My husband and my son were admirable men."

Gram laughed. "You poor delusional soul. Even when you appear lucid, you aren't."

Irma pointed to the door. "I've had enough. Get out."

Gram shook her head. "I'm not going anywhere. When you lost Jeremy, Harold, and Rachel, I thought you'd lost enough. That's why when the townspeople wanted to burn this place to the ground, Charles Hawkins and I stopped them. Looking back on it now, maybe we should've let them. Maybe Jeremy would've never been able to return if he had no home to return to."

"I remember promising that I would keep to myself and not bother anyone if you people just left me and my home alone. I've done that. I've kept my end of the deal."

"No, Irma, you haven't. You've known that Rachel and Jeremy were back. You didn't warn anyone. You told me straight to my face that you didn't care what he did to my family. That isn't an example of the peaceful lifestyle you promised."

"I don't know what day it is half the time, and you're going to hold it against me if I don't remember that my children, my dead children mind you, have returned from the grave?"

Gram narrowed her eyes at her. "Don't give me that bull. You knew what you were saying the other day when I asked you to stop your psychopathic son. What was it you said? 'An eye for an eye' wasn't it?"

Irma exhaled swiftly and sobbed. "I just want to be left alone and for people like you to stop talking ill about my son and husband. Let my poor Harold rest in peace."

Gram groaned. "Stop with the fake crocodile tears. And what is this about peace? Harold never gave anyone any peace in life. Why should we do that for him? I'm sure that wherever he is, there's no peace for him anyway."

Irma smiled deviously. "You didn't always feel that way, Edie. You just despise Harold because he chose me, not you."

Gram put her hands on her hips. "That was a lifetime ago. I'll admit that I was taken in by his charm and looks when I was young and naïve. However, I couldn't be more grateful that he chose you."

Irma put her hand over her heart. "Oh?"

Gram sneered. "I could've easily ended up like you—old, bitter, alone, and half mad. Was being with Harold Wickcliff worth it?"

"Let's get something straight. I'm not insane. I have bouts of senility. It isn't the same thing."

"Like I care. I'm just giving you fair warning. You either get rid of that son of yours, or the people of Sleepy Meadows will do it for you. I can't protect you this time."

"Like you tried to protect me by seducing my husband?"

"That was a long time ago."

"Not for me. I remember more than you think, Edie."

"I don't doubt that. You've been warned, Irma. That's all I'll say about it. Now where's Caroline?"

Irma shrugged. "Your daughter isn't here."

Gram stooped down to her level and got in her face. "You'd better not be lying."

"It would be poetic justice, wouldn't you think, if something were to happen to her? You and Charles Hawkins killed my husband. Maybe my son killing your daughter would even the score between us once and for all."

Gram stood up and groaned. "Sick bitch! I swear if you weren't so feeble…never mind, you aren't even worth it." She stormed out of the room forgetting to shut the door behind her.

"I'm not finished with you," Irma said, wheeling herself into the hallway and following her.

Gram didn't look back. "I've got nothing left to say to you."

"You can call me whatever you want, Edie, but the bottom line is that you're jealous of me. You always have been."

Gram turned around with her mouth open wide. "Please."

"It's true. I had everything you always wanted—Harold, money, power, prestige, respect."

"Respect? More like pity."

Irma narrowed her eyes. "Excuse me?"

"You've led a cold and lonely life ever since the day you met Harold. Everyone knows it. He sucked the life and the livelihood right out of you."

"That isn't true."

"Irma, look at you. You look like you're 100 years old. You've had no quality of life. He took that away from you. It's because you couldn't deal with his death that you haven't even left this house in over 25 years. Even in death he's screwing you over."

"I'm sick of your presumptions about my marriage. You have no idea what went on between Harold and me."

Gram reached the top of the stairs. "Probably nothing. You would've had to be some young, defenseless, naïve thing for him to want you. Saying no is what turned him on. When it came to sex, you didn't even know the meaning of the word."

"Me? You were the town whore. Do you even know who your daughter's father is?"

Gram smiled. "Of course I do, and I think you do too."

"What about that son of yours. The one no one speaks of?"

"Don't talk about him. Jeremy's far worse than my son ever was."

Irma let out a frustrated scream and pushed Gram backward. Gram attempted to regain her balance by grabbing a hold of Irma's wheelchair handles, but she was unable to hold on and fell backward down the stairs. Irma's chair jerked forward, and she tumbled out of it, falling down the stairs with Gram. They both screamed as they tumbled down the stairs to the bottom, landing with two loud thumps.

There was silence for a moment as they both lay on the floor at the bottom of the stairs in intense pain. They lay there moaning and then heard the footsteps of someone running across the floor towards them.

"Mrs. Wickcliff, Ms. Ford, oh my." Greta ran to the phone and called an ambulance. I watched as Gram lost consciousness. I wasn't very concerned because if she were hurt, I'd know it. She was going to be fine other than some bumps and bruises. What concerned me more was what she'd said to Irma before they fell. She implied that Mom was Harold's daughter, making Jeremy my uncle.

I refused to believe it. I couldn't believe it. I couldn't be part Wickcliff.

Chapter 24

Gram and Irma would soon be at the hospital, which made me think about Reed and Graham again. During our time trapped in the attic, Reed and I had developed a friendship. After seeing what the ancestors had done to him in the cemetery, I'd lost all hope that he'd ever be okay again, but somehow inexplicably, his body was still alive when he'd been taken out of the mausoleum.

I found Graham at the hospital sitting in a chair outside Reed's room. The hallway was quiet and dark, the smell around him sterile, and the lighting dim against the light gray walls. He barely heard a sound. He was feeling so many different emotions it was hard for me to get a lock on him. He felt fear and guilt strongly, for not knowing what had happened to Reed in the first place, for not being able to protect him and finally for shooting him in an attempt to stop Jeremy. He put his head in his hands, almost unable to deal with the rage he felt.

"I'm a decent man, God. I've dedicated my life to helping others. I've done my best to raise Reed alone after we lost his mother. I just don't understand why this had to happen to my family."

His private conversation was interrupted by the foreboding sound of footsteps on the meticulously polished floor.

"Graham?" Dr. Marsh said. "I'm sorry for interrupting your prayer."

Graham stood up. "It's alright. How is he?"

Dr. Marsh sighed. "I'm not going to sugarcoat this, Graham. It wouldn't be fair."

"Just tell me. Is Reed alive?"

"Barely."

Graham smiled. "As long as he's alive, there's still hope."

"That's just it. The only reason Reed's still alive is that he's on a respirator. Without it, he would be gone in a matter of moments. He can't breathe on his own."

Graham's legs weakened. "He was breathing before."

"Yes, but we lost him during surgery and had to resuscitate him. That has changed things a bit."

"I see. Now what?"

Dr. Marsh rubbed the back of his neck. "Do you want my opinion as a doctor, or as a friend?"

Graham locked eyes with him. "What do you think?"

"Reed's body's racked with gangrene. The cells in his body are dying, and his flesh is decomposing as if he's been dead for weeks. We're trying to treat it with antibiotics the best we can, but how did he get that way in the first place? I've never seen a case like this."

"I can't explain that now. For God's sake, Alex, tell me what's going on."

"If he were to live, amputation would be the only option, specifically his legs."

Graham rubbed his forehead. "Oh my God."

"I wish that were all that it was. Unfortunately, there's more. We did an EEG. There was no brain activity measured."

"God!" Graham sobbed. "Are you trying to tell me that my son's brain dead?"

He nodded. "I'm sorry, Graham. I truly am. Reed's in a deep coma, and there's no hope for improvement. The amputation would decrease the risk of infection because the gangrene can't spread, but it still can't address the other factors."

Graham grabbed him by the arms. "I don't believe you. You have to be wrong."

Dr. Marsh glared at his hands, and then Graham removed them. "I wish I were. I figure that as long as we keep the machines running and continue with the transfusions that Reed will require, we can keep him alive. But, you have the decision to make. Once those machines are turned off..."

"Stop right there. I won't give the consent. I won't kill my son. It's unfortunate enough that I couldn't stop this."

He studied Graham's eyes. "Stop what? What aren't you telling me?"

"I won't let you turn off the machines."

"Your son's already gone, Graham."

Graham shook his head. "No, he isn't! He's in there somewhere, and as long as there's breath in my body, I won't give up on him."

Graham whipped around, went over to the windows, and peered out. He closed his eyes, remembering how he'd held the gun on Jeremy in the mausoleum as he was about to possess Kasey. He remembered Jeremy's eyes. How they were full of fire and then the darkness that surrounded him when he pulled the trigger.

Graham rotated back to face Dr. Marsh. "You asked what happened to Reed. It was something so evil, so horrible, that it would make the devil himself cringe. As God is my witness, if my son dies, I won't stop until the Wickcliffs lose everything."

It was hard for me to listen to the doctor's bleak diagnoses, but now it made sense as to how Reed's body could still be alive. The machines kept him breathing. Reed had become another victim of the Wickcliff's twisted plot.

* * * *

I remained in the hospital after seeing the sheriff because Ethan was also waiting there. Once Rebecca had gotten back to her car and retrieved her phone, she'd called him and told him she wanted to talk to him. They agreed to meet at the hospital. Ethan looked up when he saw her limping down the hallway. He ran up to her.

"What happened to you? Why are you limping?"

She glanced down at her foot. "I twisted my ankle. It's no big deal."

"Maybe you should get it looked at."

She groaned. "I said it was no big deal! I know what's best for myself even though no one else seems to think I do."

Ethan put his hands up. "Relax. I was just trying to help."

She rubbed her face with her hands. "I'm sorry. I didn't mean to be curt. It's just that my mind's racing."

"Yeah, tell me about it."

"How's Reed?"

"Graham says that his whole body's shutting down and that he's brain dead. Dr. Marsh wants Graham to give permission to turn off the machines."

Rebecca put her hand over her mouth. "It's just so unfair. Reed's such a likable guy. Why do all these terrible things happen to decent people? Reed, your dad, Kasey's mom? Evil like Jeremy Wickcliff just keeps on living. It isn't right."

"Jeremy isn't the only evil presence in this town."

"But he may be the worst. I found Jason talking with him by the docks. Jeremy was going to kill me, but Jason saved my life. There's good in him. I believe that."

Ethan exhaled. "Jeremy found him?"

Rebecca nodded.

Ethan sighed heavily. "And so it begins then. And it's my fault."

"Ethan, you might want to sit down. That's why I called you. It's about who Jeremy's inhabited now."

He looked away. "Don't bother. I already know."

"You know about Kasey?"

"I was there after it happened."

She touched his arm. "Oh, sweetie. How can you be so calm?"

"I have to be. I'm no use to Kasey if I get hysterical. I have to stay rational if I'm going to help him."

"But he could be dying or dead by now."

"Don't you think I realize that?"

"And so could Jason."

Ethan clenched his fist. "Who gives a shit about Jason? If it weren't for that bastard coming to town, Jeremy wouldn't be holding all the cards now. He wouldn't have any family left to inhabit. His spirit would be dead by now."

"Jason didn't know what was going to happen. This isn't his fault."

Ethan threw his hands up. "Don't you dare defend him to me. If I lose Kasey, it'll be his fault and Jason will pay with his life."

"Don't say things like that. It isn't like you. You're scaring me."

"You should be scared. We all should."

Rebecca began to tear up. "Oh, Ethan."

The Possession

"I'm sorry, but it's true, and you know it." He paused. "Do you know where they went?"

She shook her head. "Jeremy said if I followed them, he'd kill me."

"Bastard. There's only one place where he can be, the Wickcliff mausoleum in the cemetery. That's where his powers are the strongest. The transfer will probably happen there. That's where he possessed Kasey. When the transfer's successful and Kasey's freed, I want to be there when he comes back to me."

"What are we waiting for?"

Ethan cocked his head. "You aren't coming."

"Like hell I'm not."

"Becca, this is serious."

She clenched her fists. "You sexist pig. You think I can't handle myself because I'm a woman, well screw that."

"That has nothing to do with it."

She put her hand up. "No more excuses. We're just wasting time here. Besides, if Jason has even the slightest bit of love for me, I might be able to get through to him when Jeremy takes over. Admit it. You need me."

Ethan thought for a moment and then nodded. "Alright. But just keep in mind that I might not be able to protect you."

"Same here." Rebecca put her arm around him. "Let the games begin."

"This is one hell of a dangerous game, Becca."

"Maybe. But all games have to end eventually, and there isn't one yet that I haven't mastered. I was married to Pit, wasn't I? When all's said and done the Wickcliffs will crumble, and life in Sleepy Meadows will go back to normal."

Ethan scoffed. "Whatever normal is for this town. There's one thing I can't figure out, though."

"What's that?"

"How do we know when it's finally over?"

Rebecca just stared at him. She didn't know how to answer his question and wondered if anyone in Sleepy Meadows could.

I wanted to know the answer to that myself. Since my suicide, I'd found out many things about who I really was and about who my family was. I'd seen things that I'd never thought I'd see including someone that looked just like me maul someone to death.

As horrific as all these visions had been, I had a feeling that they were just getting started. My instincts told me that I had a lot more that I needed to learn. There were more secrets and more revelations. What I'd learned up until now was just the beginning.

The End

Coming in the Fall of 2016 from Melange Books, LLC

Midnight's Edge: Book 3 - The Spirits of Sleepy Meadows

About the Authors:

David Chappuis was born in Waterloo, Iowa and grew up on a farm in Madrid, New York. He received a bachelor's degree in English/Writing and Art/Studio from Potsdam College. He has made a living as a professional web designer and resides in southern Virginia.

Michael Klinger was born in Niagara Falls, New York. He received an associate's degree in human services from Niagara County Community College and a bachelor's degree in human services management from the University of Phoenix. He currently resides in southern Virginia.

Authors Contacts:

Author Website: www.davidchappuis.com
Midnight's Edge Site: www.midnightsedgeweb.com
Twitter: www.twitter.com/davechappuis
https://www.pinterest.com/davechappuis/
Facebook: https://www.facebook.com/midnightsedge

CPSIA information can be obtained at www.ICGtesting.com
Printed in the USA
BVOW08s2018210716

456404BV00001BA/14/P

9 781680 462487